DEATH WAS

IN THE PICTURE

ALSO BY LINDA L. RICHARDS

Death Was the Other Woman

DEATH WAS

IN THE PICTURE

LINDA L. RICHARDS

St. Martin's Minotaur ❧ New York

A THOMAS DUNNE BOOK FOR MINOTAUR BOOKS.
An imprint of St. Martin's Publishing Group.

DEATH WAS IN THE PICTURE. Copyright © 2008 by Linda L. Richards. All rights reserved. Printed in the United States of America. For information, address St. Martin's Press, 175 Fifth Avenue, New York, N.Y. 10010.

www.thomasdunnebooks.com
www.minotaurbooks.com

Library of Congress Cataloging-in-Publication Data

Richards, Linda, 1960-
  Death was in the picture / Linda L. Richards.—1st ed.
      p.   cm.
  ISBN-13: 978-0-312-38339-8
  ISBN-10: 0-312-38339-8
  1. Private investigators—California—Los Angeles—Fiction.   2. Los Angeles (Calif.)—Fiction.   3. Nineteen thirties—Fiction.   4. Motion picture actors and actresses—Fiction.   I. Title.
  PR9199.4.R5226D427 2009
  813'.6—dc22

                                                2008030122

First Edition: January 2009

10   9   8   7   6   5   4   3   2   1

DEATH WAS
IN THE PICTURE

CHAPTER ONE

"I'D LIKE TO see Mr. Theroux, please."

The man who was still closing the office door had been surprisingly quiet for someone his size. When he crossed the room toward my desk, I was entranced by his keen blue eyes and his easy grace. He moved like an acrobat, like a dancer. He moved like someone you wanted to watch. Yet he couldn't have been much under six feet and was probably only a couple of cheesecakes shy of three hundred pounds.

"Do you have an appointment, Mr. . . . ?" I prompted, knowing full well he did not. The only way you got an appointment with Dex Theroux was by talking to me and I was about one hundred and three percent sure this guy hadn't done that. There weren't any appointments in my book, for one thing. For another, I had a pretty good idea what was on Dex's schedule for the day. I hadn't peeked in at him for a few hours, but I figured that he'd been looking at spending the afternoon with all the boys: Johnnie Walker, Jack Daniel, Jim Beam and Jose Cuervo. I'd be lucky, after an afternoon of hard drinking, if he wasn't listening to the ink stains on his desk blotter. Most of the time, that's just how it was.

The big man stopped close enough to where I sat that I could smell him. It's odd when you can notice a man's scent and still think it's kinda nice. This was like that. The big man gave off the scent of something mysterious but pleasant. Slightly floral, yet appropriately masculine. I didn't know what it was, but I wished I had the courage to ask. I wanted to get a big bottle of it. There were days things would have been greatly improved in the office if I could have doused Dex in a nice cloud of whatever scent the big man was wearing.

"I'm sorry," he said softly. "I do not have an appointment. Mustard sent me. He told me Dex Theroux was the man to see and that if I mentioned Mustard's name, you'd probably get me in without too much trouble."

He was right: he'd said a name that opened some doors. Any friend of Mustard's, as they say. "And you said his name twice," I smiled up at him. "Listen, though, I'm not sure if Mr. Theroux is free at the moment." I shot a doubtful look at Dex's closed office door. I wanted to say Dex might be free but not coherent, but didn't want to put too fine a point on things. "If you'll just have a seat Mr . . ."

"Dean," he supplied as easily as a hand over silk. "Xander Dean."

"All right, Mr. Dean. If you'll just have a seat, I'll determine when Mr. Theroux can see you."

As I headed in to Dex's office, I saw Dean attempting to wedge himself into the small space our not-so-roomy office allows for a waiting room. He was managing the operation more gracefully than I would have thought possible, given the sheer bulk of him, but it was still going to take some doing. I considered offering to pull a chair up to my desk so he could sit comfortably, then thought better of it. I might be a couple of minutes getting Dex into shape. Trying to find an acceptable position in the waiting area would keep Dean occupied for a while.

The office was small and it only took me a couple of seconds to cross from my desk to Dex's office door. Before I opened it, I shot a look over my shoulder and saw that Dean was still busy shifting this and pulling that. I slipped inside Dex's office as quickly as possible, closing the door behind me before I even looked at my boss. I wasn't taking any chances.

"What's with the cloak and dagger, kiddo?"

I noted with relief that Dex was sitting upright. More than

that, even though it was close to three o'clock in the afternoon, he looked as sober as a gas jockey's maiden aunt. And there wasn't a single sign of Johnnie, Jack, Jim or even Jose. Dex's hair was neatly combed, his chin wore only the faintest hint of stubble—not inappropriate to the time of day—and his eyes were clear and blue and weren't being chased by red rims. I blinked at him. Then I blinked again. This wasn't what I'd expected.

I knew what to do with drunken Dex. I knew who to be and how to handle things. Understand: I wasn't complaining. But neither was I prepared. It had happened before, but it wasn't something that happened every day.

"I . . ."

Dex stretched back in his chair, the racing form on the desk in front of him forgotten for the moment. He linked his hands behind his head and offered up a self-satisfied sigh. "Spill it, cookie," he said, "but I already know what's going on. You came in here figurin' I'd be soused, didn't you?"

"I . . ." I tried again. "That is, I . . ."

He laughed then, not unkindly. "Never mind, Kitty. Never mind. Don't worry about sparing my feelings. I know how it's been. But things have been better lately. Hadn't you noticed? Things have been different."

I thought about it. Was he right? Had things been different? I ran through the last few weeks in my mind. There had been cases, the usual kinds—jealous wives, suspicious business partners. Nothing exciting, but Dex had done what needed doing. And I realized that I'd been picking up Dex's ice on my way into the office in the morning, just as I always had, but I hadn't been finding any empty rocks glasses on his desk when he went out.

I looked at him then—really, fully *looked* at him. He must have seen a light dawn, because he laughed right out loud. The laughter—probably combined with his new dry state—shaved an easy ten years off his craggy looks. When he laughed like that, I saw the swaggering shadow of the youth he must once have been.

"But why, Dex?" I asked, plunking myself in one of the chairs opposite his desk, Xander Dean skootching around our waiting room like a big kitten and trying to find a comfy spot forgotten for the moment. "What's going on?"

Dex shrugged and grinned. "A lot," he said at length. "Maybe more than I wanna say."

I felt an eyebrow arch at him. "What's her name?"

Another laugh. "Naw, nothin' like that. It's not a dame. Just, you know, things have been good lately. Haven't they been good?"

I nodded warily. When I thought about it, I realized he was right. The problem was, I'd been down this road before. We both had. I'd sat right here in this very chair. I'd felt this bright spot of hope. He didn't seem to realize that now. But me? I hadn't forgotten.

"Things have been better," he continued. "We've had a pretty steady run of cases. The bill collectors have been calling less." It was another thing I hadn't noticed. It's the kind of thing you don't miss when it's gone. "I'm a grown man, Kitty. And the war? It's far behind me. I just figured it was high time I started acting my age, not my shoe size."

I could have pointed out that there weren't too many eleven-year-olds who could put away a pint of bourbon, but I didn't want to spoil his mood. If he was growing something new and fragile inside him once again, I didn't want to do anything to hurt it. That bright spot of hope again. On the inside, I could be as skeptical as I liked. But I let Dex see the part of me that shared his optimism. And I *was* optimistic, though maybe not in a way he would have understood. Just maybe, I said to myself, maybe this would be the time his good intentions would take.

I tried to imagine dry Dex, sober Dex, a cleaned-up, cleaned-out, responsible Dex that I didn't have to constantly watch to make sure things didn't go wrong. And I couldn't: it was outside of what I was capable of imagining. Still, I could work on it. If Dex was ready to try being a grown-up, I was sure as hell ready to be a secretary to one.

Imagine! Only having to type and make coffee and answer the phones. It would be a luxury to not have to do my job *and* parts of his just to make sure things kept going as they should. Because if Dex didn't do his job right his clients wouldn't pay him. If his clients didn't pay him, Dex wouldn't be able to pay me. If Dex didn't pay me, I'd have to find a new job. That's where the buck stopped—any old way you cared to look at it— because there just weren't any jobs out there to have. Not in Los Angeles in 1931, with the Okies and their trucks loaded with all their worldly goods clogging up the state lines and out-of-work men shuffling around outside locked construction sites every morning, hoping against hope they would be the one to catch a break and do twelve hours work so they could earn enough to buy their families some tea biscuits and maybe pay the power bill. Not in that L.A. In *that* L.A., I was happy enough to have a desk to show up at. Even the occasional rubber pay check couldn't put a damper on the fact that I had a job when so many did not.

I was happy for Dex, happier than I would have thought possible at the idea of him trying to turn over a new leaf. I had a bunch of questions, and maybe a couple of comments, but at that moment the door opened and I jumped guiltily at the sight of Xander Dean.

"Oh!" I said. "I'm sorry, Mr. Dean. It turns out Mr. Theroux *is* available to see you. We just had some . . . some paperwork to get through." I noticed with relief that Dex had made the racing form disappear, as was his habit, drunk or sober, when someone came in. The racing form wasn't the kind of paperwork a client needed to see.

"Kitty . . . ?" Dex said.

"Sorry, Dex. This is Xander Dean," I said, as I ushered the big man to the seat I'd been occupying moments before. "Mr. Dean, Dexter J. Theroux. Mr. Dean is a friend of Mustard's," I said, knowing that would give Dex the only introduction he'd need.

I shut the door tight behind me on my way out.

CHAPTER TWO

I WAS BACK at my desk and rolling a piece of paper into my typewriter when the phone rang. I knew who it was before I picked up the receiver. Even so, I was surprised when I was right.

"How's my favorite Kitty-cat?"

"No, Mustard. Not at all. You already know I'm not so crazy about you calling me 'Kitty.' But Kitty-cat? Absolutely not. Where's your head?"

"You don't like Kitty?" Mustard sounded astonished. "How can you not like Kitty? It's your name."

"My name is not Kitty. It's Katherine. Kate, if you must. Miss Pangborn, if you dare. But no Kitty. Got it?"

"Sure, sure," Mustard said like he meant it. I knew him well enough, though. I knew that he did not. "Dean show up?"

"He did," I said. "He's in with Dex right now."

"Good, good. Listen, if you get a chance before they work things out, tell Dex not to go easy on him."

"Pardon?" I said.

"Yeah. Did you notice his suit? And his pocket hanky: real silk."

I hadn't noticed the fabric, but the hanky I'd noticed. It was fuchsia, patterned in an even darker purple; a bright splotch on the man's otherwise conservative dark gray suit. When I thought about it, I realized that Mustard was right. The whole effect was pretty swank.

"What's his story?" I asked.

"I don't know for sure," Mustard said. "And I don't know that I'd tell you if I did."

"Thanks," I said dryly.

"Don't mention it. But this is real jack, Kitty; this is folding money. I can tell. He came recommended. Like I said, get Dex to charge all he can. The guy said he was looking for the best. He'll be expecting to pay for it."

I told Mustard I'd do what I could, but I figured I probably wouldn't get the opportunity before Dex made the deal, if a deal were to be made. I considered intruding, perhaps offering a glass of water or some coffee, but this move would have been so uncharacteristic of me, it would have left Dex open-mouthed. Anyway, once in there, I couldn't see past the tray with the cups or glasses. Would I pass Dex a note? Whisper something in his ear? Either scenario seemed out of character and beyond my job description, so I opted for another plan: I'd do nothing and hope for the best.

Dex and Dean were in the office for a long time. At least, it seemed that way to me. To fill in the time, and because Dex likes me to do it, I typed away merrily for a while.

The quick brown fox.

The quick brown fox jumps over the lazy dog.

The quick brown fox jumps over the lazy dog and falls off a log.

The quick brown fox jumps over the lazy dog and falls off a log and into a deep and extremely frightening and totally unexpected bog.

Things like that. All in an effort to supply the busy, successful sounds that Dex liked clients to hear coming from the outer office when he was in a first meeting.

The quick brown fox fell off a log and onto a brown dog and met a lavender hog in a deep, dark fog while trying to avoid falling into a bog.

But it was a long meeting. After a while, I started running out of possible scenarios for quick brown foxes and I moved on to hitting random keys at sensible intervals. Just when I was about to give even that up and start preparing to pack it up for the night, Dex's office door opened and the fat man came out. I waited, but Dex didn't pop out behind him.

"Good day, then," he said as he passed my desk. I returned his polite greeting, noticing as I did that he didn't look the least upset or perturbed. Curious.

As soon as I heard the elevator leave our floor and head down with its larger than usual cargo, I slipped back into Dex's office. He was sitting at his desk, his head turned toward daylight. He grunted in my direction when I came in, but he didn't turn away from the window. He seemed deep in thought.

"It didn't go so good, huh?" In our office, I could tell when a meeting had gone well when Dex walked a new client to the door. Then, after the client was gone, he'd stop by my desk and fill me in. But a bad meeting usually resulted in the lost potential client leaving the office in some sort of visual huff. Dex wasn't a halfways kinda guy: he usually dotted his i's and made sure people knew exactly how he felt.

Dean had seemed happy enough when he left. Dex wasn't, though. He wasn't happy at all.

"It went all right," Dex said, rolling a cigarette thoughtfully between his thumb and forefinger before lighting it. When the cigarette was lit, he flicked the match off the end of his finger— a neat trick. It did a lazy sort of triple somersault and landed in his jade green ashtray tidy as you please. "It went just fine."

Without being invited, I sat down opposite the desk in the still warm chair and looked at my boss. Dean's scent lingered, but Dex had a wrinkle in his nose like he was smelling something bad. It wasn't true that I missed the glass in front of him but I had a hunch that whatever had made him this gloomy wouldn't have had quite the same effect had it been cushioned by a bourbon haze.

"It doesn't look like it went fine," I said.

"You're not going to let up until I tell you, are you?"

"Probably not."

"Well, it's not what you'd figure, a guy like that. Not some cheating wife. Least," Dex smiled for the first time since I'd entered, "that's not what he was here for this time."

"So spill it already, gumshoe. I've got some important typing to do and you're cuttin' into it." I was trying to lighten the mood. It didn't work.

"Pipe down, Kitty," Dex said. "I'm gettin' to it. It's a hard thing to explain. Complicated. You ever heard of Laird Wyndham?"

I didn't answer. Just crossed my arms over my chest and looked Dex straight in the face. I was modern, I was in touch. I read the newspapers, went to the pictures. Of *course* I knew who Laird Wyndham was. You'd have to have been living on the moon and surviving on its green cheese for the last half dozen years not to know the name and face of the biggest motion picture star there had ever been and probably ever would be.

Laird Wyndham was tall, dark and handsome, with pale eyes that flashed charm and wit and a chin strong enough to crack nuts. Then there was his voice. One magazine article had described it as molten lava over iced cream. It was rich and deep and powerful and it was the voice that had brought stardom, in the end, edging out other actors who hadn't the vocal timbre to make the transition to talking pictures. Laird had. Laird did. And a million women, just like me, couldn't get enough of watching and hearing him.

I'd been to see one of his pictures just the week before. I couldn't really afford the nickel but, as Dex had said, things had been a bit better lately and my paychecks had been coming to me regular for the last few months.

After work, I hadn't gone straight home to Bunker Hill. Instead I'd walked over to Broadway to the Million Dollar where I'd felt like a princess in the opulently ornamented theater.

But even the pleasure in my surroundings faded away when the curtain opened on Laird Wyndham in *The Cardboard Heart*. It hadn't been possible for me to think about anything but what was on that screen.

I'd wept at the end of the film, when Laird had taken Catherine Calderon, his beautiful smoky-eyed co-star, into his arms and said, "None of that means anything, sweetheart. This fire I feel couldn't burn me, even if all I had was a cardboard heart." Then he'd clenched her even more tightly and kissed her hard on the mouth. As the music swelled and the camera pulled back, you could see that, as they kissed, the empty place between their chins and their chests together outlined the form of a heart. I'd rummaged in my handbag until I felt my hankie, then I dabbed at my eyes and nose, trying to repair any damage before it really got hold.

As the house lights came up, I'd sat alone and snuffled and sighed and wondered what it would mean to have a man want you the way Laird's character had wanted Catherine's. To feel all of what they'd felt.

Dex read my face and my body language. "So you've heard of him? OK, the guy that was here, Dean? He wants me to follow Wyndham. And report on what's what."

"What's what with what?" I asked, not understanding.

Dex sighed heavily before answering. "That's the thing, Kitty. The part where this gets sticky. Dean says the people he works for feel that Wyndham's morals are in question." He could see me get ready to interject, and he held up a steadying hand. "They want me to tail him, then report back on what he does."

I didn't say anything for a moment. I needed to think things through. It felt as though there was a part missing. Then I realized: generally, someone wants someone followed, there's a deep personal interest. A spouse, as I said before. Or a business partner. A father. Or a son. A husband. Maybe a wife. I didn't see the personal connection here and I said as much to Dex.

"So Dean wants you to keep an eye on Wyndham? Who are they to each other?"

"That's the thing, Kitty. The thing with this business that doesn't sit right with me. See, Dean is doing the hiring, but he's working for someone else. He wouldn't say who. Just 'a group of concerned citizens' was all he'd tell me."

"That doesn't mean much, does it?"

Dex shrugged. "Maybe yes. Maybe no. I mean, a 'group of concerned citizens' and they're concerned about what Wyndham does in private, that's why they want me to get a slant on him. They think a big, fat star like him hasta be above reproach, morally."

"That's what he said, Dean? 'Above reproach morally'?" I could see Dex was quoting.

He nodded. "Yeah. They figure—I dunno—maybe he's a wrong number, you know? Maybe gonna get in dutch for something and, if that happened, it would turn everyone who'd ever watched his movies into trouble boys and roundheels, I guess, 'cause he said something about 'the morals of our youth,' and how decent people shouldn't oughta hafta put up with such shenanigans, but I wasn't listening to him much by then."

I considered the things I knew about the private life of Laird Wyndham. The papers and the radio went on about him constantly, so I knew a fair amount.

For starters, he had a contract with his studio that landed him exactly one million dollars per year. And I knew that, if I had five hundred dollars, I'd be able to buy a new car. Five thousand would put me into a fairly swank house; I'd own it, free and clear. For twenty-eight bucks I could buy the coat I'd seen at Bullock's last week. The prettiest coat that had ever been. But I didn't have twenty-eight bucks for a coat, not just now. I didn't even always have a nickel for a cup of coffee. And there were plenty of men out there couldn't get enough scratch together to buy their babies bread and milk. So a million dollars.

Every year? I couldn't afford all the zeros just to write it out. It made my head swim just thinking about it.

So, OK: with a million dollars a year, Wyndham made headlines just for doing some shopping. He'd built an unimaginably expensive house in the Hollywood Hills and he owned a ranch in Ventura County, near Oxnard. He was married, too. When he was a very young actor, he'd married his first co-star, some twenty years his senior. As far as I knew, the wife had retired from acting not long after—had closed the door, as the saying went—and now spent her time out on that ranch. No one ever saw very much of her, but they saw Wyndham all right. His name had been linked to every starlet imaginable and I couldn't begin to count the photos I'd seen of him in the newspaper, at this nightclub or that one, some dazzling young girl on his arm.

I didn't know anything about aviation, but I knew he had some sort of plane that had cost a lot of money, something he flew himself and kept in a hangar at an airport out in Glendale. He had a whole stable full of cars, each more expensive than the last. He owned a yacht. Of course. He kept the boat moored out at Long Beach and quite often there were stories in the press about him roughing it at sea on *Woebegone Dream,* named for a picture he'd done a couple of years before. I'd seen a photo in the paper once: Wyndham, beaming, standing on the dock in front of what looked like a small ocean liner. He stood there wearing a captain's hat turned to a jaunty angle. Behind him ranged the white-clad crew: a half-score of handsome young men in crisp uniforms. The story said the crew had piloted the boat halfway around the world from Italy, where the craft had been built to the specifications of its new owner.

"So did you take the job?" I asked, half knowing the answer. It was written all over Dex's concerned mug.

He nodded. "I did, Kitty. So help me, I did."

I nodded approvingly. As I'm always saying, a girl's gotta eat. "I forgot to tell you: Mustard called when you were in with

Mr. Dean. He told me to tell you to charge him big. 'He wanted the best,' Mustard said. 'He'll be expecting to pay for it.' "

Dex grinned. The smile went all the way to his eyes. "Oh, I soaked him good, Kitty. The pile he gave me, I can barely fold it in half."

"So what's the problem?" Personally, I couldn't see it. A swell with a fat wallet showed up, offered Dex what sounded like a fairly cushy case and he took the job. What was there to be glum about?

"Ah, Kitty: I figured you'd see it on your own. It's the client."

"Dean?"

"No, *his* client. Whoever it is. The 'group of concerned citizens.' That kind of thing gives me the heebie-jeebies."

"Why?"

"Well, look at temperance."

"Who's Temperance?" This was getting more and more confusing.

"Not who, Kitty. What. Temperance was the movement that ended up starting Prohibition. C'mon: the Women's Temperance League. Didn't they teach you anything at that fancy school you went to up in Frisco?"

I shrugged. Of course I knew what temperance was. But it was ancient history to me: when Prohibition started, I was a little girl.

"Sure, they taught me. But we can't all be as old as you are, Dex: it was history to me, not current events."

"But it led to Prohibition. And see what a bad idea that turned out to be? Everyone knows drinking has gone way up since it started. Crime has too. There are even people that argue that the country's current financial turmoil is partly due to Prohibition."

"That's a lot of hooey," I said.

"Maybe it is," Dex said, "and maybe it ain't. My point is that the group of 'concerned citizens' responsible for Prohibition have a lot to answer for. And sometimes, groups like that just smack of people shoving their noses in where they don't belong and a lot of telling people what to do."

"But they're paying, Dex. Whoever 'they' are, aren't they paying?"

Dex nodded. Then he sighed. "Sure," he said finally, opening up his top desk drawer and pulling out a neat pile of green bills that I took to be his retainer. "They're paying. Doesn't mean I have to like what they're buyin' though." He sounded so morose that I laughed.

"Aw, Dex. Cheer up. Getting paid is good. And don't worry about it: if not you, they'd just hire some other bird. So you'll follow the guy around for however long, you'll report what you see and we'll both get to buy some groceries. What's the trouble with that?"

Dex shrugged and grinned. "I know you're right, Kitty. I shouldn't grouse. There are worse things, right?"

"Sure, Dex. Lots worse. Like not payin' your devoted secretary."

Dex gave me the ghost of a smile. His mind was clearly on other things. "I start tonight. Dean told me Wyndham is going to be at a party at the Ambassador Hotel."

"At the Cocoanut Grove?" I asked. The Cocoanut Grove was the hottest spot in the city. But Dex shook his head.

"Naw, it's in one of the bungalows. Sounds swank."

"Swank? Why they gonna let you in then?"

"Dean gave me the name and number of a girl. A contract player at MGM. I'm to pick her up on my way over. She's got the invite: I'll be her date."

I liked this setup. "Cloak and dagger."

"Yeah, well," Dex still looked glum. "I still don't like the way it smells."

"Oh, poor Dex. Forced against his will to go to a swank party with a starlet on his arm. You'd best not tell Mustard. He'd feel so sorry for you, he wouldn't know what to say."

"Enough with all the noise, Kitty." Dex was grinning, but I could see there was strain behind the smile. "If I wanted grief, I'd call up my pop and talk about the Dodgers and the Yankees. And call Mustard and get me a boiler, will ya? If I'm gonna have a date, I'll need wheels."

CHAPTER THREE

I WAS BORN in the house where I live, the house my father built for my mother when they were first wed. They weren't married long, though: my mother left the world just as I entered it. My father never recovered from her loss, though he hung about for a couple of decades longer. When he took his own life after the crash of '29, it came to light some time before he'd transferred the title of the house to Marcus and Marjorie Oleg. The couple had been with my family since before my birth, Marcus as driver and valet to my father when required, while Marjorie managed the house.

When father died, creditors scrambled for every speck of value in his estate, but thanks to my father's foresight, the house was beyond their reach. After the dust settled and my father was buried and the vultures had carried off what they could of his estate, Marcus and Marjorie left things pretty much as they had been. They didn't move out of their accommodations above the garage and they insisted I keep the suite of rooms that had been mine since childhood. However they had opened the fine old mansion to boarders. I sometimes wondered what my father would have thought of the house he built for his beloved wife turned into a rooming house. But I never wondered long. Between most of my small salary and the money that the boarders brought in, it was possible for the three of us to live. There was no money for luxuries, but we were comfortable enough. It was not a bad arrangement.

Marjorie served breakfast for her boarders in the dining room at eight thirty every morning, on the dot. I liked to be at the office by nine, so I often joined Marjorie in the kitchen before eight, having a bit of whatever was available while helping her prepare breakfast for the household. Since Marjorie was the closest thing I'd had to a mother my whole life, this part of our new arrangement was easy for both of us to get used to. After all, I'd spent much of my early childhood playing at her feet in the kitchen while she busied herself with whatever needed doing. Having me on hand behind the scenes now was just an extension of a pattern that was pleasantly familiar to us both.

"Eggs and potatoes this morning," I said as I entered the kitchen. Sun was streaming in through the window over the sink, hitting the pile of potatoes she'd washed carefully and laid out on the draining board. The basket of eggs on the sideboard was my other clue. Eggs and potatoes and sunshine. It sounded like a wonderful combination. "Lovely," was what I said.

"I wish I had a bit of bacon to go with," Marjorie sniffed.

"Never mind," I said, picking up a potato and peeling it, then putting it aside for Marjorie to chop into the tight triangles she favored for her delicious home fries. She brought me a cup of strong tea and I kept it at my elbow while I worked. Marjorie, meanwhile, began manhandling the toaster over the stove's front burner for my morning toast. The odor of carefully burnt bread soon filled the air along with her discontent.

"I'll wager you've got some bacon fat saved," I said in an effort to placate her. "Fry the potatoes in that, and give everyone a few extra wedges and no one will complain, I'm sure."

"I know you're right, Miss Katherine. And none of the gentlemen will go away hungry, but it would be nice, don't you think? It's one of the things I miss the most: meat at every breakfast. Imagine!"

It was getting harder to imagine, Marjorie was right about that. But it wasn't meat with breakfast I missed. Perhaps it wasn't what she missed either. What both of us felt the lack of was the ability to have that meat if we wanted it. Some months we had trouble paying the electric bill and getting enough groceries into the house to keep the boarders from knowing how strapped we were. Some months it was all we could do to keep going, and never mind where the next bit of meat was coming from, we were lucky to have a roof. There were an increasing number of people in Los Angeles—in the whole country, for that matter—who did not.

As was our habit, while we worked, we chatted about all sorts of things. I could not tell you what the earliest part of our conversation was made of. The marriage of one friend, perhaps. The death of another. We might have talked about the weather—it had been unseasonably cold—or perhaps the Olympics that were going to be held in Los Angeles the following year. I don't recall, precisely, because the conversation of one day blends into the chatter of the next. But then Marjorie said something that stopped my potato peeling hand in mid-stroke.

"Did you hear the news this morning Miss Katherine?"

"How would I have heard?" I said without missing a stroke in my peeling. "You know I don't have a radio in my room."

"So you didn't hear about Laird Wyndham?"

It was as though a cloud drifted over my head, right there in the kitchen. Drifted over and settled right in. Though I would have had a difficult time explaining it, her words filled me with dread.

"What about him?" I managed to keep my voice neutral.

"Why he's in jail, Miss Katherine."

"In jail?" I thought I might have misunderstood, though Marjorie tends to make herself very clear.

"That's right. He killed someone. Last night. At a party at the Ambassador Hotel."

CHAPTER FOUR

MY FIRST THOUGHT was a silly one. I thought of Dex. Perhaps dead at the hands of the man he'd been hired to watch. I dressed for the office in a hurry, toast and potato and meat dilemmas forgotten, unable to shake a feeling of impending doom.

At Angels Flight I was in for my first disappointment of the day. Though I usually took the funicular railroad to work—it cost a nickel to ride up Bunker Hill, but was always free going downtown—today I'd have to hoof it: one of the little cars had derailed near the bottom. It didn't look like a mad panic, perhaps it hadn't fallen very far, but there was a sign across the turnstile: ANGELS FLIGHT WILL BE CLOSED UNTIL FURTHER NOTICE. I felt another sigh slide out as I began to trudge down the first of the 200 stairs. It would be worse going home if they didn't get it working soon.

Though I didn't think I'd need it, habit made me stop for Dex's ice at a diner on my way to the office. Our building was on Spring near Fourth Street, a twelve-story Beaux Arts building that had for many years been the tallest skyscraper in the city, though it wasn't anymore. Dex had told me that when the building was new at the turn of the century, it had been a technological marvel, the most absolutely fireproof building at a time when fire was very much on everyone's minds. Ridiculously, my favorite bit of technology were the mail chutes on every floor. All you had to do to mail a letter was go out into the hall and place your stamped envelope in a glass-fronted chute, then watch it drop beyond sight. I didn't know where the letters went from there, only that they ended up being delivered as indicated, which is all a girl needs to know, really. But there was something almost sinfully modern about the whole arrangement. Modern magic.

From the outside, the building still had a graceful if tired beauty. Inside the ornamented front doors, however, once gracious and spacious offices had been renovated to accommodate warrens of smaller places of business. Dex's P.I. office shared the fifth floor with a slightly seedy accountancy firm, a dental surgeon with the ironic name of Payne, and a company whose door announced them to be "investment specialists" and whom I figured for their spats, the sheen on their coats, and the rough looking traffic that came and went to be the type of operation you don't ask a lot of questions about.

The only door I looked forward to walking past on my way to the mail chute or the elevator belonged to an importer named Hartounian. I didn't know anything about the man, nor did I have the least idea in what part of the world he plied his trade, but the scents and sometimes even the sounds that wafted through his office door seldom failed to put me in mind of lands so exotic I could scarcely imagine them. When he saw me, he always raised a single eyebrow in a pleasant smile.

At the end of the hall—the farthest from the elevator but at the front of the building, with an eagle's view of Spring Street— Dex did his business.

On this morning, however, when I crossed the threshold I knew right away that today's business would be dodgy at best. From the hall, everything looked normal: the gleaming wood door; the pebbled glass window with DEXTER J. THEROUX, PRIVATE INVESTIGATOR carefully lettered on it in gold and black; the brass knob I shined in idle moments.

Opening the door, however, told another story. The wave of odors were unmistakable. Even in the outer office smoke seemed to drip from the ceiling in hazy, undulating waves. It was almost as strong as the smell of the booze that rose over it.

I'm nothing like a connoisseur, but it didn't take an expert to recognize the reek of bootleg whiskey from twenty paces. A lot of bootleg whiskey. And not the good stuff.

Dex's office door was open—things in the outer office wouldn't have smelled quite so bad if it were not—but I moved forward hesitantly, afraid of what I'd find.

When I entered his office, Dex lifted his head from the desk and regarded me without recognition. His eyes were rimmed in red and shot through with blood; a roadmap to hell.

"Oh Dex," I said, putting the bag of ice on his desk. For a second, I thought he might say something in return. His mouth even opened, but all that came out was a kind of incoherent grumble that sounded something like "Grrk."

I felt a fleeting sadness for something lovely that I'd only seen for a moment on the day before. Things had been different then, that's what he'd said at the time. I could see that they were different again now.

I didn't need to spend a lot of time trying to squeeze some sense out of him to know that Dex was currently past sensibility. Most likely, he just needed time to sleep it off. Failing that, I figured I'd do what I could to clean him up and maybe get some coffee into him.

In the outer office, I put away my handbag and light coat and addressed myself to making coffee. When I'd measured out the amount of ground coffee usually appropriate to making a pot, I paused before putting the tin away, then tipped in another tablespoon for good measure. Dex was going to need all the help he could get.

While the percolator busied itself, I sat at my desk and collected myself. The sound of coffee percolating cheered me slightly. It always does, along with the smell of fresh coffee that began to rise through the office, chasing away a bit of the reek of tavern that greeted me when I opened the door.

I used the ice I'd brought to fashion a crude pack for Dex's head and brought it in to him with his first cup of joe. The coffee was strong and black with a couple of spoons of sugar. I knew he preferred a splash of cream in his coffee—sweet and blonde was what he'd say—but I didn't have any cream and, in any case, on this day, I figured he'd be best served with all the straight coffee goodness I could siphon into him.

While Dex sipped toward a more sober state, I busied myself with the office. I didn't want to spend the next eight hours soaking up the reek of smokes and booze.

I opened the windows in Dex's office wide, smiling to myself only slightly when he cringed on being hit by fresh air and morning sunshine. Next I carried his overflowing ashtray and lowball glass to the ladies' room where I scrubbed both in the sink, probably quite beyond the scrubbing point required. While they dried, I grabbed the bottle of diluted ammonia and rag I kept on hand for cleaning and wiped down every surface in the place: the desks and the phones and even the walls where I could reach, pausing only to replenish Dex's coffee when the level dropped low enough to warrant a warm-up.

It took a long time but, with Dex in his present condition, I had the time available. When I was done, the office smelled of little beyond clean and Dex was watching me with something between amusement and nausea. Either was a definite improvement over how he'd looked first thing in the morning.

"You feeling any better?" I asked, dropping into one of the chairs across from his desk.

He took a while to answer. From the look on his face, he wasn't considering his response as much as checking to make sure he still had a voice. When it came, it was gravel packed with phlegm. I tried not to shudder and I stopped myself from telling him to clear his throat. I wasn't his mom, after all.

"Better than what?"

"Better than you did when I found you."

He shrugged, kicked back in his chair so far I feared it

would fall over. "Sure. If 'better' means that the riveters in my head are on a break," he said to the ceiling.

I was pleased to see that he seemed at least coherent. Sober was ahead in the distance, but he wasn't completely drunk.

"Geez, Dex. High steel philosophy? It's not even ten-thirty."

He looked at me quizzically. "I don't get it: high steel . . . oh wait. The riveters. Like high steel workers. But it wasn't philosophy. Just stating a fact."

He pulled a cigarette from its pack and lit up, sending a plume of smoke following his glance to the ceiling. I sighed, thinking of all the good cleaning work he was undoing.

When he opened the top left drawer of his desk and pulled out a clean glass and a bottle of bourbon, I was beyond sighing. He took the icepack off his head, unwrapped the bundle of cloth and carefully plopped two of the melting cubes into his glass. He wrapped the remaining ice up again and pushed it back onto his head. I decided there was nothing I could do but wash my hands of him. I headed back to my own area to get his ashtray. If he was going to indulge in all his vices he might as well be tidy.

Once I was seated across from him again, I waited. It was a long three minutes. He didn't even meet my eyes. He mostly just sat there, letting go of the occasional sigh and rearranging the icepack on his head.

"Are you gonna tell me what happened?" I said finally.

"Whadjamean?"

"Well . . . this," I said, indicating all of it with a sweep of my arm: the booze in the glass, the cigarette smoldering in the ashtray and, most of all, the completeness of the sad sack that was Dex on this fine morning. Bleary-eyed, ill-advised hair of the dog and all.

Dex moved the ice on his head around some more and shrugged, so I went on.

"And Laird Wyndham is in jail."

Another shrug.

"And you were there, Dex. Last night. And now something is wrong." He didn't say anything so I pressed on. "You're going to have to tell me eventually, Dex. It might as well be now."

Dex plopped the icepack onto his desk and ran his hands deeply through his hair. So deeply I figured it was a good thing he was about twenty-four hours from the Brilliantine he usually pushed through it or his hands would have been slick with the stuff. He scratched absently at his jaw, and I could hear the stubble there as well as see it: a ten-in-the-morning shadow? It didn't look good on him. He watched me closely for a moment, like he might say something, make some accusation, then thought better of it. Then he sighed. Came to some decision. Took another sip. Plunged in.

"I went out to Santa Monica last night, like I was supposed to. I had instructions to stop by a gin mill on Montana to meet up with the actress broad who was going to be my ticket into the party."

I nodded. "The party at the Ambassador. You were supposed to pick up the starlet beforehand," I supplied.

"Right, right. Only she wasn't any starlet. She'd ridden the earth around the sun a few times too many to be called that."

"What did she look like?"

"Who?"

"The starlet. I'm trying to build a mental picture. Was she someone I'd know from the pictures? Was she beautiful? What was her name?"

Dex hesitated for a moment like he was going to tell me what to do with all my questions. Then he just sighed again and I could almost see him giving in. "Her name was Rhoda Darrow. I don't know if you'd recognize her. I didn't. Which doesn't mean anything, I know: you go to the pictures more than I do. And beautiful? What's that? I wouldn't have said she was beautiful. Another man?" He shrugged. "Maybe so. I'll say this: I've never seen anyone as pale as she was."

"Pale?"

"Yuh. She had on this gold kinda necklace affair? And I noticed it 'cause it was real warm against her skin. It made her look like she was glowing." He hesitated for a moment. "Oh: and she was freakishly thin."

"Freakishly?"

"Yuh. But I figured maybe it's a movie thing, you know? 'Cause they say the camera adds ten pounds."

I nodded my head, understanding his reasoning. "Right. So if you start with someone very thin . . ."

"Anyway, we didn't talk much in the car. At first, we start off and I ask her how she knows Dean and she just looks at me with these big, cold eyes like I'm something from under her feet, and I shut up, 'cause, you know. Who cares? What's she to me? When we get to the party I forget about her for a while because I'm supposed to keep my eye on Wyndham, right? Like I told you yesterday, that's what they wanted me to do. And at first it's easy enough, because there's not a lot of people there, and Wyndham just seems sort of mopey."

"Mopey?" I had a hard time figuring Wyndham for a mope.

"Yeah. And I couldn't figure it, but that was all right. What do I care if he turns out to be a mope? This big party is lining up and everyone is feeling hilarious. I figure my night is going to be eggs in the coffee, you know? Watch Wyndham, watch a bunch of dollies who aren't so hard on the eyes, put down a few drinks, scuff the rugs, then make my report the next day. It was a party, but nothing was doing, all right?"

I nodded. Sure. That made sense. "Where was your date?"

"Rhoda? She was off somewheres. And it didn't seem like we had a lot in common anyway. I figured, you know, Dean had fixed it that we go together. So she knew what that was about.

It wasn't like we needed to stay together like we were joined at the hip or anything. Which I figured was good, because she wasn't much in the hips department." He paused and smirked at this, as though he were pleased with his own joke. I motioned for him to continue.

Dex told me he'd figured that the job was going to be such a walk-through that he'd started surreptitiously taking notes, just so he'd have something to report to the client: what had Wyndham drunk and when? Whom had he chatted with? Just minor stuff, so his report wouldn't be empty. Also, since he didn't actually know what he was looking for, it seemed a good idea to watch everything.

I resisted the urge to ask Dex for details about Wyndham. What had he looked like when he was standing *right there?* What had he smelled like? How had it felt to be in his presence? Was it different than being around other men? I held my tongue, trying not to imagine the look Dex would have given me if I'd asked these things.

"An hour goes by," Dex continued, "maybe a couple. And I notice Rhoda with this other woman."

He told me he noticed the woman because she looked like rough trade. The fact that she was speaking earnestly with Rhoda Darrow was interesting, but not remarkable. In any case, the party was crowded by that time and he lost sight of them after a while, something he wasn't concerned about. Not then, anyway. After all, he was there to watch Wyndham and one working girl in the mix wasn't anything to be concerned about. Not in that particular crowd. Dex told me that the balance of the guest list seemed just as mixed, so there was a lot to keep his eyes on. He recognized some of the faces from the moving pictures and he figured that he'd maybe seen others in the papers and so on: politicians and men about town.

There were things about that party Dex did not tell me that day in the office. I'm sure of it. Things he would never tell me.

They weren't the kind of things we talked about, Dex and me. In a way, he treated me like a little sister; like someone sort of delicate. I wasn't, of course. I never was. But it didn't matter: that's how he saw me. That was the nature of the place where we fit together.

What that meant, in the end, was that there were times I had to read between the lines. I was lucky, though. Dex wasn't the best poker player. At least he wouldn't have been with me. I saw him every day, probably spent more time with him than anyone else. I knew his tells. That helped with the deciphering. Helped me understand the things he didn't say.

For instance, Dex told me about the music in the bungalow— loud, loud, loud—and the clothes some of the women wore— louder still. Naturally there was booze. It flowed like a rising tide. But there were jujus, too and at times the smell of it permeated the air.

"Is Laird Wyndham a hophead?" I asked when Dex reported this last. I imagine my eyes were wide with the question.

Dex shook his head. "I don't think so. Least, I never saw him with a tea stick." But there had been others, Dex told me. And there'd been plenty of dope at the party. "And not just the kind you smoke."

So I have a mental picture of what this party looked like. I'm not sure it's exactly right, but between what Dex told me and the stuff we heard later on, I've got a pretty good idea it wasn't far off.

My mind paints a portrait of debauchery; scenes from a bacchanalia and everything but the togas are in place. Beautiful girls running about half-clad; men leering so acutely they've got their hands full just keeping the spittle from their chins. The air is thick with the scent of hibiscus and day lilies, cigarette smoke and bootleg whiskey. Rich and glorious food glistens from tables. It spills from heavily laden plates onto thick linen tablecloths. Food enough for a hundred hungry families, but no one is really doing anything but skewering the occasional oyster, or pushing a silver spoonful of caviar onto a cracker on their way to the bar. Ashtrays are overflowing and as much drink is spilled as manages to find its way inside the revelers.

Where is Dex in all this? Sometimes my mind places him in a position of watchfulness in a corner, his hat low over his eyes, a drink in one hand, a cigarette in the other, gun out of sight in its holster.

Sometimes I paint him right in the thick of things. There's a round-bottomed girl on his lap and his head is thrown back in what could be taken as either mirth or ecstasy.

When I consider it all dispassionately, it's possible that the truth lies somewhere in between. OK: probably not the lap girl, but the joy in the debauchery. One thing I know about Dex: he can get dirty with the best of them. On the other hand, he knows what he's supposed to look like when he's on a case.

Laird Wyndham, Dex reported, was never part of this bacchanal scene. He was present for most of it, certainly, but he seemed preoccupied. At least, that was Dex's impression, because he said that, when he saw Wyndham, the actor was never joining in, just hanging around the sidelines, sometimes with the telephone receiver pressed to his ear, other times looking wide-eyed and morose.

"Sometimes," Dex told me, "he'd lift his head and seem to look around as though he wasn't quite sure where he was."

"Like he was lost?" I asked.

Dex considered before he answered. "More like he didn't know why he was there." Wyndham did not, in any case, take part in the things that were going on all around them.

The front doors of the bungalow were thrown open, and the party spilled over onto the hotel grounds, but the bungalow's two bedroom doors stayed closed, at least when Dex was looking. Dex said he noticed because with both the front and back doors wide open, the closed doors inside seemed out of place. He tried to keep an eye on them, but was unable to detect any traffic into the bedrooms in his time in the bungalow other than once, late in the evening.

Dex said he saw Rhoda appear at Wyndham's elbow while he was on the phone.

The woman indicated one of the doors to Wyndham, then faded into the crowd. Dex watched while Wyndham scratched his head, as though wondering what to do. Then he scanned the room. He and Dex touched eyes for a moment, but the actor's eyes kept moving.

Finally he sighed and headed to the back of the bungalow, closing the door behind him once he'd passed through.

It was while Wyndham was in the bedroom that Dex's date approached for a chat. He found it odd, even in the moment. Odd because she'd been ignoring him all evening and suddenly she was like a skinny cat coming to get her ears scratched, was the way Dex put it. He said it put his back up right away.

"Can I buy you a drink?" Dex said as affably as he could.

"Don't need you to buy me a drink." When she spoke, Dex remembered the used sound of her voice. He suspected the harsh caress of ten thousand cigarettes. "The drinks is free, and they're right over there." She used the filtered king-size in her hand as a pointer.

"Still," he said, moving toward the bar. "What's your pleasure?"

"Scotch soft," she said, not arguing. Dex is a bit of a looker himself, and not afraid to know it. There aren't a lot of women, no matter what age, who wouldn't like to sit across a bar from him.

"So Rhoda, you having fun tonight?" Dex said, willing to make conversation.

"It's all right," Rhoda said, looking up at him over the rim of her glass. Dex said he felt like a bug under a microscope, the way she looked at him. He said he could feel something inside himself squirm.

He chatted with her for a while. He didn't have anything else to do and he stood there, drink in hand, and felt her gently nudging him around until he was facing in the other direction. He was aware of it because he'd positioned himself in such a way that he had the front door in sight at all times. A habit with him. He liked to see who was coming and going. And now he did not. Now he faced the rear of the bungalow and he could see the two closed doors. The operation was so subtle that Dex felt another man might not have noticed these machinations at all. But he *is* a detective. And he was on a job.

These are the things he told me and, of course, by the time he did, he had reason to figure he'd been right. I believed him, too. It's been my experience that men who spent time in the trenches and came back to tell about it have a way of seeing things that others can't. Maybe that's how these few survived.

Dex couldn't remember the things Rhoda said, only that none of the words were important. What *was* important: the way her eyes pushed toward one of the closed bedroom doors every so often. The way she seemed aware of her surroundings: like that skinny stray cat. She didn't look around, but Dex had the feeling that she was aware of everything that was going on.

After a while—and it couldn't have been very long, perhaps only a few minutes after he'd gone in—Wyndham came out of the room looking as though he needed a shower. He did not, Dex told me carefully, appear disheveled or in any way frightened or excited. He went back to the bar, then back to the phone, and Dex thought no more about the incident. Until later.

Dex had a sense that, once Wyndham had rejoined the party, his date was finished with him. She stayed and chatted a bit longer but after a while, over Dex's weak protestations that he'd get it, she made as though to get herself another drink, then faded back into the party. Dex watched her go without regret.

He went back to observing. Dex enjoys watching people and this was a good place for it. There was a wide spectrum of people in attendance. To Dex, they seemed to represent all walks, from men in sober business suits to women in next to nothing at all. It seemed to him that, throughout the evening, he'd caught glimpses of studio heads, actors, agents and others from all branches of the entertainment industry and perhaps even representatives from local government, but it was hard to be sure about a thing like that. Men like that don't wear signs.

As far as Dex could see, there was a single thing that connected the group: almost to a one, they wore their entitlement and privilege like a badge. They were beautiful and affluent and careless and well fed. In the confines of these rooms it was possible to believe in a world where the county borders were not patrolled by Los Angeles policemen to keep transients out. It was possible not to think about soup lines and the crowds of men waiting for handfuls of jobs at construction sites every morning. It was possible, but Dex didn't make that choice. He maintained his position, kept his eye on Laird Wyndham—now back on the phone—wrapped his hand around his bourbon and did a slow burn.

Later Dex would figure perhaps another half hour passed before a scream broke over the din of the party. The band stopped on a gasp and the silence that filled the wake of the music seemed louder than the dance tune they'd been playing.

"Oh my God," a woman's shrill lament. "Oh my loving God, someone help me."

Without even thinking about it, Dex unsnapped his holster, making sure he could get his gun clear in a hurry. At the same time, he moved toward the source of the sound: a bedroom at the back of the bungalow.

The door was open now, light spilling onto the carpet in the hall like a puddle of blood. People seemed to be moving both in and out of the room. Fear was a rising tide. Dex could smell it, could even taste a bit of it himself.

The cause of that tide was apparent even from the doorway. Dex did not recognize the girl on the bed in that first fast look, but he saw all he needed to make his decision.

He was not at first certain she was dead, but it was clear that she was damaged. Her head was on a pillow, but at an unnatural angle. And she was absolutely still.

Rhoda Darrow pushed her way through the gawping throng and into the room and took command. She picked up the girl's wrist, took her pulse, shook her head.

"She's gone," Rhoda said. There was sadness in her voice; concern. But Dex thought he tasted artifice; saccharine on the tongue.

And then, "Where is Laird Wyndham?" It was Rhoda who said the words, but Dex heard them repeated through the bungalow, like a stereophonic echo from all corners. In seconds it was apparent that he wasn't there.

"What did you do then?" I asked, wide-eyed.

"I left," he said, inspecting the end of his index finger.

"You left?"

"Sure. There was nothing I could do, Kitty. The girl had checked out. Anyway, I figured I'd been hired to keep my eye on Wyndham and once I realized he'd vamoosed, I figured I was duty bound to follow him."

I could see the sense in that. "So where did he go?"

Dex looked sheepish. "I don't know."

"C'mon, Dex. You're no palooka. How could you have lost him?"

"By the time I figured he'd left the party and went after him, he had disappeared without a trace."

I rolled my eyes at the bit of drama, but prepared to move on. "So you went back to the party?"

Dex shook his head. "Naw. I checked the hotel grounds pretty good: from the parking lot to the pool, all the bars, the lobby. No sign of Wyndham and no one had seen him. By then I was getting a bad feeling about the whole business and, since the guy I was tailing had up and disappeared, I figured I'd just get the hell out of there. Sort it all out with the client in the morning."

"Except, of course, by morning, Wyndham had been arrested."

Dex ran his hands through his hair again. But all he said was, "Right."

"OK, Dex: I don't understand. I mean, look at you," I pointed at him with my thumb and he knew I meant the whole package: he had apparently decided to drink himself stupid at his office rather than someplace else. And though yesterday he'd been sunny and sober, today it was like he couldn't get the alcohol into himself fast enough.

"I don' know Kitty . . . it's just that . . ."—he hesitated, as though grappling with the words—"like I said, the whole business was kinda fishy from the get-go, wouldn't you say?"

"I don't know if I *would* say that."

"And the whole thing just leaves a bad taste in my mouth."

"Worse than that furniture polish you call bourbon?"

"Much worse. And it would take more than a pint of Jack to wash this away."

"Judging by the state of you, it looks like you'd be willing to see how much it *would* take."

Dex went all quiet again for a while. I could see him working things out in his head. I felt a little sorry for him. I do when he's like that; when the drink is close on him but not quite there. He can still see the shape of things then, still see how things are. But the checks and balances are injured. He can put the pieces together, but they don't always add up.

"Well, time to face the music, I guess," he said finally. "Get Xander Dean on the phone for me, will you?"

Back at my desk, I dialed the number the big man had left the day before. I let it ring a dozen or more times before I decided to try later. Determined to let Dex ripen in whatever juices he was brewing, I busied myself with various housekeeping chores in the outer office. At three that afternoon I went out for the late edition of the newspaper from the vendor who always sold his papers just a few steps from the front door of our building.

STARLET SLAIN, the headline of the *Los Angeles Courier* blared, and then, beneath it in slightly smaller letters: LAIRD WYNDHAM'S LATEST ROLE: MURDERER?

"Sad business, huh Miss Pangborn?" the elevator operator shook his head when he noticed the paper in my hand. "I just saw him in *Lake Country Cowboy* a month or so ago. I would never have suspected anything. He seemed like such a nice guy." I just looked at the young man, but didn't say anything. What was there to say?

Back at the office I brought the paper straight in to Dex. "Is this her?" I said pointing to a studio photograph of a young woman on the cover of the *Courier*. The paper said her name was Fleur MacKenzie. She looked breathtaking. And now she was dead.

"Yeah, that's her all right," Dex said, taking the paper. "But you wouldn't have known it if she was standing here next to this photo when she was alive. I'm guessin' this was taken a few years ago."

I took the paper from Dex and, uninvited, plopped myself back in the chair opposite his desk. He didn't stop me. We both knew he wasn't in reading condition and he trusted me to hit the highlights.

As I settled in I realized that there were lots of highlights here Dex probably wouldn't even want to hear about—not just now, anyway. In his current state he was likely to rush out and hurt something. He's a man who loves many things, and not all of them stuff you and I would agree with. But, at heart, he's a man who loves the truth.

From the first, I suspected I'd find no truth in the *Los Angeles Courier*. Even so, my heart sank as I read. I'd been completely in the thrall of Laird Wyndham, motion picture star. Over the years I'd spent so many hours with him in darkened theaters. I'd seen him ride into a sunset on the back of a noble steed, the virtue of the girl he loved intact due his own diligence. I'd seen him conquer corporate iniquity and overcome human greed and outdistance human hatred. I'd seen him die, gloriously and with honor. In over a dozen films I'd seen him spit in the face of all that is dark in the human heart and stand up for all that is good and gallant. I loved him for it. I loved him for what he'd helped me to believe.

And I wasn't alone, hadn't thought I was alone. So many others—millions of others—loved him for that golden light he helped shine on humanity. I would never have thought it could be different.

Yet here I was, curled into the big chair in Dex's office, not even at first aware of the tears that rolled down my cheeks as I read.

"It's like it's not about him at all," I said at length.

"How so?" Dex asked. I tried not to notice when he poured another couple of fingers of bourbon into his glass. The hard liquor slid over the ice and glinted with a mean promise.

"The man in this article," I said slowly, considering my words, "the man they describe here. He's a monster."

Dex didn't answer right away, just heaved a big sigh and took a hit of bourbon, like he was hoping the drink would add clarity. I'm guessing it did not. Finally he grunted. I took that to mean he wanted me to explain myself.

"It's just the way they talk about him. Here," I said, "listen to this: 'When the news vaults are considered, very little is known about Laird Wyndham, beyond the most basic of studio-provided information.' See? What does that mean, Dex? They've been writing about him constantly for as long as I've been old enough to read a newspaper. And now—suddenly—they don't know anything about him. I don't understand."

"Maybe they're trying to distance themselves from all the nice things they said in the past."

"I get it," I said grumpily. "Now that the chips are down, they're not sure which way they're going to land."

Dex cracked a smile. "Listen, Kitty: you're the one who went to the big fancy school up in Frisco, not me. But I'm pretty sure you've mixed up those metaphors pretty good."

"Well, you know what I mean, Dex. Anyway, it says here the MacKenzie girl was a starlet," I said, getting back to it. "And lookit: they even used the word 'dewy.' I don't think I've ever seen that word in a sentence before."

Dex snorted. "Well, it don't fit the girl I saw, that's for sure. It might have once. It didn't anymore. Last night she didn't look dewy so much as soaked. Leastwise," he added, "when she was alive, I mean."

" 'Dewy,' " I tried it out on my tongue. "It wouldn't fit a lot of people, I'm guessing. Wouldn't fit you, Dex," I laughed.

"I was dewy once," Dex said. "Woke up one morning on someone's lawn." He looked at me closely. Squinted. "Guess it would kinda fit you, though."

"Huh," I said, lobbing the sports section at his head before I settled back into my reading. He caught it deftly, nodded thanks and bent to it. I was glad to see his hand-eye coordination had recovered. Despite the fact that he was drinking again. Or maybe because of it.

The rest of the article about the MacKenzie girl was more of the same. I moved on not knowing much more about Fleur MacKenzie than I had going in. Obviously the reporter hadn't either, but had just shuffled the information available into various patterns in an effort to fill out his allotted space.

I moved on to a piece about Wyndham's background, and here things got a bit more interesting. From the looks of things, the reporter had been so busy digging up dirt on the actor he hadn't bothered spending much time on the girl. Perhaps that would come tomorrow. Meanwhile there was enough material on Laird Wyndham to keep Hollywood tongues wagging for the next two weeks.

For starters, I read, he hadn't been born Laird Wyndham. "Oh dear." I read: " 'Charles Richard Dickey.' "

"What's that?" Dex said, looking up.

"Wyndham's real name: Charles Richard Dickey."

"Chuck Dick Dickey?" Dex smirked. "That ain't good. Sounds like a clown throwing up."

"And he's not from Boston," I went on.

"Sure he is," Dex said. "Old Boston family. Tea parties and stuff. I remember reading that much myself."

I shook my head. "Uh-uh. Orchard Street. Lower East Side. Manhattan."

"Means nothin' to me," Dex said.

"Me neither. But the way they're saying it here," I tapped the paper in my lap, "not good."

"Well, I don't care. And I figure you don't care, am I right?"

I nodded agreement. "I don't care. And if changing your name meant you were a murderer, why . . . everyone in Hollywood would be in the hoosegow."

"It's true. Lotta people in that business change perfectly good names. Let alone Chuck Dick Dickey. Naw, he's no murderer. In fact, I'd put money on it. I was there. I know what I saw. And you can roll a baby in baking flour, but that don't make him a polar bear."

I hesitated, derailed for the moment by the vision of a flour-dipped baby. "Well," I reminded him hesitatingly, "there was maybe a lot you didn't see. You said the bedroom door was closed."

"Still, I saw a lot of Wyndham through the evening. And he didn't look like he was fixing to snuff out anyone's lights."

"So what do we do?" I asked.

"What makes you think we have to do anything?"

I shrugged. "Dunno, really. It just seems like you know more than most of the people that were there. And you're a professional. You know what to look for."

Dex smiled. "You're a sweet kid, Kitty. I like having you around. I don't tell you that enough. You brighten the place up. But, in this thing? I just don't know that there's anything that can be done. Least of all by us."

I squirmed a bit under the unexpected compliment. "Thanks," I sort of stammered. But I could tell Dex wasn't listening. He seemed to have gone away somewhere quiet where he could think deeply. I read while he pondered. Finally, he spoke again. "You know, this thing with the papers. It's all a bit too pat."

I had no idea what he was talking about. I said so. "I have no idea what you're talking about," is what I said.

"Well, how is it that the newspapers loved Wyndham yesterday. And they loved him all this time. Then, suddenly, he's got horns and a tail?"

"He's accused of a pretty horrible thing, Dex."

"Still. That ain't enough. The studios care for their own, Kitty. There's lots of things we don't read about in the papers. Things that'd curl your hair. The studios fix it. They hush things up. Happens all the time."

I was skeptical. "How do you know that?"

"Hell: lookit what I do for a living. And I talk to other P.I.s. It's even a job I've had on occasion: making things go away."

"So what are you saying?"

He stroked what would become a full beard if he didn't see

to it soon. "What am I saying? Good question. I'm not sure yet. I'll have to give it some more thought. Meanwhile, do you think it's possible Wyndham got on the wrong side of someone?"

I was aware of looking at Dex carefully. Of cocking my head to one side like a dog listening. Something must have resonated. "What do you mean?" was what I said.

He pulled the newspaper toward him, read the lurid headline, slapped it back down on the desk. "Well, lookit, Kitty: they're calling him a murderer. No pussfootin' around."

"So you're saying . . . what? That someone at the paper has it out for him?" There must have been a skeptical note in my voice.

"I'm just sayin' it's a possibility, is all."

"Anyway," I pointed out, aiming for a reasonable tone, "it was your job to follow him and you did that. With him in jail, I guess your job is done."

"What does it say in the paper about evidence?"

"What evidence?"

"That's what I mean. If the cops bundled him off to the can, they must have had some reason for thinking it was him."

I bent back to the paper for a bit. Scanned here and there through the stories about Wyndham. "No," I said after a while. "Nothing specific. I mean, the cops arrested him, right? You know they've got some kind of evidence. But they're not saying what it is here."

Dex looked thoughtful but didn't say anything. Everything that needed saying between us had been said.

"Guess I'll get back to work, Dex. Holler if you need anything?"

"Well you could try Xander Dean again," he said. "Other than that, I'm OK."

The second time I tried Dean's number brought the same response: a lot of ringing. I would maybe have tried again, just to make sure I hadn't misdialed, but I heard the sound of flat-foots snuffling toward the office and I replaced the receiver.

In fairness, there is probably no way I could have known it was flatfoots. But it seems to me I could hear a certain bold incompetence in those footsteps and a certain confidence combined with weakness of character. There weren't a lot of places you find such deep troughs of that combination outside Chief Roy E. Steckel's Los Angeles police force.

The cops didn't even hesitate to give me the time of day. I might not have been sitting there at all. They just barged right through and into Dex's office, without any by-your-leave. I followed hard on their heels, intending to apologize to Dex for letting them through, but it took me some time to sneak a word in even at the edge.

"O'Reilly," Dex said warmly. "Houlahan. Great to see you ladies. To what do I owe the pleasure?"

"I've got a feeling it wouldn't take you much to guess." The speaker was short and dangerously red in the face, like an encounter with too many stairs would put him in the hospital. Maybe keep him there forever. I wasn't sure if this was O'Reilly or Houlahan, I'd never taken the time to tell them apart, but on consideration, I figured it didn't much matter.

"Well, maybe yes and maybe no," Dex said affably. "Why'nt you boys come on in. Take a load off." He shifted his attention to me, standing in the doorway, not sure what to do or say. "It's OK, Kitty. I know they didn't ask your permission. You go on back and get that typing done."

I shot Dex a look he didn't see. I didn't have any typing to do and I was pretty sure Dex knew it. And I was unconvinced of Dex's need to impress the flatfoots with his busyness. Still, Dex had asked for typing so typing he would get. His was the name at the bottom of my pay checks, after all. His was the name edged in gold letters on the front door.

I scooped up the newspaper on my way out and told Dex to

holler if he wanted anything more from me. Then I left his office door open a crack. That way, I reasoned silently, I'd be able
to hear if he did indeed holler. I didn't dwell on the fact that it
also made it easier to hear what was going on in there.

The flatfoots didn't waste any time. I was still rolling paper
into the typewriter when they started up. "We heard you was
at a party last night, Theroux."

"Yeah, sure." Dex is good at seeming relaxed and comfortable around the law. It's one of his gifts. "What can I say? I like
a social gathering. Helps me hone my people skills. Maybe you
and the missus here should attend one once." I sucked in my
breath soundlessly. O'Reilly and Houlahan. We knew they
weren't the sharpest chips off the edge of a dull block. Still,
poking at them with a stick didn't seem such a good idea.

I was relieved when one of the cops picked up the conversation apparently unperturbed. Maybe he'd missed the insult. Or
maybe he was used to it.

"Party you was at? Someone got fogged."

"Yeah," said the other, "good and fogged."

"I heard," Dex said, still sounding comfortable. "It's in all
the papers."

I threw some typing into the mix here. Rapid-fire: rat-tat-tat.
I could hear them getting warmed up. I figured I may as well ful-
fill Dex's request before they got to the good stuff; and I did have
a feeling that good stuff was coming.

"People say they saw you there."

To my surprise, Dex laughed outright at this. I took the opportunity to fire another round of rapid typing into the breach.
"What's with the fishing expedition, boys?" he asked good-
naturedly. "Way I understand it, you've already landed the big
one. What the hell do you need me for?"

I was glad Dex had asked it. I'd been thinking the same
thing: Wyndham had been arrested. Why question Dex?

"You're lucky we got someone in custody, Theroux." It was

the same voice and it held an edge. I didn't much like it. "If we didn't, we'd sure as hell be looking at you more closely."

"Well, you're here, ain't you? Any closer and we'd be doin' the tango."

"Boys, boys, c'mon." I think this was O'Reilly. There was a placating note in his voice. "No need for any of that. Theroux's right, anyway, ain't he? This *is* a fishing expedition. 'Course it is."

"Yeah, well, I don't like the bait you're usin'." This was Dex.

"Well, you was there. We figured you was there for a reason."

Dex laughed. "Sure, there was girls there."

"That's not what we mean." Houlahan. I could imagine his intense face. Under the right circumstances—or the wrong ones—I knew it was a face that could scare me. "To be there, at that party with those people, we figured you had to have a special invite."

"What the hell does that mean?" Dex wanted to know. "A 'special' invite. This fishing is lost on me, boys. If you're figuring something, maybe you just oughta say it."

"Face it, Theroux," this was Houlahan again, "this ain't a crowd you run with. Too swell."

"I clean up pretty good," Dex said. "You should see me after I pull a comb through my hair and a razor across my face. Hell, even you apes could pass for human after a trip to the barber."

If either cop took offense at this I didn't hear it in their voices. Maybe they were too focused on their goal.

"Anyhow," Houlahan said, "what we're getting at is this: we figured you had to have been there for a client."

"Is that what you figured?" Dex said. I could imagine him eyeing both flatfoots as he said it. "Well you figured wrong. I mean, if I *did* have a client—and I ain't sayin' I did—but if I did, I sure as hell wouldn't tell the two of you about it. And I know I can say it all straight up and honest to you like that because you knew that before you ever walked in the door."

"OK, it ain't just that," Houlahan said.

"It never is."

"We also wanted to know what you seen while you was there."

"Say it plain, boys. What you really wanna know is did I see anything that will help you nail Wyndham. Am I right? Fact is, I didn't. I saw Wyndham on and off all night. Always alone. Sometimes with a phone pressed to his ear. But never with a girl. He looked . . . he looked like he maybe had a lot on his mind, but he didn't look crazy or anything else you might find helpful. I'd say he wasn't even drinking, or else he was drinking, but so little it won't be of use to you."

"He didn't look mad or anything? Like he was ready to snap?"

"Naw. Not even close." A pause, and then, "In fact, when I think of it, I'd say the opposite. He looked very far from snapping. More like maybe he was worried about a business deal or something. If you asked me, I'd tell you: I'd say it had nothing to do with a girl. But listen, while I got you here, the papers didn't say how the girl died."

"We're not at liberty to say."

"Ah, sure you are," Dex said. " 'Course you can. That way if I get information, I trade it right back to you, see? Otherwise, what's the point in me telling you anything at all?"

Did the two cops see how flawed Dex's logic was in this? I was guessing maybe not, because after a brief hesitation, O'Reilly replied. "Neck was broke," he said in a confidential tone.

"Broke neck," Dex commented, just to say something, I guessed, because the guys would be expecting it and because he wanted to bring them along.

"We ain't supposed to talk about that part," Houlahan reprimanded his partner mildly.

"Well that's that then," O'Reilly said. I could hear the end of the interview when a chair scraped back on the scuffed wood floor. Then another. "We won't take up any more of your time."

"Too bad I can't get the last ten minutes back," Dex said with a smile in his voice. "Maybe I'd do something useful with 'em, 'cause I sure as hell wouldn't want to spend them with you two again."

Whatever answer they might have made was lost in the smatter of rapid typing I sent into the air, hoping it would keep Dex's mind from the fact that I hadn't done much typing at all while he was in with the two cops.

"Call us if you think of anything, Theroux." The flatfoots were moving through my office area now, putting hats back on and puffing themselves back up with the importance they understood about themselves. "Anything at all that might help."

"Sure, sure I will," Dex said, escorting them out. "You two will be the first I call."

And when the door closed behind them, Dex added quietly, "when hell freezes over and Christ needs a crutch."

CHAPTER FIVE

ONCE THE COPS were gone, Dex slunk back to his office and closed the door with a nice solid thunk. Whatever life I'd managed to breathe into him with coffee and cleanup had puffed away like the angel's share on a glass of single malt. There was a grayness around his edges. Tinged with green. I figured only part of that had to do with all the firewater he'd put away.

I stayed at my desk and determined to fill what little was left of the work day with normal tasks. Clearly, there was no more typing to be done. Ditto filing. I tried Xander Dean again. No dice. I contented myself with sweeping the scuffed wooden floors, polishing the brass on the desk and the door and doing other chores that were clearly more housekeeping than secretarial. But it felt right somehow on this odd day. Anyway, it filled the time. I've never been a girl who could spend much time filing her nails and there simply wasn't any other type of filing to do.

An hour passed. Maybe a bit more. I hadn't heard even a peep from Dex. I was thinking about going in and checking on him when the front door opened and in walked Xander Dean with enough of a puff to his breath that I figured the elevator must be acting up again. Five flights of stairs will put anyone's wind back, especially someone who'd skipped as few meals as Dean obviously had.

The spiteful child who lives in each of us was sorely tempted to turn him down flat. To tell him Dex was out on a job and would he like to make an appointment? That was how it was supposed to work, after all. Not just show up like he figured Dex would just be sitting in his office with nothing really to do and never mind that this was pretty much the truth.

"I'm . . . I'm not certain, Mr. Dean," I said, and it was only half a lie. This wasn't a day when anyone was getting in to see Dex unannounced. "Please have a seat and I'll see if his schedule can accommodate you."

I didn't hang around to watch Dean shoehorn his bulk into our waiting area again. Instead I made a beeline for Dex's office, slipping through the door while opening it as little as possible, just as I had the day before.

I tried not to let Dex see the relief on my face when I found him sitting up at his desk. Though he had a drink in front of him and I knew for certain it was far from his first of the day, he looked coherent and relatively presentable.

"Xander Dean just showed up again, Dex. He's waiting to see you."

"Is he now?" Dex said, kicking back in his chair and lacing his hands behind his head. "Well, don't stand on ceremony, Kitty. Send him on in." It was impossible to read anything at all from his affable tone.

"I'm not standing on ceremony, Dex. I . . . oh, never mind," I said.

"Oh, and Kitty . . ." Dex said, just as I was about to leave his office.

"I know, I know . . . typing, right?"

"Thanks kid," Dex said, preparing to top up his drink as I headed out the door.

Dean was standing next to my desk, right where I'd left him. I guessed he hadn't wanted the challenge of trying to fit back into the waiting room chair.

"Mr. Theroux will see you now," I told him as I took my own seat. "You can go right on in."

"Thanks," Dean said, moving toward Dex's office. I was disappointed when he closed the door tightly behind him. I wouldn't be able to hear anything.

Oddly enough, not everyone *did* close the door. Most of

Dex's clients seemed to take me for part of the furniture and they'd talk away to him like I wasn't even there. That suited me fine as it meant I got to hear a lot of things with my own ears that I had no business hearing at all. Not today, though. I wouldn't be able to hear the conversation, but I knew that Dex would be able to hear typing—or lack thereof. I sighed deeply, took the piece of paper I'd been using when the flatfoots were there out of the typewriter, turned it over, rolled it back in, clean side up and started thinking about activities for quick brown foxes. And lazy brown dogs.

CHAPTER SIX

AFTER DEAN WAS gone, I waited until I'd heard his surprisingly light footsteps recede down the hall before I ventured into Dex's office. Things in there had gotten worse. Much worse. Worse than they had been for a while.

There was more grayness in Dex's face. I figured it was not entirely attributable to the booze. When I plunked myself back in my usual chair, Dex once again didn't even turn toward me from the window. That was always a bad sign. And I noted a fresh coating of booze in his glass. The smell of it was back hard in the room. Rye this time, I thought absently, not even questioning when I had acquired the connoisseurship necessary to make that determination by the vapors alone.

"What did he want?"

Dex didn't answer right away, but sighed deeply and finally turned away from the window, though I noticed he didn't meet my eye.

"I'm still not sure," Dex said finally. I didn't believe him. I told him as much.

Another sigh. Another sip. Another smoke pulled from the pack on his desk. Finally, he pulled open his desk drawer and pulled out a small stack of bills. They were green and clean and crisp. They looked good enough to eat.

"How much?" was all I said.

"Two hundred," Dex replied.

"What for?"

"He didn't say. Just he'd be in touch. I don't like it, Kitty. I don't like it one bit."

"Yet you took the money?"

Dex nodded. Something like embarrassment flitted across his face. "I did."

"But it must have been for something, Dex. He can't just pay you for nothing at all. Did he say anything else?" It was like pulling fish through a tiny hole in a barrel. I knew the fish were in there all right. It was just taking some work to get them through the hole.

"Sure. He said a bit."

"And . . ." I prompted.

Dex shrugged. Dragged on his smoke. Cast his eyes back out the window. "Wanted to know what I saw."

"What you saw," I repeated.

"You know," he said.

I nodded. I figured I did. "What you tell him?"

"Wasn't much to tell," Dex said.

"Oh," I said, finally understanding, "but you told it all, right? And you're not sure if you should have told it quite that way."

"It don't feel right, Kitty. What I saw, I mean. It didn't feel right to me then. It doesn't feel any better now."

"But you said you didn't see anything."

"I didn't," Dex agreed, "nothing I felt was significant. Xander? He's got other ideas."

"I don't understand, Dex."

"Wyndham going into the room. Coming out again, like I told you. He seemed to know I'd seen that. And he made sure I was able to describe it precisely."

"The girl, right? Your date. You said you'd felt like she was putting you in place there."

"Did I say that?"

"Not in so many words. But that was the idea I got. That you figured she was lining you up; making sure you saw Wyndham going into that bedroom."

"But if that was true, Kitty . . ." Dex's voice trailed off.

"If that were true . . ." I prompted.

"Well, it's just . . . why me? You know, out of all the dopes at that party, why single me out?"

"Well, did you look especially dopey?"

"C'mon, K: this ain't the funny papers."

"Well then, I guess it's possible she was looking out for you."

"Is it?" Dex asked.

"Seems like."

"But why me?"

"There's that extra dopey thing again."

"Kitty . . ."

"I'm just statin' the obvious. But, really, if the place was as crowded as you say . . ."

"It was."

"OK then," I stopped. Thought hard. "Well then, it would seem to follow that your date was the only person who knew you'd be there. And Xander Dean. Aside from me, of course, and I didn't tell anyone."

"You think Xander Dean told her to make sure I saw? But why?"

It was a good question. "What we're thinking is that someone wanted you to witness something. Something anticipated—or more—by them."

"That's a helluva accusation, Kitty."

"It's not an accusation. It's a thought, that's all. We're just thinking here right now."

"Anyway, I was already watchin' Wyndham. Why make sure I see what I'm already being paid to watch?"

"My guess would be that someone wanted to make absolutely sure you saw the right thing at the right time. You said there were a lot of people there, right?"

Dex grunted.

"Well," I went on, "who's to say you'd have your mug pointed in the right direction when things went down."

"Maybe," Dex said, sounding skeptical. "I guess."

"And here's something else," I pointed at the stack of bills on the desk, "the fact that he's givin' you money alone says something, doesn't it?"

"What's it say?" Dex asked. I was pretty sure that he knew and he was pretending not to get it, though I couldn't tell if the pretense was for my benefit or his own. Either way, I didn't really want to say what was on my mind: I was about one hundred and ten percent sure Dex wouldn't like it.

"Well, think on it," I said finally. "He gives you *more* money and doesn't ask for anything in return. . . ."

Dex just looked at me. Waited for me to go on.

"Well, no one gives nuthin' for nuthin', Dex."

"C'mon, Kitty: you got something to say, then say it."

I found myself looking quickly to my left and right, as though for a way out. There wasn't one. "The only reason *I* can think of that he'd give you money as described is to keep you employed by him and saying the stuff he wants you to say. I mean, he hasn't asked you to follow anyone new or anything, right?"

"You're saying he's . . . he's buying me as a witness?"

"I guess."

"Well, for someone to have wanted me to witness something, they'd have to have been cooking up something worth witnessing, if you follow."

"I do," I said, nodding. "That's what I was thinking. It's not a good thought though, Dex. Because, it means that you suspect your client of murder."

"Did I say that?" Dex asked, thought for a minute, then answered his own question. "I did not say that."

"But it's what you're thinkin'."

"Either way, we're going way beyond actual fact," Dex said. I could hear him trying for a reasonable tone. "But here's something that *is* actual. Xander pumped me for information, as much as I could give him anyway. As much as the cops asked for, too, come to think of it. Which wasn't much. Then Xander thanked me and said he'd like to keep me on retainer, which he gave me," he patted the bills in front of him. "And that's that."

"That's what?"

"That's the end of it," and then with more conviction, "that's all she wrote."

"Sorry?"

"Well," Dex said, sitting up looking suddenly brighter. I wonder if he was even aware of pushing his lowball glass to one side of his desk blotter. "I took his money, but what's to stop me from giving it back?"

"You won't do work for him anymore?" And even though I wasn't sure it would be as easy as washing your hands, I had no doubt it was the right thing for Dex. He looked better already just thinking about it, like he was getting over the grippe.

CHAPTER SEVEN

BY FIVE MINUTES after nine the following morning I was at my desk and on the telephone. I didn't know where Dex was but I figured that, like most days, I'd be lucky to see him before eleven.

Not long after I got to the office, I finally managed to get Xander Dean on the phone. He answered himself with a crisp "Hullo." I explained that Dex was requesting a meeting and we sewed one up for two that afternoon. I figured that Dex would be sober and sitting in his chair by then. I hoped so, anyway. Sometimes hope is all we have.

Xander Dean showed up at two minutes of two, exactly on time. Dex, on the other hand, didn't wander off the street until two fifteen.

To his credit, Dex hadn't actually known when his appointment with Dean would be, but he'd been the one to request it. And he hadn't checked in. So he was late.

Though he showed no outward signs of impatience, I could tell Dean was less than happy at being kept waiting. I didn't blame him. Not only had Dex not shown up on time for a meeting that he himself had called, the best reading material I could offer was the July 1929 issue of *The Cunarder*. It was the magazine of the Cunard Steamship Company and I couldn't imagine how a copy had ended up in our waiting room, let alone one more than two years old. Xander flipped through it fixedly, as though determined to wring some value from this lost time, but he rechecked his watch every few minutes as he sat there.

When Dex finally breezed into the office, he pulled with him the scent of sunshine and an air of ease. I was relieved to see he had recently shaved and was wearing a fresh collar. And he looked quite sober. I was relieved about that, as well.

"Why Xander Dean!" he said, moving toward the big man with his arm extended, then patting him on the back two or three times while they shook. "It's good to see you, sir! And to what do I owe the pleasure on this fine afternoon?"

I rushed in with an answer before Dex had the chance to make things worse. "Why, you asked that I make an appointment, Dex. You remember, I'm sure."

"My apologies, old chum," he said to Xander. "Of course I remember. Of course I do. But it's a beautiful day with a lot in it. You'll forgive my tardiness? And my forgetfulness, as well?" He pounded him again on the back, guided the big man to his feet, then led him into his office.

When Xander closed the door behind him, I allowed myself a sliver of disappointment. Though I understood why the door was closed, a part of me had hoped to eavesdrop on what I was sure would be Xander and Dex's final meeting. I didn't have long to think about it, though, because, pretty much as soon as the door closed, the shrill voice of the phone demanded my attention.

"Good afternoon, Dexter Theroux's office. How can I help you?"

"I'd like to make an appointment with Mr. Theroux, please." The voice was male and neither especially old nor young. From the precise way he'd phrased his words, I'd have guessed the caller was educated. Beyond that, I had no clues.

"Certainly," I said, pulling Dex's appointment book toward me while I spoke. It was tundra clean and just as white. "Let's see what we have available. When did you want to come in?"

"That's just it. The appointment isn't for me; it's for a client of mine. And he wouldn't be able to come to the office. He's being held at Number 11."

"You mean the new jail?"

"That's right, in Lincoln Heights. So it will have to be during visiting hours. But it can be at Mr. Theroux's convenience."

"Oh, I see," I said. "No, wait, I guess I don't see. Sorry. What
is it you feel Mr. Theroux can do for you?"

"Not for me, I told you," the man said, though there was
patience in his voice, "for my client. My name is Steward Sterling. Esquire," he added, as though it were an afterthought.
"I'm a lawyer. He asked that I make this call on his behalf."

"He who?"

"Who what?"

"You're not making this appointment for yourself you said.
But for someone. A he, you said. And I said . . . 'He who?' "

"Ah, right. Yes. It's for a client."

"I see," I said again. But I did not. We were getting nowhere
fast. "Is . . . is your client someone Mr. Theroux has met with
before?"

"No. I don't believe that to be the case."

"OK then," I said.

"I'm sorry to be so opaque," the man said, reinforcing my
thoughts about his education. The whole idea of opacity can be
somewhat tricky. "It's just that . . . well, it's a fairly sensitive
matter."

"Sensitive," I repeated.

"That's right. You see, my client is . . . well, quite high profile, put it that way. And if you sense I'm being careful," I could
hear him inject a smile into his voice, "it's because I am."

"All right. Fair enough. But you've called to make an
appointment—one that won't be held at Mr. Theroux's office—
and yet you're being, as you yourself said, quite opaque."

"Yes, yes," the man said. Sounding friendly and careful all at
once. "I suppose I am. It's just . . . well . . . you're right, of course.
I suppose Mr. Theroux would need to know my client's name?"

"He would. He does. He's funny that way." I was getting a
bit impatient with him just bumping his gums down the blower.

"All right then. But you'll not tell a soul?"

"Of course. It's our business to be discreet."

"Fair enough. I understand. All right then. Laird Wynd-ham."

"Pardon?" I said, though I'd heard him perfectly well.

"That's who Mr. Theroux is to meet at Number 11: Laird Wyndham would like to see him as soon as possible. But in confidence. You understand."

"Of course," I said. And this time, I actually did.

CHAPTER EIGHT

I WASN'T SURPRISED when Dex and Dean's meeting didn't go as long as the previous ones had. It was less than fifteen minutes before Dex's office door opened, though no one came right out. Instead I heard Xander Dean's voice fully inflated for the first time. It was firm. Loud and firm. And he wasn't quite yelling, but he had the volume dialed way up.

"I don't know what sort of racket you run here," was what the big man said in his biggest voice, "but you're not playing it with me. When I hire someone, they stays hired." Anger had slid the culture off Dean's voice. It was not reassuring.

"I told you, Mr. Dean . . ." Dex began but Dean didn't let him complete the thought.

"No. I told *you*: we ain't finished here." Though while he was telling Dex they weren't finished, he started moving toward the door. "You give some thought to what I said. Just see as you come up with the right decision."

He didn't quite slam the door on his way out, but he closed so hard that the glass window with Dex's name stenciled on it rattled in its frame.

I continued to sit at my desk for a moment, letting everything sink in. While it was sinking and I was thinking, Dex poked his head out at me, gave me a sheepish grin.

"Well that's that done," he said.

"I don't know, Dex. That didn't sound done to me."

Dex shrugged. "It's as done as I can make it. He's not my girlfriend, Kitty. And, even if he was, I told him straight out. He's just going to have to figure that no means no." He cracked a silly smile. I could tell he was liking his analogy just fine.

"And you two broke up just in time," I said with a smirk.

"How so?"

"Guy called while you were in your meeting."

"When my ears stop ringing, maybe you can tell me who."

"Said a client of his wants to meet you." I didn't get the response I wanted out of Dex, so I pushed on. "He said he was a lawyer, Dex. And his client is being held at Number 11."

At that Dex raised his eyebrows at me, then rested his behind on the corner of my desk as is his wont at times of great thought.

"Hmmm," was all he said.

"Hmmm? That's it? No big guess?"

"I could make a guess, all right," Dex said, "but it's so foolish, I don't even want to say it out loud."

"It would be the right guess," I said quietly.

Dex just lifted his eyebrows some more.

"And the lawyer wants you to meet him during visiting hours which, I gather, is pretty much any time you want to go. And I'm coming with you," I said as though it were an afterthought. Though, of course, it was not.

"You are?"

"I am," I said with confidence.

"Look, I can't have little sister tagging along all the time," Dex began, but I didn't let him finish.

"Last time I let you go on your own and I've had cause to regret it. But this time? Well, you'll have figured this out already, but there's just no way I'm going to let you go meet Laird Wyndham on your own."

CHAPTER NINE

IT WASN'T AS simple as all that, of course.

Even though Dex had ended his official relationship with Xander Dean and was theoretically clear to take on a different one, there is such a thing as conflict of interest. Viewed from certain angles, there were a couple of places where such a conflict might figure here. Dex didn't seem particularly concerned about such things, so I had to worry for the both of us.

Though Dex had told Dean he wanted out, it didn't seem like Dean was going to take no for an answer. At least, that's how it seemed to me. Both of these things seemed cause for concern, though neither appeared to bother Dex. The only thing he seemed at all troubled about was how he was going to get up to Lincoln Heights.

If I'd been making the trek on my own, I would have taken a streetcar or, with enough time on my hands and without a lot of ready cash, I would have walked the three or so miles. Dex considered neither option; instead he had me call Mustard for a car.

When I got him on the phone, Mustard told me I'd just caught him on the way out the door. He said he hadn't planned on heading toward Lincoln Heights, but that dropping us off wouldn't be far out of his way. That meant Dex and I would be on our own on the way back, but I didn't point this out to Dex. We could jump that hurdle when we got to it.

When he arrived at the office, Mustard looked sportier than usual. He was wearing plus-fours, no jacket and a shirt with no tie and the top few buttons undone. Garters held his sleeves up and off his forearms. His head was bare and his ginger hair curled gently, as though it had been recently washed. He looked amazingly crisp and fresh. I almost didn't recognize him.

"What are *you* dressed up for?" I demanded when I got a load of him.

"Golf," he said.

"Golf?" This was Dex, standing in his office doorway, pulling on his jacket. His tie was nicely done up and he had his hat in his hand. He and Mustard couldn't have looked more different. "When did you get to be a swell?"

"Ha," Mustard said crisply. "I've always been a swell. I've just been hiding it from you. Guess you're not shamus enough to catch on."

"Not bloody likely," Dex said with a grin.

The car Mustard led us to was of a red so dark it was almost black. Dex let out a whistle.

"You know I'm not much of an automobile buff, Mustard," Dex said as we got in. I hopped into the backseat, letting the boys sit together up front. "But this one changes my mind. This is the prettiest car ever rolled. Dussie?"

"Naw," Mustard replied while we got going. "Marmon Sixteen. They call it the world's most advanced car."

"Wow," Dex said.

"It's not brand new. Looks it though, don't it? The guy I got it from . . . well, let's just say it was suddenly more car than he could afford."

Unobserved in the back seat, I felt my eyebrows raise, but didn't say anything. I'd never seen anyone who owed Mustard money. Not with my own eyes. But I figured it probably wasn't a position many wanted.

It was only a couple of miles to Number 11 and, before we even knew it, Mustard was pulling up in front.

"Who are you seeing?" Mustard asked as we got out.

"You don't wanna know," Dex said with a grin, "and I don't wanna tell, so I guess that works out about even."

"Huh," Mustard said cheerfully. "Well, that's a fine how do you do. I'll remember that the next time you ask a favor." With that the dark red Marmon growled powerfully away from the curb. Dex looked after it longingly. "Golf," he said with a shake of his head as we watched the car disappear. "Imagine!"

Mustard's banter and his jovial presence had danced my attention away from the business at hand. Now Dex and I stood on the pavement outside the imposing exterior of Number 11, and I felt the apprehension I'd been unconsciously suppressing rise like a live thing.

Dex must have seen my discomfort. "You sure you want to go through with this?" he said. " 'Cause you don't have to, you know. You're the one who wanted to tag along. You could sit out here in the sunshine if you wanted. Wait for me."

"I know I don't have to," I said, conscious that we were already moving toward the building, approaching an imposing front entrance via a half score of stairs. "Like you said, it was my idea to come. Anyway, if I'm not there, who would hold your hand when things get rough?"

Inside, you could tell the building was so new the paint had yet to dry: you could smell it thick on the air. The building was even newer than that, it wasn't quite finished and, as soon as we passed through the large front doors, we could see teams of workmen completing details. The Los Angeles City Jail was so new it had yet to be officially opened. But it was so badly needed and so overdue that, even before its opening, the brand new six-story building was moving toward capacity.

The officer on duty at the front desk was approaching middle age, but was beyond middle size. He filled his uniform near to overflow and the cloth tugged unmercifully at the brass buttons that cinched him up in front.

"We're here to see Laird Wyndham," Dex said without embarrassment or preamble, just as though Wyndham's fans hadn't been constantly trying to get in to meet the star almost from the moment he was arrested.

"Are you now?" the officer said. His eyes slid over Dex but lingered on me overlong. I didn't like to wonder if it was insult or invitation, nor did I have to. I could see where the eyes stopped, where they rested. He didn't bother raising them to our faces as he spoke. " 'Fraid you're gonna hafta do better n' that," he said.

"His lawyer asked me to come down here," Dex said. His voice a low growl. You didn't have to know him to figure it was a dangerous sound. "I'm Dexter J. Theroux."

"The shamus?" the man said, to my relief meeting Dex's eyes.

"That's right."

"Let me see your ticket."

"Here you go," Dex said as he produced a billfold and handed his license across.

"OK," the cop said when he'd scrutinized the thing as close as could be. "This looks jake. But what about the frail?" he said, jerking a thumb at me.

"This is Miss Katherine Pangborn," Dex said, drawing out the syllables and holding them taut. "She is my secretary and I require she record my meeting with Mr. Wyndham."

"Record, huh?" the cop said skeptically. "That's a good one. Lookee here Theroux, your name is on the list." He did indeed have a list and Dex's name was on it. Wyndham's lawyer must have fixed things, just as he'd said he would. But he'd had no way of knowing about me. "But see? No Kathleen Pambo, or whatever it was you said. 'Fraid she's gonna hafta wait right here." His eyes leeched across me again. "But she'll be OK," he said. "I'll keep her company."

I suppressed a shudder. Visible revulsion didn't seem absolutely politic.

Dex took out his billfold again and drew out his license, fiddling with it quickly but carefully before handing it across once more. "I don't think you looked closely enough at this, officer. Here: have another gander."

I saw the cop reach out and take the license, the confusion on his face clearing as soon as he touched it. The folding money Dex had pressed to the back of the license was in his pocket so quickly, I almost thought I hadn't seen right, but the cop's change of opinion convinced me I had. He started singing a different tune straight off.

"Well I guess you're right. She's just a little thing. I don't see what harm it'll do. Follow this hallway down until you get to the staircase, then go up two flights, then hard left until you see a guy at a desk. Tell him Officer Stacey sent you and sez it's just jake for you to see Wyndham."

"Architect forget to scribble elevators on the plans?" Dex asked before we got underway.

Stacey shook his head. The guys are workin' on them today. We're not even supposed to be open yet. You're lucky you don't have to climb a rope."

That rope was starting to sound good before Dex and I got to the part of the building that Stacey had sent us, the place where they were holding Laird Wyndham. I found the building eerie. From outside it was beautiful. Teal-tinted concrete in the most moderne style. From the outside it looked like a museum. Or a bank. Something noble, something regal. It seemed almost funny that a building where so many police officers would work should look so respectable.

Inside the building things looked different: it could have been a government-run structure anywhere. I followed Dex silently down gleaming corridors, up new-smelling stairwells and then down some more corridors until we came to the place the desk officer had described.

At the desk, Dex had to go through pretty much the whole thing again with another officer. Once again, I saw a small donation disappear into a uniform pocket. I was getting the idea that it was possible to get just about anything you wanted, provided you had the right greenbacked motivation and an inconspicuous way of presenting it.

We were finally led to a long white room, lit by the dozen or so windows that lined one wall. The room reminded me of a cafeteria filled with poorly made tables and chairs, all too new to bear any but the most exploratory marks of abuse and defacement. At some of the tables prisoners sat talking in low voices with family, friends and lawyers. Many of these had ashtrays in front of them and a haze of blue smoke decorated the room as though for some unearthly holiday.

I squelched the dual step my heart made when they brought him in. He looked just like the Laird Wyndham I'd seen so often on the silver screen, somehow undiminished at mere life-size. He didn't look dashing. Not today. He looked precisely as I would have expected to see him if, say, he were preparing for a role as a prisoner. If that were the case, I knew he'd be unjustly accused and would likely save the warden's infant daughter from the rubella during the time he was forced to spend in the clink. Tragic and beautiful in a masculine way. My heart did another double-step at this thought.

"Steward said he'd try and get hold of you," he said, pointing to an empty table and inviting us to sit, as cordial as though we were in one of his mansions or on his boat. "I'm glad to see he did. Thanks very much for coming." The sound of his voice thrilled me. I chided myself for it. So familiar. So much the same. Yet humanized here, unamplified. His next words nearly made me faint, combined as they were with his cool, blue glance. "And who have we here?"

"Laird Wyndham, this is Miss Katherine Pangborn, my secretary. She'll be recording the proceedings today." To my mortification, I felt myself make a small curtsey. Apparently Mrs. Beeson's School for Young Ladies would never, ever die in me.

"How do you do, Miss Pangborn," his grip was soft—not

a workingman's hand—and neither warm nor cold. His eyes gently amused. I made myself remember the details, it seemed likely I'd want to take them out later and replay them.

At a gesture from Wyndham, Dex and I took the two seats opposite him, the table between us. Dex looked as comfortable as he always did and I tried to follow his example. This was not, however, a normal day. Laird Wyndham was sitting directly across from me. Close enough, I realized, that if I stretched out a leg, I'd be able to touch him with my toe. Close enough that, with the right crossbreezes, I'd be able to catch a whiff of his scent, and he—I thought headily—mine.

I was so caught up in thoughts of toe-touching and possible scent exchanges that I missed the earliest part of the conversation. Nor did I later regret it. How often, I reasoned, would I have Laird Wyndham practically almost to myself in this way? I knew what they were talking about anyway, or thought I did. The small talk that marks the earliest part of human interaction: I'm here because of this, you're here because of that.

But his hair.

Up close—this close—I could see the irregularity of his part. And I could see that while his hair did not appear especially thick, there was a lot of it, dark chestnut in color, waved back so neatly it looked almost creamy. Thick, dark cream. A lock of it fell over his forehead and dipped toward his left eye.

"She's not taking notes." I'm not sure if the words themselves stirred me or the fact that they were about me. Probably both. There was amusement in Wyndham's voice and I found myself only lightly mortified that he should have found me out so quickly. It was likely not the first time a young woman had finagled her way into his presence.

"Hear that, Kitty? Your lack of note taking is inviting concern." I smiled timidly at Wyndham, then cast Dex a disapproving look. He paid no attention.

I could feel color hitting my cheeks. "Sorry," I said stammering a bit, "it's just . . . sorry." I took out a notebook and wrote "Wyndham Notes" across the top of the page. "I'm ready now," I said with more confidence than I felt. "Please. Continue."

I was relieved when their attention was diverted by another arrival at our table. The man who joined us was dressed perfectly and expensively, from his crisp collar down to his spotless luggage-brown wingtips.

"Steward," Wyndham said warmly, rising and clasping the other man's hand, "good of you to join us. Thanks for setting this up." Wyndham introduced us to his lawyer, Steward Sterling, and I receded as far as possible into the background, feeling a bit silly taking notes where none, strictly speaking, needed taking.

The three men spoke lightly at first, feeling each other out. Dex seemed to like both Wyndham and his lawyer almost instantly. Wyndham didn't seem at all the spoiled star the papers made him out to be, and there appeared to be real affection between Wyndham and his lawyer: the two men were obviously friends as well as colleagues.

I noticed that the tightness and suspicion I'd seen in Dex's face when he spoke to or about Xander Dean was absent. I could tell Dex felt that these were men he could trust.

"What I don't quite understand," Dex was saying, "is how you think I can help. Or even, to be perfectly honest, what I'm doing here. What Kitty and I are doing here," he amended.

I saw the two men exchange a glance before either answered.

"You know the bare facts in the case." It was Sterling who spoke first. "You understand . . . that is, you've heard and read and so on, you know what Laird is accused of and how the papers say it came to be."

Dex nodded. Grunted slightly. "And I was there," he pointed out.

Sterling nodded agreement. "And you were there. Right. That's one of the reasons we wanted to talk to you."

"How did you know that?"

"What? That you were there? Let's just say you are not inconspicuous in a crowd like that. Laird here saw you. Asked around."

"Yes," Laird confirmed. "And then when . . . when all of this happened, I realized you were someone who might be in a position to be helpful to me. Someone I could talk to."

"I'm listening," Dex said.

The two men exchanged another glance. This time it was Wyndham who spoke. "We think there's more going on than meets the eye."

"How do you figure?" Dex asked.

"It's the only thing that explains . . . well, everything," Wyndham said. "The way the press has been since my arrest and . . . the thing itself."

"Unless you did it," Dex said matter-of-factly.

"Right," Wyndham nodded, meeting Dex's eyes. "Unless I did it. But I did not."

Dex nodded. "OK," he said. "Though maybe you can clear something up for me. Something that's been bothering me. That night—the night of the party—you were on the phone a lot and when you weren't, it looked as though you were waiting for someone. Can I ask who?"

Wyndham and his lawyer exchanged a glance. I did not see Sterling shrug and encourage Wyndham to explain, but I felt it just the same.

"I was waiting for Sterling here."

Dex kicked back in his chair, stretching his legs out in front of him. I knew what this meant: he didn't believe this answer. Yet. But he would listen to all of it. He said as much. "I'm listening," was what he said.

The two men exchanged glances again. I could tell they were weighing their answers, wondering how much to say.

Finally Sterling said, "We'd had words."

"Pardon?" Dex said.

"Words, you know. We'd had a bit of a falling out."

"About what?" Dex wanted to know.

Another shared glance.

"It doesn't matter," Wyndham said.

Sterling nodded. "Not relevant," he added in lawyerly fashion.

"So let me get this straight," Dex said, "the two of you had some kind of . . . what? Disagreement?"

He got a brace of nods. I gathered that his choice of the word "disagreement" was a good one. "All right," Dex said with the air of someone who was letting something go. For now. "Still, someone did it. The girl is dead. And if not you, then who?"

Both Steward and Wyndham shook their heads. It seemed an unconscious show of unanimous innocence.

"That's the rub, I think," Steward said. "And that's why Laird felt he wanted you here. We don't know who did it and the police aren't looking because they think they do. Laird got to thinking that if someone—say, you—could discover who *did* do it . . ."

"Gotcha," Dex said. "You wouldn't have to prove your innocence if someone else was guilty."

"Right, right," Wyndham said. "So you'll take the case?"

Inexplicably, Dex looked at me. "What do you say, Kitty? Do we take the case?"

I tried to glean what Dex wanted from me just then: it seemed he wouldn't have asked this particular question if he didn't already have an answer.

"Umm," I stammered. "Uh . . . yes?"

"There you go then, boys. You heard the lady. I'd like five days in advance. Plus expenses."

Wyndham looked pleased. Sterling stuck out his hand, pumped Dex's. "Cash OK?"

It was.

"One thing I need to know," Dex said, "was what happened from Laird's perspective."

"What happened?" Wyndham asked.

"Right. What did you see? I saw a woman—Rhoda Darrow—point out the bedroom to you. I saw you go in. I saw you come out. Next thing you know, the girl is dead. And I'm gathering from the fact that you're claiming you're innocent that the girl was alive when you left the room. . . ."

"She was," Wyndham said emphatically. "She certainly was."

"Still," Dex prompted. "Something went on in there. . . ." He left the sentence dangling, willing Wyndham to finish it.

Wyndham looked to Sterling, who nodded, approving this portion of the tale.

"Well, like you said, that Darrow woman came to me. I didn't know who she was right off, though her face was familiar."

"We've figured it out since, though," Sterling interjected. "They'd worked together on a film, maybe five years ago. Right, Laird? Five?"

"Right. I remember because we weren't talking yet. No hint of talking, so I'm thinking '26 or thereabouts."

"So she looked familiar . . ." Dex prompted, obviously not that interested in Rhoda Darrow's resume at this point.

"Right. And all she says was, 'The messenger is waiting in the larger bedroom.' And she says it like that's going to have meaning for me, you know? Like I'm going to know what it is."

"And did you?" Dex asked.

"No," Wyndham said right away.

"So why did you . . ."

"Go into the bedroom? Well, it was, like I said, the *way* she said it: like I was supposed to know. And I figured . . . I figured, I don't know anymore. So much has happened since . . ." Wyndham tugged at his hair distractedly. I noticed this of course because I was endlessly fascinated by his hair.

"Well, I figured, maybe it was Steward. Or maybe a message from Steward. So I went."

"Lemme guess," Dex said. "Not a message?"

"No. No message. There was just this . . . this girl. And she was in the bed when I came in. Not wearing much of anything at all."

"And you didn't know the girl?" Dex asked. "Not like, say, with the Darrow broad? You'd maybe worked with her or something?"

"No, no," Wyndham said quickly. "Nothing like that. So I come in the room and I close the door behind me."

"Why?" Dex wanted to know.

"Why'd I close the door? Just because, you know," he cracked a smile, "I'm Laird Wyndham. Sometimes people want to lurk around. Hear stuff. It's a habit I've gotten into."

Dex nodded. "OK. So you close the door . . ."

"Right. And the girl on the bed? When she sees it's me, she's on me so fast . . ."

"Has this ever happened before?"

"Strange girls on beds taking their clothes off and attacking me?" Wyndhan's smile was wry.

Dex just nodded.

Wyndham nodded. "Yes, actually: it happens all the time. But this . . . I don't know if I can describe it properly, this was different."

"Try," Dex said. "Tell me what was different."

"Well there was a . . . I guess you could say there was a hunger on her."

"She wanted a sandwich?"

"You do like to break things down to their most simple bits, don't you, Mr. Theroux?"

"Call me Dex."

"Okay, Dex. And no sandwich. But, to be honest, it wasn't like she was after sex either. Or at least, not just sex. Or even sex for the sake of it. I know . . . forgive me if this sounds arrogant, but I know what that looks like. This was something more."

"So you had sex with her?"

"No!" Did the word come out too quickly? I couldn't decide. Maybe Wyndham thought so too because he tried it again, "No. I just extricated myself as well as I could and got the hell out of there."

Which was pretty much in line with what Dex had seen. He'd told me that Wyndham had come out of the room looking like he needed a shower. Though, when I thought about it, that was a look that could swing either way.

"And that's it?"

"Pretty much," Wyndham said. "I was . . . well, I guess I was a bit upset by it. I'm not sure why. There was just something . . . well . . . dirty about the whole scene. I decided I wanted some air and slipped out when I thought no one was looking."

"It just happened," Sterling picked up the story here, "that I was arriving as Laird was leaving the bungalow."

Wyndham nodded. "That's right. And we had . . . well we had some things to clear up. We went someplace quiet to talk things out. We drove down to the marina in Long Beach where I keep my boat. And we were sitting there, on the aft deck, just chatting into the night and, next thing I knew I was being arrested for murder and I ended up here. You know the rest."

"Well," Dex said, "as much as there is to know, I guess. At least, among us. And for now. We'll try to discover the rest. I'll need your help with that. Do you have any enemies, Mr. Wyndham? Anyone who would wish you harm?"

"Call me Laird, please. And no. Nothing like that at all."

"I'd like you to give it thought, please, sir. Careful thought.

And if you can't think of anyone now, that's all right. We'll be talking a few times over the next few days. Anything comes to you, you can fill me in then or you can always call the office. Most likely talk to Kitty here, if I'm not around."

I blushed.

"All right," Wyndham said.

"So . . . no enemies you can think of right off the top of your head. Here's another thing to ponder then: you're both saying you didn't do it."

"I didn't!" Wyndham said quickly.

"OK," Dex said. "We got that part. But if not you, then who? Someone did, that's clear as rain. What's not so clear right now is who *did* do it. You got any pet theories?"

The two men exchanged another glance, but I couldn't read anything into it. Looking at Dex, I figured he couldn't either. It was Sterling who spoke.

"One thing we've been discussing is the likelihood of one of the service people having done it."

"The service people?"

"Yeah, you know: busboys, housekeeping staff, even catering people."

"I know what service people are," Dex said. "It just seems a bit far-fetched, is all. I mean, let's face it: we've got a bungalow crawling with all sorts and you're thinking—what?—the butler did it?"

Wyndham looked embarrassed. "I was just thinking they might have had access, is all."

"Don't take this the wrong way, OK?" Dex said, looking from Wyndham to his lawyer and back again, "but, the next few days, all you're going to have is time to think about what happened. Maybe that kind of meditation will shake something loose. Meanwhile, here's what I'm going to do. I'm going to go away now and over the next few days, we'll nose around some, see if there are any clues the cops are overlooking because they're so confident they've got their man."

"That's wonderful," Wyndham said effusively. He looked as though he might clasp Dex's hand gratefully once more, but Dex stopped him.

"Hold on though," Dex said looking directly at Wyndham. "Not so fast. There's something I want you to do for me."

"But what can I do? I'm stuck in here."

"I just need you to think about that night. And about who might have wanted to put the frame on you. Make notes on anything that jumps into your head that you figure might help me, even if it doesn't seem like much of anything at all. OK?"

Wyndham laughed. It had a hollow sound, though it wasn't unpleasant. More like hopeless, the way hopeless looks on a man who is used to having his dreams come true. "I can do that, all right. Like you said earlier, I got nothing but time on my hands." And he said it rough, like he might have done when playing the love-struck cowboy in *Border Dove*.

"For starters, though, I'd like you to scratch out a fast list now so that I can get Kitty here right to work on it when we get back to the office."

"Who should be on that list?" Wyndham asked. "Possible enemies?"

"Sure," Dex said, "that's a good place to start. But also I'd like the names of some of the people closest to you. People who work for you. And friends. Your inner circle. See, we'll start by building a profile, in a way. We'll put together a big picture. And then we'll see what we've got when we're done with that and think about what to do with the information we've gathered."

"I can do that," Wyndham said.

"Good. I know that there will be names that escape you this first go-round. So, like I said, I'll drop back in a couple of days and let you know what, if anything, I've got and you can give me the more detailed list you're going to work on. One way or another, we'll make some sort of progress."

"What about now?" Wyndham said.

"Pardon?" Dex replied.

"I mean what if I can think of things—now—to help you?"

"I guess I'd expect you'd tell me."

"Well, I'm just thinking about the Masquers' annual ball. It's tonight. That might be a good starting point for you. Short notice, I know. But I'd planned on attending. And, as you can see," there was a bitterness in his tone, slight, but present, "I now have other plans."

"Sorry, Wyndham, that's a new one on me. I've never heard of the Masquers' Ball. What say you fill me in?"

"The Masquers? You know: 'We laugh to win.'" He looked from Dex to me, then back again. "No? Nothing? Never heard of it?" Wyndham seemed completely astonished.

"No, Wyndham," Dex said firmly. "Never heard of it. If we need to know about it now, you'd best tell us."

"The Masquers are a, well a sort of secret organization," Wyndham said.

"It being secret might be why we never heard of it," Dex said.

"Not *that* secret," Wyndham said. "Least, we've never expended much effort to keep it from people."

"But what sort of organization is it?" I said.

At the sound of my voice, Wyndham looked at me as though he'd perhaps forgotten I was there. He smiled, not unkindly. "Why, I would have thought the name made it apparent: Masquers?" he looked from Dex to me then back again. "No? All right, then: actors. It's an organization of actors."

"Like a guild?" I asked. "A union?"

"No," he said, "not really like that, though there are some who would make it so. No, the Masquers are more of a social club. We have a clubhouse on North Sycamore and any member can go there any time at all and always know friends are

there. And we have dinners commemorating great accomplish-
ment of our members. We have revels about once a month. . . ."

Here Dex stopped him. "Revels?"

"Oh. Sorry. Performances, I guess you could say. But it's
more than that, too. A revel is a theatrical evening with members staging plays and the like. It's quite entertaining."

"And the ball, is that what it is?" I asked. "A revel?"

"Oh no," Wyndham said. "Nothing like that. The Masquers'
Ball is an evening of mystery," he said theatrically. "Everyone
must wear a mask, so all who come are anonymous. Because of
that, everyone is more willing to step outside themselves and be
something more or at least different than they normally are."

"That's why you think they'd talk to us?" Dex said. "You
think people might be more willing to talk about things than
might normally be the case?"

"Quite right," Wyndham said. "That's just what I think. Plus
it's the only time you'll find so many prominent people from the
movie business in one place. Well, short of the Academy Awards,
of course, but that wouldn't be a good evening to engage people
in conversation. But the ball, that's different. And you can go not
as a detective but as a party-goer. An invited guest."

"So this shindig is open to everyone?" Dex asked.

"No, that's the beauty," Wyndham said. "That's what
brought it to mind. The event is open to members only, along
with their invited guests. The fact that you're even there—that
you even know about it—implies a level of intimacy. People
will talk more freely because they'll assume you're a member,
or close to someone who is."

"But they'll see me, right?" Dex pointed out. "They'll recognize that they don't recognize me."

"No, no. As I said: you'll be wearing a mask."

"And Kitty, if I bring her along"—my head shot up from
the notes I was still making a big show about taking. I hadn't
even thought about asking Dex if I could go.

"That's right: Miss Pangborn would need to wear a mask as well. Everyone wears one to the annual ball."

"Where would we get them?" I asked. "And how would we know the right kind to get?"

"Sterling knows," Wyndham said. "He can bring one for each of you to your office. And an invitation, so you'll be all set."

"What kind of costume would I have to wear?" Dex asked. "Would I have to dress like King Tut or something?"

"No, no, nothing like that. Just normal evening dress. Black tie for you, Dex, and ladies long."

"Well, that's settled then," Dex said, startling me. I hadn't thought anything was settled at all. "All right, Miss Pangborn." I blushed at the way he said my name. Intimate, in a way. And playfully at the same time, even with the honorific in place. Dex rose and clasped Wyndham's hand, then, "Come along. We've got a ball to attend."

CHAPTER TEN

"I CAN *NOT* go to a ball."

We were in a taxi heading back to the office. I knew we'd be there all too soon—it was not a lengthy ride—I figured if I was gonna talk, I'd better do it fast.

" 'Course you can," Dex said calmly. "You can and you will."

"Please, Dex . . ."

" 'Please, Dex,' " he mimicked me. I wanted to slug him right in his smug mug, but I did not. And not just because he's several times bigger than me. "It's just the ticket, don't you see? This isn't the sort of thing a dope goes to stag, kiddo. You heard Wyndham: it's their big once-a-year affair. And those actors have got their pick of dames standing in line waiting to be asked to this thing. No, no: I can't go alone."

"OK then," I said, trying for my most reasonable tone, "why not ask someone else, then?"

"A real girl, you mean?"

"Yeah, a *real* girl," I said biting back all of the more obvious retorts that sprang to mind. None of that would have been productive. "Isn't there someone you're sweet on? Asking her to this might be just the thing. Like you said, dames stand in line to go to a shindig like this."

"Well," Dex said thoughtfully, "there are a few I might ask, but I'd be afraid they might get the wrong idea."

"And you're not afraid I'll get the wrong idea?"

Dex looked at me and smirked. "Kiddo," he said, "that would be about the furthest thing from my mind."

"Thanks," I said a bit huffily, settling myself more deeply into my seat.

"You're welcome," he said back. I didn't like him much right then for his grin. "Ah, don't be like that. You know I'm just kiddin' around with you." I didn't respond, so he went on, "Here's what I figured: if I take a date—a real date—to this thing, my head might get all full of her instead of full of the business at hand. And, anyway, she'd be hangin' off me like a wet blanket. How am I supposed to detect with some dame always asking for a drink or a dance?"

"And that won't happen if I'm there instead? Geez, thanks, Dex."

"C'mon, Kitty. Whaddayawant? You can't have it both ways," he said, sounding suddenly more serious than before. "And I know you don't want it both ways anyway. We've got a good thing, me and you. We wouldn't want to mess that up with any funny business."

I smiled at him then. A real smile. Because the truth was, the last thing I wanted with Dex was . . . funny business. On the other hand, a girl likes to know she's considered someone you'd want to be funny with, if you get what I'm saying. I didn't want Dex to feel that way about me—I really did not. Yet, on the other hand, I did. I could see the duality in that, but it didn't change the way I felt.

"OK. There's another reason." We were nearing downtown now.

"OK," Dex said. "Shoot."

I found myself sitting up straight in my seat, looking ahead and past the driver out the window, very focused on the line painted down the middle of the road.

"I have . . ." I stopped. "Promise not to laugh."

"Sure, kid. I promise."

"I have nothing to wear to a party like that."

Dex broke his promise. Maybe he'd never meant to keep it. He laughed a big, deep, murderous laugh. "And *that's* why you don't want to go?" he asked.

I just nodded.

"Well hell, Kitty. That's easy, why didn't you say something? Wyndham's paying our expenses." He told the driver to stop the car right there and, when he pulled over I noticed that though we were still a few blocks from the office, we were on Broadway only half a block or so from Blackstone's Department Store. Dex brought out his wallet and fished out a fifty. "This cover it?" I felt my eyes go all wide. Dex knew damn well that with fifty bucks I could buy a used car. Not a good one, but that wasn't really the point.

"Pretty much," is all I said.

"Good. So buy something to wear to a ball, Kitty. Something just as nice as you please. And don't worry about the price: unless it's more than fifty bucks. And if you got any left over, you keep it."

Even when the big car had pulled back into traffic, I stood on the pavement and watched it. I actually had a fifty dollar bill clenched in my hand. *Fifty.* I could take a steamship to Hawaii. I could buy groceries for the whole house for a year or take a luxury train trip to San Francisco and stay at the Fairmont Hotel for a week. I could *fly* to New York in a clipper plane. With the fifty bucks in my hand, I could do almost anything. For just a moment, there on the sidewalk outside Blackstone's, the possibilities took my breath away.

My mission was pretty clear: Dex had given me the fifty bucks and told me not to bring him any change. I knew he meant it. He'd asked Wyndham for his daily rate plus expenses. And Wyndham was loaded. I knew he wouldn't give Dex any trouble with laying out fifty bucks for a new get-up for me so that I could accompany Dex to the ball.

No, the source of the money was okey-dokey, no problems there. The problem came from my end: fifty bucks was a *lot* of money. The fifty bucks pressed tightly into my hand was too much to spend on a dress and maybe some shoes.

The department store was filled with the scent of newness. Why had I never noticed that when I was a child? Newness and possibilities. I inhaled deeply and considered. Prosperity, that's what I smelled. It lingered still, in here.

I wandered around for a bit, entranced by the scent of prosperity and possibilities and, in the end, I fell in love with a dress being worn by a haughty looking mannequin on a plinth in one of the aisles. It was an ivory sheath dress covered in gold beads. So glittery. I wanted it instantly.

A salesgirl saw me admiring it. "It's the last one, you know."

"Is it . . . is it very expensive?"

"You know," she said, "for how beautiful the workmanship is and how well it's made, it's not very expensive at all."

I looked at her out of the corner of my eye. She was wearing a perfectly tailored little suit over a beige blouse, her hair permed to a perfect blond nimbus around her head. Even if she understood the full meaning of the word "expensive," she would not let on to me.

"How much?" I asked cautiously.

"Well, it was $49.95," she said. She must have heard me gasp, because she added, "It's Jean Patou, you know. But, as I said, it's also the only one left. It was going to come down today anyway. I can let you have it for," and here she looked at me shrewdly, perhaps sizing me up and estimating what I might be able to pay, "um . . . $19.95."

It was *still* a lot of money. More than a lot. There were dresses that would have done quite nicely for half that. But none were actual Jean Patou—even last season's—and once I'd tried it on I knew that none of them would have fit me so perfectly, or sparkled so prettily when I walked.

I managed to find a pair of shoes to go with the dress and a hooded cape affair to wear over it for another three bucks each. Then, with money still in hand and strict instructions not to give any back, I bought two attractive dresses for the office, one for three dollars and another for five and a nice new leather handbag for Marjorie for three. I knew that later, when I got home, I could in good conscience give Marjorie her new purse and a few dollars toward groceries and keep a couple emergency dollars for myself while still knowing I'd followed Dex's instructions to the letter.

I was tired, but happy.

I felt like Cinderella.

I was going to a ball.

CHAPTER ELEVEN

THERE IS NO feeling quite like the one you get emerging from a department store with your arms fully laden, knowing that you've spent a great deal of money exceedingly well. I almost can't explain it. Your arms might be tired from carrying all those packages, but your heart is light and satisfied.

There are those who will scoff at such fancy, others who feel such thinking is flawed or wrong. I don't care. Shopping can be restorative. It can be like time in church. Shopping can lift your spirit and your heart. They say gambling is addictive. Those who say it have not truly shopped.

The lightness of mood I felt after leaving Blackstone's followed me all the way to our building and even to the elevator where I wondered if I would show Dex my dress right away, or make him wait until he picked me up that evening so that he got the full golden-beaded effect. I found that, silly though it was, I liked the possibilities available to me. I liked pondering these questions. It made me feel young and girlish. And I was both those things, but the times and my troubles sometimes pushed that reality aside. I found myself looking forward to the ball far more than I'd anticipated I could when we'd first heard about it a few hours before.

My mood continued thus—light and girlish—until the moment I passed Hartounian's door and our own came in sight. It stood open to the hallway. The sight of it stopped me in my tracks for a moment. I tried to get hold of myself. Was an open door really so odd, I asked myself? Yes it was, I replied instantly, then hurried along.

At first, aside from an open door on an empty office, I could see nothing amiss. Then I spotted one of Dex's shiny black broughams toe-up on the floor, peeking out from behind his desk. When I looked more carefully, I could see that there was still a foot inside the shoe. I dropped my packages next to my own desk as I passed, hurrying to Dex, splayed on the floor next to his.

He was perfectly still and there was an awful lot of blood. My hand on his wrist reassured me: he wasn't dead. I could feel his pulse, but when I tried to rouse him, I got no response at all.

I grabbed the phone on Dex's desk and dialed Mustard's number from memory. I knew Mustard had gone golfing, so I didn't have much hope I'd get him at his office. When he answered I almost felt like weeping in relief. I told him what was happening in as few words as possible.

"What should I do? Should I call the police? Or an ambulance? Maybe Dex needs medical attention? Oh, but if I called the police, they could decide—"

"Hold your horses," Mustard interrupted my stream of possibilities. He sounded like he was already in motion. "No police. No nuthin'. I'll be there in eight minutes. Seven if traffic is light. Then we can decide." And he was gone. I stood looking at the phone, biting my lower lip, wondering if I'd done the right thing, but knowing that Mustard would probably get here faster than the police would have in any case.

I spent a bad eight minutes. Maybe it was five. Or ten. It certainly felt like much, much more. In that time, even though the wound on the top of Dex's head that had bled so profusely had slowed, I used a clean rag to staunch the blood. By the time Mustard got there with a couple of his men, the bleeding had stopped altogether, but Dex still hadn't woken and I was frantic. After a cursory glance at Dex, Mustard reassured me.

"I think it'll be OK, Kitty. Head wound like that can produce more blood than seems likely. But Dex has got a head like an engine block. You'll see, he'll come 'round in a bit."

From speaking to me—reassuringly, gently—it was almost comical to see Mustard switch gears when he turned to his thugs. At the sound of his voice—grim and serious—I looked up from where I'd squatted on the floor next to Dex. I wanted to see if what I heard in Mustard's voice was also in his face. The voice hadn't told any lies: Mustard had about him the look of a man who would cause a death if given the chance. I had always suspected he wasn't someone to mess with. The look on his face confirmed it.

He conferred with the two men quickly, before both of them left the office. I could tell it wouldn't be long before Mustard followed them—he just had that look—but first he bent back to where I sat next to Dex on the floor to see what needed doing. His face held its usual cheerfully gentle look, the murderous intent banished, at least for the moment, while he looked at his friend.

"He hasn't come 'round yet?" Mustard said, stating the obvious.

I shook my head.

"OK," he said rising. "Let's try something." He crossed to Dex's desk and pulled a bottle of bourbon out of one of the top drawers. Then he took his handkerchief and doused it with a splash from the bottle, which he then dabbed gingerly across the cut on Dex's temple.

What Mustard had done seemed like magic when Dex protested with a yelp of pain.

"Now we're cookin' with gas," Mustard said sounding satisfied.

"Huh!" Dex said. "I don' know what you're cookin', but I think you just dumped some of it on my head." He sat up, pressing his fingers gingerly to the cut, then pulling them away quickly. It seemed likely that the cut wouldn't be the worst of it: a bruise was already forming under the skin.

Now that he was awake and moving, we could see that the cut on his head wasn't Dex's only injury. He held his right arm painfully at his side, moving it as awkwardly as a heron with a damaged wing might have done. His eye was going to settle into a shiner in a few days time and the way he moved his body—carefully and without full motion—made me suspect other injuries.

Mustard had seen it, as well. "Looks like you got yourself beat up pretty good."

"You think?" Dex said sarcastically while he pulled himself to his feet.

"Looks like they took a little waltz across your suit while they was at it."

Dex pushed his fingers experimentally into his side, his abdomen, his upper thigh. "Musta done. I don't remember. Must have blacked that part out just after they put their dancin' shoes on."

"Huh," Mustard said. "Probably a good thing."

"It's all right, I guess," Dex said, still poking.

I took a breath that felt like the first I'd pulled in half an hour.

"Who was it?" Mustard asked. I could sense his urgency returning. His friend was all right—would live, in any case. Time he was out with his muscle, chasing down whoever had done the damage. I knew the signs. "Did you recognize them?"

"Seems to me there were three or four of them altogether. But I only recognized one of them: Xander Dean."

Mustard's eyebrows rose, then ducked back into position so quickly I doubted having seen them lift in the first place.

"Little I saw of him," Mustard said, "he didn't seem the type."

"Ha," Dex said mirthlessly. "I think mebbe you had him pegged wrong."

"I think mebbe you're right," Mustard agreed. "Where'd he go?"

"Wish I could tell you. But I think they were careful not to say. Or maybe they *did* say, and I was too busy listening to the floorboards."

"What was it about?" I asked.

"He wanted to know had I changed my mind about what I told him earlier," Dex said. "I told him I hadn't."

"What had you told him?" Mustard asked.

"That we were parting company."

It was clear to me that there was as much here that Dex was not saying as what he chose to share. It must have been clear to Mustard, as well, because he didn't pursue the matter; didn't press for greater detail. I resigned myself to the fact that Mustard and I would never know exactly what had happened here this afternoon. But the upshot? That much I knew: Xander Dean had been even more unhappy than we'd suspected that Dex had left his employ. He'd put some pressure on Dex to prevent it happening. That hadn't worked. Could never work. Not with Dex who, in the end, truly didn't care what was done to him. You got that with Dex before long. It was hard to frighten someone who figured that nothing worse could happen to them than what already had.

"When did it happen?" Mustard wanted to know.

"I'm not sure, to be honest. But they were waiting for me when I got back to the office and they worked on me for maybe half an hour."

"He would have gotten back to the office close to two hours ago," I supplied. "If he came back here right after he dropped me off at Blackstone's."

"I did," Dex said nodding.

Mustard nodded crisply, all business. "All right then. So you were out for an hour, Theroux? That ain't good. You wanna make sure you keep an eye on yourself: see you don't go all loony or anything after bein' out that long."

"Yeah," Dex said dryly. "I'll do what I can about that, old hoss."

Mustard seemed not to have heard the irony in Dex's voice. Or maybe he just chose to ignore it. With Dex, that wasn't always a bad idea.

"I'll go poke my head out," Mustard said, "see what I can see and if the boys have picked anything up. I have a hunch there won't be anything. Not today. They had too big a lead. Still . . ." and with that he plunked on his hat and left the office without another word. The air about him swirled as though it knew it followed a man on his way to fix something.

"I need a drink," Dex said, dusting himself and his bourbon off and righting the chair behind his desk before dropping himself into it.

The office was a mess. Dean's toughs had seen fit to upend every single chair in the place, including mine. I wondered mildly what they had against chairs.

A couple of file drawers had been opened, their contents strewn on the floor around my desk, but I got the idea that no one had been looking for anything, that whoever had done it had just wanted to make sure their message was delivered loud and clear. Dex's ashtray and the contents of the coffee pot had been dumped in the middle of the floor together. This was more irritant than anything. Since our floors were battered hardwood, one more mess wasn't going to make that much difference, but it wasn't going to be much fun to clean up, either. And though Dex's blood would mop up easily enough, the trick would be tracking down all the places he'd left it. Judging from the blood spatters I found all over the office, they'd really bounced him around a bit.

I let Dex nurse his bruises, his battered ego and his bourbon while I put the place back together. The toppled chairs and tobacco soup messes were easy. The most difficult part would be organizing the files. I decided to just press everything neatly into an empty file drawer for today: I could sort things out properly over the next week or so, whenever I had time in the office that needed filling up. It wasn't like we hit those files on a daily basis anyway.

My tidying was interrupted only once when Steward Sterling popped by as promised with masks for the ball, an invitation and the address.

He whistled when he saw the place. "Wow," he said pleasantly, "what a dump! Tell me it's not always like this."

"It's not always like this," I repeated as instructed. "Only when we're anticipating going to a ball."

"There's a story, I'd imagine," he said.

"Yeah. I just don't know that I feel like telling it right now," I said taking the small package he'd brought. "You could try your luck with Dex, though," I said, indicating his closed door.

"Naw, that's OK," he said. "Maybe you two will feel like filling in the details next time I see you." And with a smile and a bit of a bow, he was gone.

Once I'd tidied things up to the point where it no longer looked as though a tornado had hit the place, I poked my head in at Dex, Steward's package under my arm.

Dex was sitting upright in his chair with his face turned toward the window. There were about three fingers of bourbon in the glass on the desk, but he wasn't touching it. His ashtray was sitting just as I'd left it after cleaning: no butts marred the jade-green surface. It always scares me when Dex abandons his vices. Sometimes it can be the calm before the storm, sometimes it can be the storm itself but, whatever it is, it's usually not good.

"Want some company?" I said now.

"Sure," he replied, pointing one long index finger at my usual seat.

"Thanks," I said, taking it.

"Drink?" he said once I was seated, using the same index finger to indicate the bottle.

I shook my head. He knows I don't care for spirits, but he's also dead polite.

"What do you figure?" I said after a while. I was trying not to notice the angry color the flesh around his eye was turning.

"I've got a bump on the noggin, but I figure I'll live. And they didn't dump my bourbon, so that's good news."

"But what do you figure it was about?"

"You know as well as I do, Kitty. And you called it right, too, didn't you?"

"I guess," I said, not sure that I had.

"I honestly figured I'd quit Xander Dean and that would be the end of it. It seems he has other ideas." He paused for a moment, deep in thought. "You were right about something else, too," he said, finally.

"What's that?"

"Well, you figured maybe Dean didn't hire me to follow as much as he hired me to see what he wanted me to see."

"I said that?"

Dex nodded. "More or less, yeah, you did."

"OK," I said, unconvinced. "Let's say I did. What makes you figure I was right?"

"It's in how mad he was at me wanting to part company," he said, as though thinking it through for the first time. "You know: you hire someone to do a job and they don't do it. What do you do?"

"I don't know. Hire someone else, I guess."

"Exactly right. That's what you do. Easy as pie in this day and age too, ain't it? You open a door and holler, someone'll come running to do the work that needs doin'."

"Pretty much I guess."

"So why break a sweat if I don't want to do it? Unless the job, such as it was, is already done. And the thing you're paying for is what was *already* seen, if you follow."

Unfortunately, I did. "He was hoping for corroboration," I said softly. "That's what you're saying."

"Right. Corroboration. Trust you to find a ten-dollar word," he said, not without affection.

Dex saying it like that—out loud and in plain language—made me think of something else. "If that's true, Dex, if you were hired not to follow but to . . . to witness, then maybe you weren't the only one."

Dex looked at me for a while, as though if he looked closely enough he might see a more complete answer. He took a sip of his bourbon. Lit a butt.

"And if I wasn't the only one," he said finally, "it'll make our job that much easier."

"How so?"

"All we have to do is find the others."

It might have sounded easy to him. To me it did not. To me it sounded like needle in a haystack time.

"Not first, though," I said.

"Huh?"

I looked at Dex's bruised noggin, at the careful way he was holding his arm. "Well, I don't know if you're still feelin' up to it, but before anything else, Dex, we're supposed to go to a party."

CHAPTER TWELVE

BEFORE I LEFT the office for the night, I called Mustard and arranged for the use of a car. Dex would stop by and pick it up after he left the office, at which point he'd come and collect me and we'd go to the Masquers' Ball together.

Dex arrived right on time. I opened the door myself. When he saw me, Dex's eyes went wide. It was gratifying and a little scary, too. "Why, you're all grown up, Miss Pangborn." We stood at the door like strangers. Me on the inside, backlit by the house. Dex on the stoop bringing with him the scent of evening and the sound of cicadas and the city at night.

"I've decided to take your remark as a compliment, Mr. Theroux. I take it you approve of the purchase you had Mr. Wyndham make?" I spun around theatrically, with more élan than I felt.

Dex smiled. "I do, Miss Pangborn. You'll be quite the belle of the ball."

"You look pretty dashing yourself, Mr. Theroux. You cut quite the fine figure in your monkey suit." He did, too. And I was glad to see that, though his face was bruised and somewhat the worse for wear, and though he held his arm gingerly, it looked battered more than broken. You had to be glad for small favors. From what I'd seen that afternoon, it could have gone either way.

He nodded at me formally, then handed across a white mask. It was beaded and in a pale champagne color that didn't entirely clash with my dress.

Dex hooked a black mask from his breast pocket and popped it on. "Say: I'm starting to think we might just have some fun at this shindig."

"Miss Katherine, do invite Mr. Theroux inside," Marjorie said, poking her head into the foyer from the dining room.

"Well, hello Mrs. Oleg," Dex said, taking off the mask and popping it back into his breast pocket. "Lovely evening we're having, isn't it?"

Marjorie just scowled at him. Even though she'd extended her invitation, you didn't need to be a detective to know she was suspicious of Dex. In a way, I understood that quite well. When my father was alive, Dex was not the sort of man who would have been welcome in our home—at least, not when anyone was looking. Since he'd died, though, I'd had reason to wonder about some of the secrets my father had kept.

Dex wasn't put off by her coldness. "And you're not to worry about Miss Katherine, Mrs. Oleg," he said, just as though she had greeted him in return. "I'll have her back to you all in one piece in a couple of hours."

"Thanks, Dex," I said once we'd settled into the big car. I had the cape I'd bought at Blackstone's around my shoulders to ward off the evening's chill. The beaded dress had been built for beauty, not warmth. "Marjorie is never very nice to you. I'm sorry about that. Nothing I say or do seems to change her mind."

"It's all right, Kitty. I understand. She's afraid I'm a danger to you. I can see it in her eyes. And I guess I am." I would have protested, but he barged right through. "No, no: really. Look at the danger you face on a daily basis." I laughed at that because, truly, there were whole weeks where we didn't see a single paying customer and I doubted I was in danger from the mailman. "Well, she sees danger even where you and I do not, Kitty. It's just the way of things."

I knew that, in a way, he was right. Yet that was a part of it all I enjoyed, though I don't think I would have admitted it out loud to Dex or anyone else. And I was quite sure I could never have made Marjorie understand.

Working for Dex wasn't like working for a doctor or a lawyer. Perhaps those jobs had their points of interest, as well. But from where I was sitting, I couldn't see it. And where was I sitting? In a big car, at the side of a handsome man. I was wearing a pretty dress made by a famous designer and purchased by a movie star. We were on our way to a masquerade ball—a *ball*—being thrown in the clubhouse of a secret organization of actors.

No, really: it was difficult to imagine this happening to a girl who worked for Hartounian the importer or in an accountancy firm.

"Have I told you that you look swell tonight, Kitty?" I smiled. Thanked him. Controlled the melt of lipstick and the flutter of wings in my gut.

CHAPTER THIRTEEN

THE MASQUERS WERE headquartered on North Sycamore
Avenue in Hollywood, just a couple of blocks off Hollywood
Boulevard, a couple more from Sunset. Their clubhouse was in
what had once been a grand private residence. From the street
it looked like a normal, if lovely and huge, home. It was finished in the Tudor style, the grounds carefully maintained and
closely clipped, the house an island in a huge man-made oasis.

I didn't know what I had expected, but it was different from
the reality. As we wandered up the front walk, our masks in
place, the music got louder, the cacophony more pronounced.
The front door was open, as were many of the windows, perhaps letting in the cool evening air but also allowing plumes of
smoke and sound to escape into the night.

Once we'd put our masks on, we stood in a larger foyer momentarily flummoxed, not knowing quite what to do with ourselves or what to expect beyond this point. Stairways led up and
down, though the largest wave of music and noise came from a
pair of double doors on one side. They were closed just now but
one imagined that, when they were thrown open, it would have
been difficult to talk or even think.

"It's all a bit much to take in, isn't it?" the speaker was about
Dex's height, a tall man with broad shoulders under an evening
jacket of good quality. He had medium brown hair, dark and
laughing eyes but, almost inexplicably, it was difficult to tell
anything more about him because he was wearing a tidy black
mask that, like ours, covered only the area around his eyes. You
wouldn't have thought that small black mask would make so
much of a difference, but somehow it did; completely obscuring

the essential something that would have made the man an individual to me. I knew that our own masks would have the same effect.

His voice was surprisingly deep, even for someone of his height, and it was warm and welcoming. I figured that might be the reason he'd been given the assignment to greet people at the door. "It's early yet, though you're certainly not the first to arrive."

Dex handed over our invitation. The man gave it a cursory glance and handed it back.

"I'd start in the ballroom," he said, indicating the direction we should follow. "You can get a drink and look the food over. But you'll find most of the house open tonight, and the gardens, as well. Follow your pleasure and have a wonderful time."

Once there, I guessed that the room our greeter had described as the ballroom served many functions at different times. With very few modifications, it could have been a large dining room—with row upon row of masquers raising toasts—or even a theater suitable for live productions, the revels Wyndham had told us about. In its ballroom function, however, a ten-piece orchestra commanded the far wall. I couldn't see who tonight's orchestra was from my vantage on entry but it was immediately apparent that they were wonderful.

Small tables and stools flanked the walls, providing places for people to sit and chat and perhaps have a drink while watching the dancers. It was early yet—just nine o'clock—so there weren't many dancers when we arrived. I suspected that would change as the night wore on, though, while the champagne—and other drinks—flowed and inhibitions loosened. Food was already laid out, though. I could see the tables from across the room and I looked forward to a closer inspection.

On one side of the room a series of doors led out onto a verandah and from there to a garden. Lanterns were lit and food and drink were laid out there as well. Beautifully dressed masked couples flowed in and out of those doors like so much liquid.

I made a bee-line for the eats. Dex pressed a glass of champagne into my hand while I looked the food over. Seeing all that food made me a little sad. If only Marjorie could have been there to see and enjoy it, I thought. It was so beautiful. Almost too beautiful to eat, though I didn't let that stop me.

One platter alternated eggs and small artichokes, both filled with crabmeat and shrimp and arranged so prettily it looked like modern art. A molded fish salad glittered on its own platter, the salad an iridescent green, with flakes of salmon apparent through the gelatinous surface. The whole was covered with a lovely cucumber sauce and the green against green took my breath away.

An iced bowl held a pile of glistening black caviar. Next to the bowl were tiny pancakes *a la russe* and soured cream. I thought of making myself a confection of these ingredients as indicated, but feared I'd get the order wrong.

There was one beautiful tray that featured bite-sized tomato aspics filled with cream cheese and anchovy and I helped myself to one of these. The salt of the one perfectly complimented the creamy texture of the other while all those glorious flavors were encased in softly flavored glossy red. In that moment, it seemed the most perfect bite of food I'd ever enjoyed. These things—and more—were all served in the buffet style: one could go as often as one liked and eat as much as one could hold. But there was more food yet. Masked serving girls bearing trays moved among the guests, some offering glasses of champagne, others hot canapés with creamed oysters, crabmeat as well as tiny little perfect sandwiches featuring pineapple with ham, egg with almond and other clever combinations.

"You gonna stop eating when you're full," Dex asked, "or

when your arms get tired?" He stood over me and grinned while I helped myself to a small plateful of the molded fish salad drizzled with some of the cucumber dressing.

"A girl has to keep up her strength," I said a little hotly once I'd finished my mouthful. "So what's your big plan?" I asked, thinking to divert him from my snack.

"Well, here's what I figure," he said, taking a crab-stuffed artichoke off my plate and nibbling it with surprising delicacy while we spoke, "everyone is going to be busy playing at being something they're not. You and I will mosey around on our own and just see what we can see. Talk to people. Don't worry about being found out: we got our invitation right enough. It's not like we had to sneak in."

I nodded, glad he'd reminded me of this. Despite the fact that I was both hungry and eating, I'd been somewhat shy about this whole escapade. Although, it wasn't like you could tell that from the way I was stuffing my face.

"Let's do this," Dex said, "we'll mosey around on our own, like I said. But we'll meet back here in an hour, compare notes. OK?"

"Sounds good to me." Before I shoved off, though, I risked it: I took one of the tiny pancakes and delicately dropped about a teaspoon of the shiny fish eggs on it, topping the whole with another teaspoon of the soured cream. Dex watched while I popped this in my mouth and chewed thoughtfully.

"Not bad," I pronounced, reaching for my champagne. "Salty." Dex pulled a face that said you couldn't pay him to stick that in his mouth and headed in the direction of the foyer. I had a hunch he'd poke his head in downstairs, just to see what there was to be seen. I headed over to one of the windows that led to the verandah and the garden, wanting a gander of what was beyond all that expensive glass.

The verandah was host to cigar smokers and couples who looked as though they'd like to find a place to tryst. Though I've no fondness for cigars, I joined the smokers: I hadn't brought the right sort of decoy to be playing at the other.

"Would you care for one of my Cubans?" Though the mask made it difficult to judge accurately, I gauged the man's age to be between fifty and sixty, though dapper. The kind of man used to making headway with girls my age. He was nice-looking, too, I could see that, mask or no. There was something vaguely familiar about him: something in the shape of his head, I thought. And maybe the cut of his shoulders. I couldn't place it, though. Nor could I shake the feeling.

"No thank you," I said. Then, lowering my voice, "I don't actually smoke," allowing him to draw his own conclusions. He did.

"Ah," he said. "Out here to escape someone." It wasn't a question. I just shrugged, noncommittal. He accepted it as a positive reply, which was fine by me. "But say," he said, "you look familiar to me."

"I was just thinking the same about you."

"Have I seen you in anything?"

I shook my head. "I'm not an actress."

He arched his eyebrows at me. That is, I could not actually see his eyebrows due to the mask he was wearing, but the rest of his face stretched around the way faces do when eyebrows are raised.

"You're not?" said he. "What then?"

I touched a finger to my own mask. "There's a reason we're wearing these, is there not?"

He laughed, taking my meaning. "There is. All right then, can I at least know your name?"

"You can . . . you can call me Kitty," I said, inexplicably reaching for the detested nickname rather than my real name. Something about the mask called it up.

"All right, Kitty," he extended his hand, "I'm Baron."

I shook the hand he offered, but my mind was reeling. *That* was why he looked familiar. Of course. Baron Sutherland had been a major star when I was a child. He still got roles now, but they were secondary ones—bad guys, fathers, bank presidents. In person I could feel the presence that had made him a star. There was a kind of subdued intensity about him. You had the feeling that, most of the time, he got what he wanted.

"You should maybe have made up a name, Baron. That's a pretty distinctive moniker. So now I know who you are, mask or no."

He laughed again, sounding unconcerned. "There are worse things." Then, "Walk with me?" he said, not waiting for an answer, but steering me down the verandah stairs and into the garden. I trotted along obediently. A movie star, I thought. Imagine! I took his arm as we made our way around the garden path, trying not to look as though I were hanging on his every word.

He chatted as we walked. "Anyway, you're the one who was cloaking herself in mystery, not I. Let's face it: for someone as old as I have become to have a chance with someone as young and beautiful as you," he stopped and took my hand as he said this last. Raised it to his lips. "I need every bit of magic I can muster. Are you impressed? Well, that's just fine." He smiled at me. Winked. I could see that wink through his mask. "That's just what I want." Then he led us on again, back down the garden path.

I laughed, as well. Drawn to him despite myself. None of this was getting me what I'd come here for. But—oh!—I was having a wonderful time.

"So, hmmmm," he was saying. "You won't tell me what you do. Will you tell me who you came with?"

I cocked my head at him, the mystery of the evening washing me in an unfamiliar coquettishness. But it was all the answer he seemed to need.

"All right then," he said, "I'll have to guess. Look at you:

tall and reed slender. Elegant, certainly. Aristocratic if I hold my head in a certain way. So I say . . . you're a princess—from Russia—and you don't dare tell me your identity. You're here in exile and have been since babyhood."

"Oh, good guess! Quite, quite good. Only I was born right here in Los Angeles. And I have no Russian blood."

"Born right here in L.A.? Well, that's something. One of the three, then?" He kidded.

I looked at him blankly.

"Well," he said, motioning dramatically around the verandah, "everyone's from somewhere else, aren't they? Go ahead and ask. I myself was born in a small town in Michigan. We're all from somewhere else. But one in three . . ."

"Ah, I get it. Though it's a shrinking number, isn't it? I'd wager that, these days, it might even be one-in-six. Or more. I'm an aberration now. An outsider, almost, in my own hometown."

"An outsider? Oh, princess: look at you. Never an outsider. Not here or anywhere."

The level of champagne in our glasses had grown low and we'd left the girls with trays behind on the verandah. Baron settled me on a bench under a palm and went off to find full glasses. As I watched him go, I took myself to task. He was twice my age—maybe more—and I was enjoying his company more than was appropriate. When he came back with our drinks, I determined to steer things around to business if I could. If I couldn't, I'd go off and find someone else to talk to.

"There you go, your ladyship," he said when he returned, passing me my glass. "Your most royal highness."

He extended his hand to me and I took it, rising. We continued our walk, deeper into the garden. I couldn't see much of it, but what I *could* see—and smell—was lovely. A lush, tropical oasis with a footlit path. We walked on.

"Thank you," I said, "I feel just like . . . I feel like Catherine

Calderon in *The Cardboard Heart*. Have you seen it?" I asked
in what I hoped was a guileless manner.

"Seen it?" he said laughing. "I was in it."

"You were?" All coquettishness was off me now. I was genuinely astonished. "Perhaps it's not polite to say, but I don't
recall that."

He sighed and then he shrugged. "That's the thing, isn't it?
A decade ago, it would have been me kissing the lovely Miss
Cat in that movie." I wondered if I heard a trace of bitterness
in his voice. "Ah well. No, I was the sheriff. In the scenes in the
town?"

"You were?" I said, trying hard to remember, carrying with
me only the impression of someone grizzled and beyond prime
years. A cutout of a sheriff, then. A character without weight or
substance. "I barely remember you there. But it's not your fault.
It was a silly role for you. I think you should still play leads." It
came out sounding juvenile and ridiculous, yet I meant it. He
could see that straight off.

"Ah, that's sweet, princess," he said, obviously touched. I
thought maybe the bitterness I'd heard had been my imagination. "Balm to an old man's heart to hear a pretty girl—a Russian princess no less—say things like that. You oughta be careful
with your powers. A man could fall in love with a girl who said
things to him like that."

He'd stopped next to a small bamboo grove that sheltered
us from the house. There was a low table there, and a bench,
though we did not sit. He took my glass and placed it on the
table with his own. Then he moved in close, close enough that
I could catch the woody citrus scent of *chypre* on his jacket. My
stomach fluttered in a way that made me feel as though I
might fall over with it. I felt literally weak in the knees.

We didn't speak for a moment and then he reached out—
ever so gently—and touched my chin, lifting it softly between
thumb and forefinger. And even as he bent his head, even as he

kissed me and all the sensations were swirling around me like a movie vampire's cape, I felt myself wonder at the art of this seduction. Though such things—stolen kisses by handsome men—had been rare enough in my life that I had practically no experiences to recollect, I understood even while it was happening that the same could not be said for him and that even as he made me feel rare and special—a princess fallen across his path—such occurrences were, for him, neither rare nor especially unique.

I understood these things with the part of my brain reserved for calm judgment. And I did not care. In fact, I felt my neck extend further into him, felt an instinct overtake me and my body, my mouth, my heart respond to him. And a part of me felt ridiculous. And a part of me felt swept away. The two parts were somehow not at war.

It was he who finally pulled away, not I. He held me at arm's length, peered into my eyes. "Were it not practically considered a sin here, I'd reach over and pull off that mask. I so want to see your face. And I want to see your face regard mine."

"What would you see?" I said, matching his tone. Meeting it, as though both of us were in some lighthearted film brimming with romance.

"Why," he said, more honestly than I'd anticipated, "perhaps I'd see my youth."

I shook my head. "Perhaps not. Perhaps you'd see something to frighten you. Something to make you run away."

"Ah, princess. Not that. Never that."

I was surprised when, despite his words, he pushed me away from him, gently but firmly. When he righted his hair and the items of clothing that had become slightly askew in our gentle tussle, I was surprised because, had it been left to me, I would not have made that decision. I blush to think of it now but it's possible that, in those few heated minutes, I would have followed anywhere he led.

"Forgive me, Princess, because I *am* loath to leave your side." Fully and expertly repaired, he reached across and picked up our half-full champagne glasses, keeping one and handing me the other. I took mine gratefully. Sipped carefully. I was parched, though I didn't think much more alcohol would do me a great deal of good. "But I came here with another," he continued. "And I suspect that you did too." He looked a question at me and I shrugged, again allowing him his own conclusions; knowing at which he'd arrive.

He got us moving again and we traveled the footlit path in companionable silence. Sensing I might not get another opportunity and sensing also that our time together was drawing to a close, I decided without anything ventured, there could be nothing gained.

"Am I right in thinking you were one of the founders of the Masquers, Baron?"

He smiled down at me as we walked. Sipped. "I was."

"Then you know Laird Wyndham."

"Yes, of course. Poor chap."

"Why poor?"

"Well, that business? With the girl? So tragic." Yet it seemed to me there was something in his voice that said he didn't find it tragic at all.

"Yes," I said. "I only . . . I only know what the papers said. Sounds awful."

"Indeed." For a moment, Baron seemed lost in thought and when he spoke, I wasn't sure he spoke to me or simply to express his thoughts aloud. "He always had a streak in him though, Laird Wyndham."

"He . . . he did?" I said.

"Well, not so just anyone could see it." Were the words spoken too quickly? A recovery from a near-fumble? Or was my imagination running away from me? Jumping at shadows. "But a darkness, you understand. When I heard the news, I wasn't surprised."

"Really," I said, prompting. "How so?"

"Well, we worked together many times over the years, Laird and I. Hell, I guess you could say we were friends for a time, of a sort."

"A sort."

"Well, I was the leading man and he was the pup, coming up. And then, slowly, you understand, a shift came."

"A shift. And then he became the leading man?" I asked the question, but I didn't have to. We both knew what had gone on. One day your name was on the marquee, in lights. And the next? You were the grizzled sheriff. The father. The town barber. You were someone with less lines, less money, less fame. "That must have hurt."

We had come back to the foot of the stairs that led to the verandah. Baron stopped and looked down at me carefully. The look must have reassured him. After all, what did he see? A slip of a girl not yet in her mid-twenties, a pliant girl with soft lips. I could not blame him for not seeing anything else. I had not intentionally brought him to this spot, but I was not now sorry that I had.

He took a sip of his champagne and leaned into the base of the concrete banister gracefully. It was a casual movement, easy. But I could see it masked deep thought.

"Hurt? Hurt is not the word for it, Princess. It scorched my soul, in a way. It burned."

Now it was my turn to look closely. Did his eyes swim at the words, just a bit? But it was impossible to tell protected by the twin shields of the dark and the mask.

"I'd want to do something about it." I said the words quietly. I addressed them to my shoes.

I felt rather than saw Baron move his hand to the top of my

head. It seemed to me he caressed my hair the way he might have done with a dog. Or maybe it was just that I was seeing him differently now, differently than I had in the garden. When I would have followed him anywhere.

"You'd want to," he said absently, as though his mind were far away, "but you'd think very carefully before you did."

"Were you at the party?" Did I move too quickly with this question? But no: I was not a detective, after all. Just a slip of a girl.

"At Laird's party at the Ambassador? Sure. I wouldn't have missed it. Why? Were you there? I don't remember seeing you."

"Maybe you wouldn't have seen me," I said, not answering his question but not even sure where I was going with my remarks. "Maybe you would have been busy?"

"That could be. There were a lot of people there, that's for sure. But listen, Princess, I've known Wyndham a good long time. We've worked on movies together. We worked on this place together." He indicated the gardens we still stood in and the house that loomed above us, alight with party noise and golden light. "And I'm a man who prides himself on being able to judge a character, do you understand?"

I nodded. "I think so. Yes."

"So I stand more or less side by side with Laird Wyndham for a dozen years and now someone tells me he murdered a girl. Brutally and without care. And that's *not* the Laird Wyndham I used to know," he said flatly. He'd put down his champagne in order to slap the back of one hand into the palm of the other. "But maybe—just maybe, mind—maybe he's changed."

"People don't change," I said, repeating something Marjorie said often enough.

"Don't they, Princess?" He smiled at me—indulgently or with respect, I couldn't tell. It was a little too dim in the garden for visual nuance. Still, all things considered—soft lips, champagne and the tendrils of moonlight I could now begin to see poking around the edge of the house—my money was on the former. "Oh, but I think they do."

There seemed to me something chilling in those five words.

I tried to get more out of him, but he wouldn't budge. And I had the feeling it wasn't just the conversation he wanted to get away from. I had the feeling he had gotten nervous and was keeping an eye out for someone, a feeling that increased when he led me back up the stairs and onto the verandah.

Just as we'd reached level ground, a girl appeared framed in the doorway. She was devastatingly beautiful, with hair the color of honey and limbs so long they gave her a coltish appearance. Her dress was silk and looked as though it had been poured onto her while warm, settling into every groove as the material came to body temperature which, on her, probably hovered around the melting point of bronze.

"There you are, Baron," she said. Her voice was like honey, as well. Deeper than I'd expected, but feminine just the same. "I've been looking everywhere for you." Seeing us chatting, she smiled at me, but her eyes were cold. "Let's go in, shall we? I've been speaking with the Hutchinses. They want us to come with them on their yacht this weekend," she said in a voice that indicated yacht trips were possibly a daily occurrence. "Just a day trip to Ensenada. I told them we would, if you'd like to go."

"That sounds lovely, Beatrice. Look . . . we were just talking a bit of business. I'll meet you at the buffet table in two minutes flat, all right?"

"Of course, darling," she said sweetly enough, though her eyes, when they scraped me, would have swatted me dead if she'd had her way. A girl knows these things. A girl can feel them tickling her blood.

"So, Princess," he said to me when Beatrice had gone back inside, "that's how it is, OK?" His voice, when he said it, was kind enough, though maybe he was taking the extra minute to be certain I wouldn't cause him any trouble.

"Sure," I said, as though the whole thing had been a lark. And, truly, what had it been if not that? "I can see that. That's just how it is."

As luck, fate, kismet or karma would have things, Dex chose that minute to stick his head out the door. "Everything OK, angel?" he said, looking from Baron to me then back again. I silently blessed and cursed his instinct in a single breath, then went to him straight away.

"Yes, of course darling," I said, linking my arm in his. "Mr. . . . Sutherland was just going inside. Do come out and enjoy the night air with me for a while."

Baron said good-night to both of us quickly, then ducked inside, leaving me stuck with a gawking Dex.

" 'Darling'?" he said, feigning astonishment. "I should shave and play dress-up more often. That's the second time someone has called me that this evening."

"Well, don't get used to it," I said, dropping his arm.

"What was that all about?" he asked.

"Research. Gathering evidence and clues and whatnot."

"Ah. Really, that's what I thought when I looked in the garden for you a while ago."

I felt color rush to my cheeks. Not the pretty kind, either— the kind that makes your brain feel hot and your cheeks about to explode. That may not be quite right, but it's not in any case a pleasant sensation.

"You saw?" I said. My voice barely above a whisper.

Dex just nodded, then patted my shoulder awkwardly. "It's all right, Kitty. These things happen. Just a few kisses, nothing to get worked up about. High time you had some fun."

I pushed my hands over my eyes and steeled myself not to cry which, in the face of Dex's sympathy and understanding, was nearly impossible.

"You won't . . . you won't tell anyone?" I said, without lifting my eyes from my hands.

"Naw, Kitty. I won't tell a soul. How did I even know it was you? You were wearing a mask. Could've been anyone."

"Thanks."

"Really, Kitty, you have to try and be a little less serious. Now c'mon: you've been out here working up an appetite long enough. Come back in and get some more fish jelly or some damn thing. Though, maybe in your case, no more champagne."

I did as he suggested and had some more of the molded fish salad and some other stuff as well. I felt better for it, too. Even though I *did* have more champagne. What more, I reasoned, could happen this night? Why did I need my wits about me? Turns out I had no idea.

CHAPTER FOURTEEN

THE BALLROOM HAD gotten more crowded in the hour or so I'd been outside. Dex managed to find us a small table anyway. He held it while I got myself another plate of food, then we both sat down to swap notes and figure what came next.

Dex told me that directly under the ballroom there was a sort of basement, partially below ground level. There were a couple of mechanical rooms down there as well as a gaming room, including two billiard tables. All I'd seen of the main floor was the ballroom, but Dex had also scoped his and hers bathrooms, a kitchen equipped to cook for a platoon, a couple of offices meant for the men who ran the club on a day-to-day basis, and a sort of smoking lounge, done up in men's club style, complete with deep leather chairs, a mahogany bar, and probably one of the best collections of illegal booze in the Southland. This had impressed Dex most of all.

"You stand there, in front of that bar," he said, a sort of wonder in his voice, "and you don't think at all about Prohibition. You can't. You just see all the beautifully arranged bottles and think you're in Paris. Or Vancouver. And it's all classy stuff. None of that coffin varnish you get at the speakeasies." There was a wistfulness about him when he said it. A wonder. It almost made me sad.

Another level had been added to the house since the Masquers purchased the property. Dex said they'd built a deck on the roof where lunch was served every day. I reported on the verandah and the garden while avoiding looking at Dex. We agreed that, from what we'd seen, the place was pretty impressive.

Dex didn't probe about Baron Sutherland, and I was grateful. I figured I'd fill him in on the little I'd learned later, when the earlier part of the episode didn't feel quite so raw.

"Now what?" I said when we'd exchanged everything that seemed necessary for the moment and the last of my fish salad was gone.

"Well, more of the same," Dex said. "Seems to me, we're doin' all right. It's not even eleven o'clock and the party just seems to be getting started." He looked around. "The booze and the food certainly haven't eased up any. They're obviously expecting people will be here for hours."

"Meet back here in another hour?" I asked.

"Sounds about right. But listen, Kitty, try to keep the evidence gathering to a minimum, okey? We don't want any love-struck actor type following you home like a lost puppy." Then he sauntered away. Before, I guess, I could collect my wits enough to talk back or sock him.

This time, it was Dex who headed out to the verandah and the garden, which suited me fine. I decided I wanted a peek at that roof deck. Getting there meant passing through the second floor where I saw that the rooms were smaller: mostly bedrooms and small sitting rooms, with the occasional bathroom thrown in for good measure. The carpets and the walls were a deep, almost lurid crimson—although that adjective might have come from the present context: the use and abandon of a masquerade ball and the sound of giggles and muffled ecstasy that floated out from behind a few of the closed doors. I wondered if there were still masks in place behind some of those doors. I figured perhaps there were.

At the end of the hallway at the back of the house, a second stairway headed up. This one was more austere than the one that led up from the foyer, but then its purpose was different as well.

Like the verandah, the patio had been decked out for a party. I imagined that on a normal day, the tables would be set up at generous intervals, allowing room for either privacy or thick groups of friends. One could almost see them smoking and laughing with the sun on their heads: a perpetual picnic where the food didn't come in baskets and the booze flowed free.

However, for this party, the tables had been pushed to one side, making room for another orchestra—though this one was smaller than the one in the ballroom: just six pieces playing Rodgers and Hart's "Dancing on the Ceiling," which seemed ironic considering where they were. The bar was set up directly opposite. Apparently one could not have masquers without also having a bar. This made sense to me.

A little dance floor had been cleared in front of the orchestra, but just now, no one was dancing. Instead there were thick clusters of masquers in conversations I didn't feel welcome to intrude upon. Some heads rose as I joined them. I could see them looking me over quickly, cataloging where I fit. A few eyes lingered but no one beckoned me over and I quickly retreated back into the house.

Passing through the corridor of bedrooms and sitting rooms, I saw that one of the doors was open. I stopped and peered inside. A thickset man of about forty wearing an expensive evening suit sat on a nubbled sofa the color of oxblood. The suit was slightly rumpled, his head was in his hands, his mask a bit askew. I could see he'd had too much to drink. More. I hadn't spent all this time with Dex without learning a thing or two about recognizing signs. The man on the oxblood sofa was looking at his life and he wasn't much liking what he saw.

At a different time, I might have been afraid of him, sitting there so deeply into his cups. But there was something rumpled and forlorn about him. I was aware of no fear, only simple human concern.

"You all right?" I said from the doorway.

He lifted his head without interest, regarded me dispassion-ately. To him I might as well not have been there.

"I'm counting my sins," he said through his drink, though his voice was quite clear and pure. It surprised me.

"And you can't count that high?" I said gently, making a guess.

Now he looked at me more closely. So closely he narrowed his eyes to slits.

"What do you mean?" he said at length. "What do you know?" I suspected he thought that I was not real. The mirage of a drunken man. A mirage in a beaded dress.

I entered the room cautiously. Here is what I knew: judging from his profile and his girth the well-dressed man on the oxblood sofa wasn't an actor. That combined with his age and his dress and his location made me guess he was an executive of some sort, therefore someone in a position to know a thing or two. Just the sort of person Dex had suggested it would be good to chat up. But something more basic drew me to him and my response came just as strongly because I understood he was a human in despair. That's not something I've ever been able to walk away from, nor really even tried.

"I don't know anything," I said. "I know nothing at all. But men counting sins . . . well, let's just say you look like someone who wouldn't need even a quarter hour to give to despair. Yet here you sit." Without even knowing I was going to do so, I en-tered the room and sat on the other end of the sofa, the side closest the door. I was far enough away to make a hasty escape if I needed to. Close enough that he would understand that an-other human had heard the despair in his heart . . . and had stopped to listen.

"Bah," he said, a tiny explosion of sound, accompanied by more air than was strictly necessary. But he made no move ei-ther away from me or in my direction so I held my ground.

"That's the thing about sins," I said, "they don't need a lot of room for you to be able to pile them real high."

He looked at me out of the corner of his eye then. Shot me something like a smile. "What's your name?" he said.

"Kitty."

"I'm Joe. You want a drink?" I started to say no, then realized if I'd opted to share a bit of his misery I should also share some of his poison. It felt like part of some unwritten code.

"All right," I said.

He hauled himself up and moved across the room to a makeshift bar. There were spirits here only, I noticed. Ice in a bucket. A bowl of nuts. And the most basic types of mix. No champagne.

He poured himself a couple fingers of scotch, hesitated, then added a third. Neat.

"What'll it be?" he said.

"Gin and tonic, please," I replied then added, with a smile, "heavy on the tonic, though. It's starting to feel like it's been a long party."

"I know what you mean," he said, mixing my drink. Then, almost as an afterthought, he added another finger of scotch to his own glass before joining me again on the couch. The activity seemed to have jolted him a bit, despite all the new scotch. The activity and, perhaps, my presence seemed to have brought him slightly out of the morose place in which he'd been hanging his head.

"The thing is," he said when he was seated again, "everything I've done, I've done for the good of it all, do you know what I mean?" He looked at me earnestly, like my answer mattered. And truly? I did not know what he meant. It was all too oblique.

"I . . . I guess," is all I said.

"And we ask ourselves that, don't we?" I didn't even start to answer this one. It sounded rhetorical. "We ask ourselves if it's more all right when only good was meant. After all, what part do intentions play in all of this? If you *intend* no harm, yet harm comes, is it just as bad? Or do the intentions cancel out the sins themselves?"

I did not answer this. That rhetorical thing again. Or rather, I did not answer out loud. But do intentions matter? Sure they matter. Does one cancel out the other? Maybe. It all depends on the nature of the sin.

"But the industry is in a mess," he lifted his head once again, met my eyes. What I saw there cut me. It was like a window into a place I did not wish to see. Yet he wanted me to. I could see that, as well. Here I was: anonymous, non-threatening, dubiously connected. And, anyway, he was drunk. He required less of a reason to unburden than a sober man would have done. It's why people with secrets do better when they stay off the sauce. "I had to do something, didn't I? I did. And, like the lady said, 'what's done . . . '"

". . . cannot be undone," I said, picking up the quote and remembering as I did so that the words belonged to Lady Macbeth in the one of Shakespeare's works that our drama teacher at school had always insisted we refer to as "the Scottish play" for fear of—I wasn't quite sure what—creating a haggis famine or a run on bagpipes or oatcakes or some such.

"But what . . . what did you do?" I asked it so softly, at first I thought he didn't hear. When he hesitated before he said anything, I pressed on. "It's probably not as bad as you think."

He looked at me closely again. "Do you recognize me?" he said after a beat.

I shook my head, confident I'd never seen him before.

He lifted his mask. "How about now?" There were glasses under the mask. They magnified his eyes, they were blue shot through with red. His nose was crossed with spider-veins and his lips fit into his face like a pair of German sausages. He was not an attractive man, unmasked. And I did not recognize him.

I shook my head again.

"I'm a very important man," he said. They were boastful words, but he did not say them boastfully. Rather, he sounded broken as he said them. Sounded as though he was aware of their cost.

"I'm sure you are," I said softly.

"I work at the Hays Office, directly under Mr. Hays himself." He watched my face as he said this, waiting for the import of his words to sink in.

I offered no reaction. I didn't have one. If I'd heard of the Hays Office before, I didn't remember it now. That seemed entirely possible. After all, I hadn't remembered Temperance and even Dex had berated me for that.

"You haven't heard of him or me, have you? I can see that in your face."

I shook my head. "Sorry. No. I haven't."

"Motion Picture Producers and Distributors of America?"

"*That* sounds familiar," I said. "So you distribute movies?"

He shook his head. "We're the governing body of the people that make and distribute the movies."

"My," I said, "that *is* impressive." I wasn't trying to be patronizing. But I would allow that it may have sounded that way.

"Well, see. . . ." He withdrew a silver monogrammed cigarette case from his breast pocket, offered me one and, when I declined, fumbled one from the case for himself, then expended some mental energy on getting it lit. The process seemed to demand almost more of his motor skills than he currently had available.

"On paper, it *is* impressive," he said. "Real impressive. But the thing is, the studios put it all together to get people off their backs."

"What people?" It struck me that there was a thread of something in what he was saying that might be of interest to me.

Special interest. But that's the thing with thread: if you look at a lot of them altogether, it's tough to see where one ends and another begins. From a distance, it all just looks like a whole piece of tapestry.

"Oh, you know, govnmint. Churches. That kind of thing."

"So, wait: who hired you?"

"Will Hays."

"No, I mean, churches? Or government? Is that what you're saying?"

"No, no. I'm saying it wrong." He drew on his smoke and slurped his drink thoughtfully, as though figuring the best way to explain.

"See, at the beginning of the twenties, some people—like I said, govnmint and churches mostly—they got the idea that the movies were showing too much of the wrong kind of things."

"Oh-kay . . ." I said doubtfully. He seemed to be digging in to give me a history lesson. And this part of his story I knew already. Everybody kinda did.

"They figured Hollywood was gettin' out of hand, you know? The movie stars were gettin' too big for their britches and something oughta be done."

"And that's where you came in?"

"Not quite. See, the studio bosses figured it would be better if they could keep being the boss of everything. So they got together and made a kind of club and *that's* who I work for."

"A club?"

"No. The Motion Picture Producers and Distributors of America, like I tol' you." He looked at me closely then, like he thought I might be a little slow. I got up and retrieved a bottle of scotch, filled his glass, banked on the fact that he wouldn't remember I was drinking gin and made a show of filling mine, then sat back down.

"So that worked out then? That fixed everyone's concerns?"

"Not even close. See, we made some rules about what could and couldn't be showed. But no one listened. What do you do when no one listens?"

"Um," I fumbled, "say it louder?"

"That's kinda what we did, I guess. But they still don't listen."

"Who? Who doesn't listen?"

"The studios. Yeah, they pay their dues. They come to meetings. But then they just send whatever pictures they want out into the world like nobody's business." He sounded injured as he said this last. He said it as though it rankled.

"So then what do you do?"

"Well, that's it, ain't it? Something had to be done." He said this with the air of someone set to justify himself. Sometimes that's the only way that we survive all that needs to be gotten through: by believing whatever actions we performed were right and justified and the only way to proceed. " 'Cause now the League is at us about it and our hands? They're tied!"

"The League?"

". . . of Decency. Lookit, I don't know why I'm talking to you like this. If it's boring you so much you don't wanna hear it, just say and I'll shut up."

"No, no. That's not it. It's just . . . well, it's complicated, isn't it? It's an easy story for you to follow. You know all the ups and downs. This is the first time I'm hearing any of it." Then, as an afterthought, because it was and because I wanted him to keep talking, I said, "And it's fascinating."

"Well, all right then," he said, sounding slightly mollified, but like it was still gonna take some work for him to be completely over the personal injury he'd seen looming. And he moved a bit closer to me on the sofa. At least, it seemed to me that he did. I wasn't quite sure.

"So this League," I said, prompting, "I don't really get their place in all this."

"Well that's 'cause, officially, I guess they don't have one. But here's the thing: they're mad as hell. They say—all hoity-toity like—that we'd better do something or they'll pull their support. That's just how they said it."

"Would that matter?"

"It matters! Jeepers creepers. It matters. Times is tough, girlie, or haven't you noticed? People ain't going to the movies anymore like they used to. Oh, they wanna. But they don't always got the nickel for it. And the studios? Their revenues is down. But the League? They say they're gonna make things worse. Preach it from the pulpits: Hollywood is evil. Don't go to the movies."

"I can't imagine that would make a difference."

"What? Preachers telling their flocks not to give us their nickels? Not to give us their nickels or they'll go to hell? Sure. That would make a difference."

"You think people would listen?"

"Sure, sure they would. It's already started. Oh, not in places like L.A. Not here. Not in New York, either. But in other places. Sure. People there will listen. *Are* listening. And we see it in the receipts: fewer people going to see the movies we make out here. An' that's bad for everyone."

As he said this last, he moved still closer to me. I was sure of it this time. And he let his hand rest in the small amount of space left between us. I ignored this slow advance, for the moment. But I kept an eye on him.

"So what do you do?"

"Well, we gotta make it right, don' we? And that's happening now. I mean, it's the Depression what's doing it. But those religious types have the keys to the tower. We give 'em their way, they'll see to it that things go back the way they were."

I heard the words but I doubted them even while he said them. You can't really ever go back, no matter how much you might want to and how much you put into getting there. I said none of this. What I did say: "But how do you do that?"

"Well, the Production Code is a start. We've got that now. So it's just a matter of getting everyone to toe the line and obey it. So all *we* have to do is keep convincing the industry it's in their best interest to show a sunnier face to Chicago."

"Chicago," I said. "What's in Chicago?"

"Why the League of Decency for crying out loud. Haven't you heard anything I said?"

Chicago. "And this Production Code? What's that?"

"Jay-sus, girlie, but you ask a lot of goddamned questions." With that he got his hand in motion. I saw it but it happened so quickly, it was in my hair before I even knew what he had in mind. By the time he pressed his sausage-y lips to mine, I had my wits back about me.

It was easy to shake him off. He was drunk enough that I wondered if he would even have tried it sober. If he had, he would have been stronger, though. As it was, the drink had sapped both his brains and his strength.

I moved as far away from him as I could, a little dismayed because he was now between me and the door. I worried mildly that he'd try something again, but I was more repulsed than frightened. The door was open and people were nearby. It seemed likely to me that someone would hear me scream. If it even came to that. As drunk as he was, I somehow doubted that it would.

I was right. Within seconds of my revolted rejection he pulled himself to his feet and started shuffling for the door. The remorse and despair I'd felt on him earlier had gone as though they'd never been. I'd felt sorry for him then. It was why I'd stopped and talked to him in first place, before I'd even known he'd have anything of interest to say.

"If I wanted rejection," he said as he moved through the

doorway, "I could have got it at home from my wife." With that he was gone.

I carried my drink over to the makeshift bar and left it there, grabbing a clean glass and filling it with tonic, straight, which I carried back to the sofa. I sat there for a while, just letting my revulsion pass and everything the man had told me swirl through my head.

I felt as though I needed a scorecard, or at least a pen and paper to help make sense of it all. I didn't know how it all fit together, but I had a feeling that a connection was there. Somewhere. It just had to be found.

CHAPTER FIFTEEN

I FOUND DEX in the arms of another woman. This was not a problem for me. After all, turnabout is fair play and I had no claim on him. In fact, I didn't even feel a twinge seeing the voluptuous redhead wrapping herself around my boss like a serpent feasting on a rat in the very corner of the garden where Baron had kissed me not two hours before.

Well, I *did* feel a twinge, but it was one of impatience. It had been a long night and I'd had enough. I poked around at the buffet table but even that could no longer hold my interest. And not because I wasn't hungry. I was. But all the food on offer was either very rich or very empty and pretentious. Excepting, of course, the foods that were both rich *and* pretentious. And despite all I'd eaten that evening, I found I was slightly hungry. But I wasn't hungry for any of this.

"It's starting to look a bit tired, isn't it?" The speaker was a woman, perhaps five years older than I chronologically, but a lifetime older in sophistication. She was hovering near the blinis and caviar, elegantly putting them together then delicately packing them away. The hunger combined with a light sheen of sweat on her skin made me think she'd been dancing.

I could see her sophistication in the way she dressed—as though everything she wore had been made for her in Europe—and in how she wore it. Her lips were carefully rouged and her eyes were artfully kohled and every bit of what she wore bespoke care and money as well as the knowledge of what to do with them.

"It *is* looking tired," I replied. "But then, to be honest, I'm tired as well."

She smiled a bit at that, liking the words or their honesty, I couldn't be sure which.

"These parties: they bore after a while, don't you think?" She'd said it out loud, but she needn't have; boredom was in the delicate slouch of her shoulders, the moue of her beautiful lips. Even in the way she sprinkled a bit of crumbled hard-boiled egg atop the caviar on her latest blini and then nibbled at it absently, as though she was only doing it because no better idea had struck her yet. She embodied boredom, though somehow it looked good on her.

"I don't come to enough of these things to be bored," I said truthfully. "I've had an exciting evening. Though I could see how it could become tiresome if one went to a great many events like this." I could, too. The empty—bored—people all as concerned with how others saw them as with whom they saw. The empty rich food. The endless rivers of booze. All exciting to me who had never experienced an occasion like it. But now I'd done it, I wasn't sure I'd want to do it again.

"How charmingly candid," she said, sounding like she meant it when she could as easily have just made fun. "I'm Rosalyn Steele."

"Really?" I said, still more candidly. "What a wonderful name! How lucky you are."

"Luck had nothing to do with it. This is *Hollywood*." She leaned in close to me and stage whispered, "And, anyway, 'Rosie Stein' would have an entirely different wardrobe, don't you think?"

"Rosie Stein would have a different *everything*. You're an actress then?"

"I am. It doesn't seem to come overnight though. At least, not for everyone. You didn't say your name."

"Katherine," I said. "Katherine Pangborn."

She raised her eyebrows, looking impressed. "Little Miss

Coy," she said, though there was laughter in her voice. "You've hit on a pretty good one yourself."

I laughed. "I'm no actress: I come by that one naturally."

"Really? Wow. No Stein for you?"

I shook my head.

"So, you're not an actress. What are you doing here then?"

I actually thought about telling her, but knew Dex would have quashed the idea. We were meant to be under cover, as dramatic as that sounded to me. But we were meant to be here on the QT, even if the truth, in this case, felt as though it would have been easier than lying. I settled for a partial truth by omission.

"It's too complicated to get into. But my boss . . . my boss has done some work for Laird Wyndham."

I had anticipated that this small piece of truth would provide an ice-breaker. After all, Rosalyn had said she was an actress, Wyndham was an actor and a well-connected one at that. If nothing else, it would give us something to discuss, or so I thought. As soon as I said his name, though, I was surprised to see a change wash right over Rosalyn's face. It was like a curtain fell over my new friend's eyes. Her expression was unchanged and a smile still lingered on her features. But it was not the same. I could see she was acting.

"Ah," she said, pushing her current blini and caviar into her mouth and masticating gently, "well," she said. And then, "well," again. She moved toward the place on the table where a new molded fish salad glittered in place. This one was rose-colored and a beet sauce completed the visual ensemble. Rosalyn focused all her attention on removing her slice of molded fish salad, drizzling sauce over it artfully and ignoring me altogether.

"Excuse me? Rosalyn? Miss Steele? I . . . I don't know what I said, but I do apologize if I said it badly. It . . . well, it wasn't meant."

"It's just . . . well, I didn't realize you were friends with Laird."

"Oh, no, hardly friends," I said. "I've only met the man once myself." I watched her for a moment while she continued to ignore me, then decided I had nothing to lose and plunged right in. "You don't like him," I said.

"That's not possible, is it?" she said sarcastically. "Everyone *loves* Laird Wyndham."

"Not now," I said. "Not anymore. And, apparently, not you."

Rosalyn kind of snorted and dumped another hefty spoonful of beet sauce on her fish. It occurred to me that, though she was playing coy, she clearly had something to say. In the same moment I recognized that, if this were the case, I was going to need to be the one who got her to say it. A table near us opened up and I grabbed a couple glasses of champagne and steered Rosalyn and her fish plate toward it.

"Now tell me," I said when she was sitting, "what did he do to you?"

"Do? Ha!" she said, eating a forkful of fish and sauce with more relish than was strictly called for. "It should be so simple."

"I don't understand," I prompted.

She sighed, then sat up straighter and looked around. We were in a crowded room, but no one was paying us the smallest amount of attention. We were hidden in plain sight. Seeing this, she seemed to relax slightly. She grabbed a corner of the table in each hand and straightened her back. As she did this, all that hair seemed to collect in a honey-colored flame. Her eyes simmered with a pale blue intensity. Had all that intensity been directed at me, I would have been frightened.

"We were . . . we were lovers. I thought we were in love. Though that turned out to be wrong."

"When?" I asked.

"A year ago? Perhaps a bit more. He told me . . ." I could

hear her voice move toward breaking. She stopped. Collected herself. In that pause, I wondered why she would continue. What would possess her? I was a stranger, after all. I realized that was probably the why of the thing. Sometimes you can tell things to a stranger that you wouldn't want your best friend to hear. No attachments, no judgments.

"What?" I said gently. "What did he tell you?"

"He told me he was going to leave his wife for me. That we'd be together. Always."

"And you believed him?"

She looked at me fully then. Perhaps for the first time. "Of *course* I did. How could I not?"

She was right, of course. There was a reason Laird Wyndham was one of the leading actors of his generation. You believe a man like that when he tells you a thing.

"And that's why you hate him?"

"Well, that would be enough, wouldn't it? But, no: that's not it. It's for what happened when we broke up." She lowered her voice still further. Leaned closer to me. "He hurt me."

"Of course he did. I'm sorry. It would have been a very hurtful thing," I said.

"No, no," she said. "You don't understand." She moved closer still. Spoke more quietly. "He lost his temper. The day we were breaking up. His wife was coming. Or his lawyer. I can't remember which: they're almost indistinguishable anyway. We were in his apartment at the Knickerbocker. I'd spent the night." She looked as though she might blush if I showed the smallest sign of disapproval. I held all expressions and she went on. "We'd had a wonderful evening, and a beautiful morning—room service in bed—and then the phone rang. It was either the lawyer or the wife and, as soon as Laird was off the phone, that was the end of it: I needed to get out *now* because the real people were coming."

"He used those words? Real people?"

"No, actually, he didn't," Rosalyn admitted, her chin low. "But that was how it felt. Anyway, I told him he couldn't just give me the bum's rush like that. I was somebody. He couldn't just treat me like a hoor. And you know . . . you know what he said?"

I shook my head.

"He said, 'If you act like a hoor, you'd better plan on getting treated like one,' and he grabs my stuff and throws it into the hallway and he picks me up and carries me and throws *me* out into the hallway after my stuff. And I . . . well, I was *mad,* I tell you. I stood in that hallway and—nekkid as the day I was born—I stood there and pounded on that door. 'Let me in!' I sez. 'Let me in or I'll be standing right here when your wife shows up.' And what do you figure he does?"

"Calls the concierge?" I guessed. "Has you thrown out?"

She laughed. A mirthless sound. "Well, yeah: that's what you'd figure. That's what a normal person would have done. I mean, I was just mad, right? I didn't actually want any trouble. But my heart, you understand. It was *breaking*. So I'm pounding. And I'm hollering. And he comes to the door and opens it and, too late, I see he's got the ice bucket in his hands. And he throws it at me, half melted ice, half frozen water. And he says, 'You going to act like a bitch in heat? I'll treat you like one,' and he pulls me back into the room and he pops me."

"Pops you?"

"Yeah, you know," she pantomimed a boxer. Her meaning was all too clear.

"Jesus," I said.

"Yeah," she agreed. "It wasn't hard, you know. It wasn't so's I fell down or anything. But still . . ."

"Still . . ."

"Yeah, that's just how it was. And then he made a phone call and someone came and got me—and my stuff—and drove me home in a limo. And I never saw him again." This last was said with such sadness, that I looked at her more closely. The story made me realize that she was still in love with him. And, it was possible that, despite all his special detecting skills, Dex didn't know quite what he was dealing with. Yet.

I could see Rosalyn regretted telling me her story as soon as it was out in the air. Without even bothering to say good-bye, she nodded to me archly, collected herself and stalked toward the nearest exit. I watched her go until a voice—low and masculine—reverberated in my ear, so close it made me jump. "You ain't too good at makin' friends, are you kiddo?"

"Dex! Do you hafta sneak up on me?"

He laughed. "Gotta keep my stealthy moves in tip-top condition." Dex just stood there and stared at me.

"What's with givin' me the up and down, gumshoe?"

"You know, Miss Pangborn, all dolled up like that you make me look almost respectable."

"Jeepers, Mr. Theroux," I said, momentarily flummoxed by his words, "take it easy heaving around the compliments. You wouldn't want to pull a muscle you never use."

"You're right," Dex said, "let's get out of here before I sprain something."

CHAPTER SIXTEEN

HOW CAN ANYONE not love Philippe's? I've heard tell of a few people who didn't, and I just don't understand it. Or them. I mean, really, what's not to love? The wonderful warm fatty smells. The jostle for a place to sit. And then the food itself. Abundant, delicious and cheap. I've never varied my order at Philippe's, not since I was a little girl. Marjorie and I would go when we were downtown. In the middle of our day, when we were tired from shopping and nearly transparent with hunger, we would tramp into Philippe's. I'd get one of their famous French-dipped sandwiches, with hand-cut coleslaw on the side. You can say what you like, but nothing settles a hunger like Philippe's French dip.

I've always liked the story that goes with the sandwich, though I suspect it may be one of those apocryphal things. The original Philippe—a Frenchman, hence the fancy name—was making a sandwich one day in 1918. I'm not sure why, but the year is always given with this story. Does the inclusion of the year make it sound more true?

In any case, this Philippe was making a perfectly normal sandwich in his respectable but normal Los Angeles eatery when—lo!—he dropped a French roll into a roasting pan that happened to be sitting around with roast drippings inside. Being, I guess, a thrifty sort of Frenchman, rather than the spendy kind who are rather more famous, Philippe offered it to his customer, and the customer, a policeman, took it anyway. Likely at a discount if I know L.A. cops.

The next day, the cop came back, with a couple of his cop buddies in tow, and asked if they could get some more of those

French-dipped sandwiches and a new taste sensation was born. Either that or it was something else entirely. I like this story, though, and I certainly love the dipped sandwiches. Philippe sold the place in the late twenties and has gone off to be thrifty someplace else, but the name and the sandwiches remain, and I'm glad.

On this evening, Dex and I got lucky and ended up with one of the trestle tables all to ourselves. This was practically unheard of at Philippe's, where sharing the table with strangers is the norm. But it was late—nearly closing time—and the crowd had thinned somewhat. Philippe's is an eatery, pure and simple. Not at all the sort of place you go for a festive evening out on the town. In case we were in doubt about that, a few of the people still in the restaurant looked me and Dex over pretty carefully when we came in. One man seemed especially taken with the sight of a woman in a beaded dress being escorted by a gentleman in an evening suit. "What's a matter?" Dex said to the gawker. "Ya never saw a penguin on a date before?"

When the time came to order, I, of course, asked for a beef French-dipped sandwich with a slice of American cheese and a side order of macaroni salad. It just seemed too late at night for cabbage. Dex's sandwich was either pork or lamb—I didn't ask which—with a side order of coleslaw *and* a pickled egg. He was, I guess, undaunted by the thought of late night cabbage.

Once we'd secured our food, Dex didn't waste any time.

"You learn anything useful?" he asked around his sandwich. I quelled the feeling of annoyance that rose when he dipped a mouthful of coleslaw into the little pot of au jus. Beef-dipped *cabbage?* But I let it go.

I nodded. And then I shrugged. And then I nodded again.

"I *think* so," I said. "But it's a little hard to tell."

"How so?"

I told him what Baron had said about his relationship with

Wyndham: how the older actor had been the bigger star until Wyndham supplanted him as Hollywood's most significant leading man.

"So you think Baron Sutherland set this whole thing up?" Dex asked, clearly incredulous. "You think he made it look as though Wyndham killed someone because he was—what?—jealous of his old rival's success?"

"When you put it that way, it *does* sound pretty lame. On the other hand . . . I don't know, it seemed like it might be a theory worth exploring, is all. A jealous older actor, displaced by a young hotshot. It *could* spark things."

"Say, I saw Baron leaving with that blonde."

"Beatrice," I supplied. Somewhat sourly, I'll admit.

"She was gorgeous, kiddo. Legs on her all the way to *here*," he made a chopping motion just under his chin.

"Stop it," I didn't raise my voice.

"I'm only saying."

"I *know* what you're saying. But it's not like that, Dex. I'm not suggesting Baron did it because—what?—because he left the party with his girlfriend. I'm not even saying he did it at all. Just, I don't know. When he was telling me about Wyndham—about what they'd been to each other—I thought I could hear something in his voice."

"This was before whazzername, Beatrice, showed up?"

"It had *nothing* to do with any of that, Dex. Just stop it. It's not even a feeling, really. Not even a hunch. Just a thought."

"Well Kitty, all due respect? I don't think it's a thought that holds water. If jealousy were the motive—and I mean professional jealousy here, not just the kind with a broad—why, we'd be having to look at every actor in Hollywood. It seems to me that they're all real willing to step on each other's heads just to get to the top."

"Even so," I said.

"Even so," Dex said back to me with a smirk.

"Is that what that redhead with the serpenty legs was doing with you in the garden? Trying to get ahead?"

"Ha! If so, she was barking up the wrong tree. But that Mildred," he said with a low whistle. "She's something, ain't she?"

"Listen, Dex: I know sometimes it *seems* like I am one of the guys. But I am not one of the guys." I let the thought go unfinished.

Dex continued as though I hadn't interrupted. "Yeah, she's something all right. I'll be seeing her again."

"Is it the quality of the sound in here?" I said. "Can you hear me? At all?"

"And I had a drink with this guy, Samuel Marcus. Do you know the name?"

I shook my head.

"He was pretty interesting. He was like us—kind of in disguise? But he's a reporter with the *Los Angeles Courier*."

"No kiddin'? Was he there because of Wyndham?"

"Naw. Near as I can figure, he just managed to wangle an invitation, like we did more or less. And he figured maybe there'd be a story to do: and then he found the free booze. And then I found him. Anyway, we got to talkin'. And I asked him about my theory. You know."

I shook my head. "What theory?"

Dex polished off his pickled egg before he answered, carefully wiping his fingers on the cloth napkin while he spoke. "You remember, when the papers all seemed to get so nasty, so fast? I wondered if someone might have it out for Wyndham."

I remembered. I also recalled that I'd felt Dex had sounded vaguely paranoid when he'd broached it, but I didn't bring that up. "What did he think?"

"Well, like I said, he wasn't working on a story about Wyndham, so he couldn't say, per se—that was the way he put it. But he said he'd look into it even though he figured there was nothing to it. He's gonna call and let me know if he finds anything."

"That sounds promising. I guess," I said.

"Well, it's something and, other than that, I don't figure I had as much luck as you."

"Oh."

"I did talk to this one guy. But that didn't go so well."

I sighed over the last of my beef dip. It had been that good. "How so?"

"Well, after Sam left the bar, I got to talking to this guy was in there said he was a friend of Wyndham's."

"That sounds like a good lead," I said. "What happened?"

"Well, he said they'd worked on the clubhouse together."

"Baron told me the same thing. I gather a bunch of those movie star types built the place with their own hands."

"Yeah. Except I guess this one day it didn't go so good. This guy said Wyndham near threw him off the roof. Said he managed to get down to the garden, but Wyndham followed him and laid into him pretty good: broke a couple of the guy's ribs and blackened an eye." Dex told me all of this without expression. I couldn't tell if he believed the story or not.

"I heard something like that too," I said. I told him about Rosalyn Steele and how Wyndham had encouraged her to go home. I figured there were elements in the story Dex had told me that Rosalyn would have recognized. "What was the fight about? Did the guy say?"

Dex shook his head. "Not really. That was the funny part. Or a bit of it, anyway. The guy sort of clammed up when I asked him. But I gather it was about a girl."

"Geez. OK," I said. "Well, that's not good. It seems our gentle movie star has a bit of a temper."

"Still," Dex said loyally, "that doesn't prove *anything*."

"No, no, of course. You're right. It doesn't prove a damn thing. But it does kind of make you think."

I could see he bought my point.

I told Dex about my talk with Joe, the guy I'd met on the second floor of the Masquers' clubhouse. Dex listened closely while I spoke, then was quiet for a minute, considering all I'd said.

"All interesting enough," he said finally, "but I don't think it's got anything to do with any of this. Do you?"

"I don't know, Dex. I just don't know at all anymore. Sometimes I hear something—like the thing Baron was saying?—and I feel a glimmer of something. Then that feeling passes, too. So, is it connected? I don't know. Everything's connected I guess."

Dex looked at me. Grinned. "Now who's gettin' philosophical?" he asked. But I knew the question was rhetorical and I didn't reply.

"So what have we got?" Dex asked after a while.

"Got?"

"You know: we did all of this and we did all of that. Where are we now?"

"Well, we're getting nowhere fast," I said. There was a smile in my voice, but I knew I was only half kidding.

"You figure? I don't know that's so." He held up one elegant index finger. "We got a good friend for a long time, says Wyndham's got a streak in him."

"Yeah," I said. "A darkness."

"That too. Then we've got two old friends say he's got a violent nature."

"Rosalyn and your roof guy."

"Right. We got an overworked 'zecutive says the world is ending."

"That's not quite what he said."

"And we got a newspaperman don't know nothing, but will get back to us when he does."

I grinned despite myself. "OK."

"And we've got a redhead . . . man. You see the gams on her!"

"Dex. Please!"

"OK. So . . . what have we got?"

I just looked at him uncomprehending. He didn't say anything, so I crossed my arms and looked at him some more.

"C'mon, Kitty: What. Have. We. Got?"

"A mess?" I tried. "A big, disconnected mess?"

"Naw. Geez! Didn't they teach you the no quit spirit at that college in San Francisco?"

"It wasn't college. It was high school. And . . . um . . . no quit spirit was not a part of the curriculum."

"Oh fer cryin' out loud. I gotta draw you a picture? OK then. Picture this, here's what we've got: a foundation for various truths. A foundation on which we may build."

"You sound like a daisy."

"This isn't like following some poor sap's cheating wife, Kitty," Dex said, suddenly serious. "It's not even like tracking down an embezzler or some bum who's hanging orphan checks. I hate to say this, Kitty, but this feels . . . it feels bigger than me. Bigger in a way than the both of us."

I looked at him then. Looked at him closely to check for signs of another joke. What he'd said sounded like a line from a movie, a corny romantic movie at that. But he wasn't smiling. It wasn't any joke. And he was right: the thing we were dealing with was so large, I was beginning to get the idea we couldn't see the whole thing in one glance, even if we had all the facts, which I was fairly certain we did not.

"So what are you saying?" I asked.

"Oh, Kitty, I dunno, you're right. We got nothin'. Yet. But, hell: it's a start."

CHAPTER SEVENTEEN

DETECTIVE WORK IS a series of educated guesses ideally aided by good information from a paying client and resulting in the discovery of the desire of said client's heart. That's not a direct quote from my boss, but it's close enough for the kind of jazz we play around here. Least, that's the way Dexter Theroux puts things often enough when he feels like having all the answers and doesn't actually have too many.

Me, I'd put it another way: Detective work is a series of fits and starts put together in moments of sobriety stolen from the demon drink. It comes together at the place where good, blind luck meets up with the angel who guards drunks and small children.

Now, all of that said, the day after the Masquers' ball was filled from front to back with detective work—real detective work. You could take Dex's definition or you could take mine and either would apply.

We had the list that Wyndham had made for us the previous day. It needed to be worked through. One of the theories Dex had decided to pursue was that all of this might have happened just because the actor was well known and at the top of his game in a visible profession. Another pet theory suggested that someone had a bone to pick. Either way, Dex figured that for someone to go to all the trouble of framing Wyndham up, there might just be a grudge or two swimming somewhere close by. That's how he put it, too: "swimming." And Dex figured there was enough of a chance that it was worth looking for.

So when he headed out to follow some in-person leads, he

gave me Wyndham's list. He told me to just go down it and call people up on the phone and ask those who were closest to Laird Wyndham what they really felt about him. Did anyone hate him? Had he done somebody wrong? Were there people who were jealous, for one reason or another? People he'd thrown over, passed over or somehow emotionally worked over? Or even, was there someone who would profit from Wyndham's misfortune? Someone in whose way Wyndham had stood, even accidentally? Dex told me to pay close attention to the sound of their voices. He told me to listen as hard to the things they didn't say as to the things they did. I wasn't sure I totally understood him, but I told him I'd give it a try, even if it sounded pretty impossible to do all those things at once. It wasn't like I had a lot else to do so I set to.

Dex instructed me on how to expand the list Wyndham had given us, asking the listed few if they knew of anyone I should talk to or could think of anyone Wyndham had done wrong and so on. Though these phone calls might not strictly speaking have fallen under my job description, I didn't mind the extra work. In the first place, it was Laird Wyndham. He was a movie star. That made him interesting from the get-go. In the second place, it could get pretty quiet around the office. It was good to have something to fill the time. I welcomed anything that would let me put off righting all those mixed up files I'd stuffed into the file drawer. That was going to be no fun at all.

Looking over Wyndham's list, I saw one glaring omission: Wyndham's wife, Lorena Duvall. I wondered how we were expected to get a full and proper picture of Wyndham's life if we couldn't talk to her. But we hadn't been given a contact number. It was something I was sure belonged at the top of the list.

Meanwhile, I'd work with what I had.

Before I could get started, Mustard came in with a lot of noise and plunked himself into the waiting room chair. He looked at me without saying anything.

"What's up?" I asked when it became obvious Mustard wasn't about to volunteer anything.

"Been following up on those thugs what roughed Dex up yesterday."

"It was a bit more than a roughing, I'd say, Mustard. You make it sound like he got a light sandpapering."

"OK, so he had a whole carpentry team work on him," he said a bit hotly. "I didn't say they were teaching him the Lindy Hop."

"More like they were fittin' him for a pine overcoat. So no luck, huh?"

Mustard shook his head. "At this point I'm not even sure Xander Dean is the guy's real name."

"Who makes up 'Xander Dean' though? It's not like Joe Blow or something."

"Either way," Mustard said, "I can't find him. He just seems to have disappeared off the face of the earth. Come from nowhere, gone back to nowhere. Dean seemed on the level, though. I would never have sent him to Dex if he didn't."

"I know that, Mustard. Dex knows it, too. These things happen that way sometimes."

"Not to me, they don't," he shook his head as though trying to clear it, then headed down a different track. "I'm going to get to the bottom of it, though. I'll talk to the Chicago contacts what sent him to me. I've got a hunch something's going on, Kitty. Something I don't know about. But it stinks like last week's catch of the day."

"But why would he do that, Mustard? Why would he hire Dex, rough him up when Dex quit on him, then disappear? It doesn't add up."

Mustard shook his head. "Whatever it is, we'll get to the bottom of it. You'll see."

After Mustard left I forced my mind off his business and onto my own. I had a list of people that needed phoning and lots of questions to ask them, though I soon discovered that just being on a list wasn't enough to ensure participation. Despite the things that had been said about him in the newspapers since his arrest, the people on the list that Laird Wyndham had supplied to Dex were disinclined to be completely candid about him, at least to me. I could feel them holding back. This made sense, though. It was Wyndham's list. So I ended up talking with his immediate support people—the girl who did his hair, the man who captained his boat, the woman who attended to his wardrobe. These were people fairly close to Wyndham who depended on him for their living. Talking to them you got the idea that people as famous as Wyndham didn't have friends so much as they had people they employed, only maybe they'd forgotten the difference.

On the other hand, the man who looked after Wyndham's horses sounded a little dodgy.

"Things isn't always what they seems to be. I'm not sayin' it's agin the law, mind. Not of man, though perhaps of God," was all he'd say in his smoke-stained voice. But he said it several times in similar ways.

When I couldn't budge him to say more, I made a note. If things didn't go well for Wyndham, this was someone we'd be able to talk to when more time had passed. I'd sensed that there were moments the man had been close to telling me something and I figured maybe Dex or even Mustard could have pushed it all the way home. But I lacked the experience—and probably the necessary weight—to move him.

I had more luck with people whose contact information I got from those on the original list when I'd asked, "Do you know anyone close to Mr. Wyndham I could talk to? Someone who might have the kind of information I'm looking for?" Maybe because this next layer weren't in Wyndham's inner circle—less loyal, further from the warmth of his direct sun—a few of them were quite willing to speak their minds.

"I never really thought he was all he said he was," sniffed a thin-voiced woman who had been employed by Wyndham's wife when she still lived in the city. She was now working as a nanny in Hancock Park. "I always felt he had the potential for violence."

My ears perked up at that. "You did? Did you see him . . . Did you ever see him shouting at Mrs. Wyndham? Or threatening her? Perhaps you saw him threaten her?"

"No, no. Nothing like that," she said hastily. "He's actually a very quiet-voiced man. No, I never heard him shout, per se . . . I just . . . it's just that . . . I always somehow knew . . ."

"What, Miss Laverntine?" I pressed. "What did you know?"

"Well Miss Duvall—Mr. Wyndham's wife—she had a somewhat delicate constitution. A lovely woman. Mr. Wyndham would never do anything *overt* you understand? Nothing you could even point right at. But it seemed to me sometimes that he'd push her."

"Push her?"

"Yes. Cow her, in a way. I don't know how else to explain it. There was just something so big about Mr. Wyndham. And something so small in his wife. So delicate. She's a lovely woman," she said again, "inside and out. But I think he made her feel . . . less."

"They're still married," I pointed out.

"Well, it's not like that would make any difference, the way he always carried on. Married. Not married. I can't imagine he cared either way. That's the thing, you understand. There was a *bigness* about him."

"A bigness."

"Yes," I could hear her struggle to explain. "Almost as though his life was larger than other people's. Larger than, say, yours or mine. It was as though, the rules that apply to me and you? They didn't apply for Mr. Wyndham. He made his own rules. Always."

"Maybe that's how you get to be a star," I ventured.

"Maybe," she allowed. "But it's not the easiest thing to live with, I can tell you that for sure. I can tell you another thing, as well," there was a definite catch in her voice now, "I *loved* Mrs. Wyndham. I love her still. And married to *that beast*, poor thing. And him running around and leaving her alone to rot. Always out on that yacht of his with his *friends*. What . . . what will she be doing now without me?"

Miss Laverntine didn't seem to have much in real information to add to what I knew and I ended the conversation not long after. Still, in a certain way, I felt as though I'd learned a lot. A picture of Laird Wyndham was emerging that differed quite sharply from the one he presented to the world, the one he had crafted for me and Dex to see.

Even so, it was a big jump from arrogant movie star to killer, one I couldn't quite make. Was Laird Wyndham capable of being thoughtless? A jerk? Of hurting people's feelings? Of riding roughshod over their hearts? Absolutely. Was he capable of murder? That was something else again. I thought about what I'd tell Dex. I made my notes. And then I moved on.

CHAPTER EIGHTEEN

THOUGH THINGS HAD not been going swimmingly with my telephone calls from the start, they got worse from there. The fact was simple: it was not a good week to talk about Laird Wyndham. Those that were close to him and cared about him had been listening to the radio and reading the papers. They weren't about to let their guard down. Those that didn't like him knew he was safely out of the way and made no bones about talking badly about him. Neither picture felt authentic. Neither extreme rang true.

I was glad when, deep into the day, Dex called to say he'd paid another visit to Wyndham and had gotten a more complete list from him as well as permission to go out to Oxnard to talk to his wife.

"So call Mustard and get me a machine for tomorrow morning, please."

"He was just here an hour or so ago," I said.

"Well, call him anyway. Wyndham said she doesn't have a phone. So I thought I'd just drive out there and take my chances that I'll catch her home. From the sound of things, she doesn't venture very far out."

My eyes widened at this, but I didn't say anything. It hadn't taken long to realize that movie stars seem different from you and me because . . . well, because they are different. The only thing regular about them might be their bowels, and I wasn't in a position to vouch for that.

"Sure, Dex, sure," I said. "But what do you want me to do for the rest of the day?"

"Rest of what day?" Dex said. "It's six o'clock already. Pack it up."

It had been a long day and I'd gotten a lot accomplished. Between partying with movie stars the night before and trying to get a picture of Wyndham on the phone all day, I was exhausted, plain and simple: emotionally, physically, plus I was discovering that this whole shamus business was maybe a bit tougher than it looked when executed by a half-sozzled expert.

At dinner that night, Marjorie presented her boarders with baked fish, creamed vegetables and scalloped potatoes. It was a feast and I raised my eyebrows at her even while I enjoyed every tiny bite while she did nothing but beam her lady-of-the-manor smile at me. I knew she had a secret, but I couldn't discern what it was.

Dessert was cherry whip, which I suspected meant we'd have scrambled eggs with our breakfast in the morning. Marjorie wouldn't like to waste the egg yolks when she'd used the whites for the whip. I like cherry whip just fine, but it's not one of my favorites. Perfectly good canned cherries whipped into a froth with gelatin and egg whites. It always seems a little empty, like there should be something more to it than just cherries and air.

As was our habit when I was at home, I moved into the kitchen with Marjorie to help with the washing up after our meal.

"Marjorie, what on earth," I said to her almost as soon as the door to the dining room was closed behind us. "Did you win the Irish Sweepstake?"

"Whatever do you mean?" she said, the picture of innocence while she tucked leftovers into waxed paper for future consumption. She made tidy little packages, then secured them with rubber bands she saved for the purpose. She was pleased with herself about the dinner; I could tell. So I played along.

"That fish dinner. It seemed so extravagant. It was like Christmas Eve or something."

"It did seem like that, didn't it?" she asked, smiling, pride in her eyes. "But no, alas, no Sweepstake. And the fish was . . . well, it was really very cheap."

"Cheap?" I said. "How could that be?"

"Marcus . . . oh, Miss Katherine. You simply mustn't tell. Do you promise?"

I shrugged. Nodded. "Sure." Who would I tell, in any case? I doubted that either Dex or the newspapers would care very much.

She lowered her voice, almost to a whisper. "Marcus caught it. At Santa Monica. At the pier."

"He did not," I said, suddenly paying close attention.

"Oh, but he did," she said.

"But Marjorie, those weren't little smelts or pile perch. I know: I ate it. That was the flesh of a large, white fish. What on earth could he have caught—at Santa Monica? At the pier—like that?"

Marjorie looked around conspiratorially, as though someone might be hiding in the kitchen to hear her revelation. Satisfied we were alone and unobserved, she leaned toward me and lowered her voice still further.

"Well it could have been halibut. But it was not. And it could have been queenfish or guitarfish. But it was not, either. Not this time, at any rate. No, that tonight," and here she dropped her voice so low I had to lean in to hear her, "that was shark."

"What?" I asked, certain I'd heard incorrectly.

"It was shark, Miss Katherine. Marcus caught a mudshark."

"And we *ate* it? Whatever were you thinking?"

She didn't look abashed, as I thought she might have done. Rather she faintly glowed with pride—though if it were in herself or Marcus's abilities as a fisherman I could not have said. Perhaps both.

"I was thinking right enough, Miss. You said it yourself: it was like a feast day."

I couldn't argue with that. But I had to think again about the times in which we now found ourselves. And I had to think about my father, as well. Was he spinning now, I wondered? Was he spinning in his grave while his old housekeeper fed his daughter the flesh of a fish he would have considered inedible? And if I were to tell the truth, I'd not only eaten it, I'd enjoyed it: and it was the fullest my stomach had been in months. From the looks of things, too, there might even be fish sandwiches for lunch tomorrow. Maybe even fish omelettes for breakfast.

"Well, fish omelettes might be pushing things too far," Marjorie said when I mentioned it. "But look what I found," she went to the cupboard and brought out a tiny bottle filled with an evil looking brown substance. "It's liquid smoke, Miss Katherine." She sounded terribly pleased with herself. "If all goes well, we'll have kippers with our breakfast."

"Mock kippers?"

"Quite," she replied, nodding her head in satisfaction.

I embraced her then, a fast impulsive hug. There were not many people who would have found joy in our predicament, but Marjorie did. She found joy wherever she looked. It was a trait I decided I'd have to try to learn.

CHAPTER NINETEEN

IT SEEMED AS though I closed my eyes—my stomach full of illicitly procured white fish, my head full of shadow figures and unpleasant possibilities—and fell asleep instantly. And then what felt like five minutes later I was brought back to consciousness by the self-righteous screaming of a nearby bird with an overbalanced sense of propriety. And he was right outside my window.

I opened my eyes to full light and the inexplicable sense that I'd missed something. The squeal again. So apparently what I'd missed had not been the bird.

In the kitchen, Marjorie still looked vastly pleased with herself.

"You look like the cat what swallowed her canary," I said to her, still thinking of that noisy bird.

She smiled—Cheshire-like this time—and nodded and said, "You'll see."

I'd overslept and was doubtless going to be late getting to the office, but I decided coming in late just this once wasn't going to hurt anything. Especially since Dex pretty much left it up to me to decide when to open things up in the morning. It's not as though he was ever there at the crack of nine.

On this day, Marjorie wouldn't let me help with the breakfast service, but asked that I join the gentlemen in the dining room. She was like a mother arranging a surprise for her children. I could feel her anticipation and her glee and decided to play along.

And then breakfast. It was beautiful. It reminded me of the breakfasts of my childhood on those rare occasions when we'd had a house full of guests. Marjorie carried too much food out of the kitchen on serving plates overflowing with home fries and scrambled eggs, thick slices of Marjorie's home-made bread turned into golden browned toast and . . . kippers. I had a hard time not laughing out loud in delight and wonder at her creation. The creamy white flesh that we'd had with dinner the night before had been cunningly tinted a beautiful caramel color and artfully shaped to resemble the salted fillets of the much smaller fish.

Even though Marjorie never shared how close to poverty we were with her boarders, I often had a sense that everyone knew. We were all in boats of similar creation. The same boat, in a way, even if there were to be differing destinations, different ports of call.

So we reveled in this feast, all of us. We laughed and we chatted emptily about happy nothings and we ate until we were full.

At one point, I looked up to see Marjorie regarding me with a secret expression. She touched a finger to her lips, winked at me. I winked right back. Far be it from me to give away her kippers as the flesh of the carnivore shark or, more to the point, the fish that was free at a time when real fish was very dear.

Walking toward Angels Flight, I found the day coldish, but I minded it less than I might have done on another day this chilly. I knew that this was partly because I'd been so well fed two meals in a row: I generally didn't have much extra in my body to sacrifice to the cold, so I felt every drop in the temperature.

Today, however, I felt pleasingly the way a fat seal must feel slicing through Arctic waters: I felt protected from the bitter cold and even invigorated by the world that came with it. As I boarded Angels Flight, I noticed clouds pulling themselves sluggishly through a dull gray sky; the other riders on the little railcar were bundled against inclement weather: overcoats and even scarves and hats. Someone from Chicago or even San Francisco might have laughed at the sight because, truly, by those standards, it was not *that* cold. But by Angeleno standards, it was a day to bundle up. A day to stay at home and sit by the fire if that was an option.

At our office door, I gave a start: the door was unlocked. I moved inside cautiously, afraid of what I might find until I recognized the smell of coffee in the air. Dex. I checked the clock on the wall. Nearly an hour before ten and my boss was at his desk. I got the feeling that floats to you when you play with the idea of miracles and unlikely endings. It was more than I would have wished for and I wasn't quite sure what to do with it.

"I didn't even know you knew how to use that thing," I said, motioning toward the percolator.

"I don't," he said, looking at me and grinning. "But not to take anything away from you, Kitty? It was pretty self-explanatory."

"So you really *are* smarter than you look," I said, knowing that it's one thing to figure out the mechanics: what goes here, what goes there. Quite another to put it all together in the expected way. We'd give it a few minutes, then see how it all turned out.

"What are you doing here anyway?" I asked, taking in his smoothly shaven chin, his clean shirt and collar, his favorite silk necktie.

"The rats and the cockroaches kicked me outta my apartment," he said. "Told me not to come back until I came up with the rent and an armload of groceries."

"That may well be," I said adopting the same tone, "but you seldom get here before me. What made them kick you out this early? You snore? Sing in the shower?"

"Hold off on the thumbscrews, will ya? You're not exactly the early bird today."

"You've been working me plenty hard, shamus. Girl's gotta get her beauty sleep."

"By the look of things, you've been gettin' more than your share."

"Don't be gettin' all soft on me, Dex, or I'll be playin' you a few bars of chin music." I raised my fist in a mock pugilist salute.

Whatever Dex might have said next was cut off by the sound of our front door opening. It was the kid who worked in Mustard's office dropping off the heap Dex had ordered. I tipped him a short bit. He grinned his thanks and disappeared.

"Wanna come with me?" Dex asked when the kid was gone.

"Out to Oxnard?" I asked. "Why?"

"Dunno. Keep me company, I guess."

I agreed readily enough—it was an adventure, after all. Something to keep me away from those files.

In the car, though, Dex admitted he had an ulterior motive. "And it's not that I don't want your company, either," he said as the big car rolled up the Roosevelt Highway toward Ventura County. "Just, you know, another woman. I thought it might help, is all. And it's a long way."

It *was* a long way. Having a back-up plan—even a slightly lame one—didn't seem like such a bad idea. I thought about this as we drove past the burned-out husk of Malibu Potteries. I'd read about the fire a few months before but it was worse than I'd imagined. Very little had been left unscathed. As thoroughly burned as the place had been, the owners seemed to be persevering. A tent had been erected not far from the burnt-out building and judging by the buzz of activity, it was business as usual.

North of Malibu, even the little bit of traffic thinned out until it was possible to follow the new highway for several miles at a time without seeing another traveler. At that point, Dex opened the big car up and it ate the asphalt in hungry bites. I felt I could have watched the ocean sail past the car windows endlessly: sand dunes here, tree-studded cliffs there, and everywhere mile upon mile of sand. As we neared Oxnard the highway veered away from the ocean, and the sandy cliffs and white-capped vistas gave way to countless acres of cultivated fields.

"Sugar beets," Dex said, noting my interest.

"You mean like pickled beets?" I asked, thinking of the jars of jewel-like vegetable Marjorie put up each fall.

"Well, I guess," Dex said. "But mostly, they use them to make sugar. Hence the name. And for some reason, I think these aren't red, but white."

"Oh," I said. I'm a city girl. I always have been. I tend to find unfettered nature and blatant agriculture a little disconcerting. It was, therefore, a relief when the endless fields began to give way to signs of civilization. A diner here. A gas station there. A residential neighborhood where one perhaps had not been ten years before.

The town of Oxnard itself was lovely: imagine a sweetly self-satisfied little city in a perfect setting at the edge of the sea and that would be Oxnard as we found it on that day. I could see it all so well because we spent some time driving around it. While I looked at everything with interested curiosity, while enjoying the day, I could feel Dex's mood slipping and his temper flaring. He didn't say anything, though. Just drove about with his brows pulled into a single dark line above his eyes and a scowl marring the strength and cleft of his chin.

"Are we lost?" I asked after a while, knowing as I did that it was probably exactly the wrong thing to say.

"Naw. We're still in California."

"OK," I said. "Well, *that's* reassuring. Something's wrong, though."

"The address Wyndham gave me," Dex groused. "It doesn't match up with anything we've seen."

"Look," I said, pointing. "There's a Richfield station. Why don't we just stop and ask?"

Dex shot me a look, but did what I'd suggested, pulling the car up to the pumps and asking the kid who worked there to clarify our directions while he filled 'er up.

"Oh, I can see why that would have confused you," the kid said when told the address. "That's out Port Hueneme way." Leastways, that's what I knew the word to be. What he actually said came out sounding more like Port wye-NEE-mee, but we knew from the signs along the way that it was not. Dex wasn't in the mood to hang around debating pronunciation and before the windshield even dried from its wash, we were underway again.

Once we were headed in the right direction it didn't take long to find what we were looking for. As the gas station attendant had told us, the road snaked around until it came nearly to the ocean, where it ended at Silver Strand, Wyndham's estate. Both Dex and I were struck dumb at the sight of the place, which was saying a thing: me having been born in luxury and Dex used to putting a façade up and his nose in where it did not belong.

You could see the house from the place where the road met the grounds, but only just. Right at the water's edge, Wyndham's country place was a modern mansion, with gardens, a pool and garages for the motion picture star's cars. Away from the ocean, it looked as though the estate might go back for miles and board-fenced paddocks housed Arabian horses who frolicked in equine abandon, their tails held high in the air. I watched the horses play as we followed a long tree-lined driveway. When we came to the house Dex pulled our borrowed car under the porte cochere. I looked around for some lurking servant in a uniform but didn't see one, though it was the kind of swank joint where a liveried footman or six wouldn't have been out of place.

There was no activity—no cars coming or going, no planes on the airstrip we could see beyond the pasture, no horses being taken to or from the barn—so we left the car where it was and headed for the door.

That door was massive. Easily twice my height and made of wood that was a deep mahogany in color and heavily figured. It looked to me like it might have been cut from a single ancient redwood, felled for the very purpose of the creation of the new California. I wasn't sure if that made me sad.

We looked around for some type of ringing or knocking device and, seeing nothing, Dex extended his hand and gave the door a good rap with his knuckles. It hurt my ears just listening to the bone hit the wood, but Dex didn't even blink.

We stood there for a long time. I became aware of the scrawny sun heading toward a noonday sky and the taste of salt in the air. It's always cooler by the ocean than it is even a few miles inland, and I noticed that now, wishing for the protection of a light coat or even a cardigan on my bare arms.

A minute passed. Maybe two. I could feel Dex preparing himself to move off when the door scraped against its frame as someone pulled it open from the other side. The sound of wood against too-much wood, the door perhaps swollen due to the humidity that comes off the ocean.

The door didn't swing wide—it opened only a foot or so—but I still got an instant whiff of what was beyond. It sailed out on a slender column as though it had been waiting for the opportunity. It took me a while to name what it was.

It was dark in there—I could see that as well as feel it—and dank. The fingers of a chill. I'm being dramatic. I know that. Yet what I saw directly after didn't alleviate those feelings at all.

"Yes." It was a single word, not formed into a question. Spoken by a woman. We could not see her face. The voice was neither old nor young, but it was deeply used.

"Miss Duvall?" Dex found his voice first, directed it at the opening that wasn't nearly big enough to support a conversation. "How do you do? I'm Dexter J. Theroux and this is . . . this is my associate, Miss Katherine Pangborn."

I murmured a greeting. Dex pressed on.

"Miss Duvall, I don't know if you've had contact with your husband over the last few days . . ."

"Laird?" the voice said softly, making me wonder if she actually had so many husbands that she needed to verify the identity of this one.

"That's right," Dex said reassuringly, as though he were perhaps trying to gentle one of those frolicking horses. "He gave us this address and told us we'd find you here."

"You're here to talk to *me*?" she sounded as though she didn't quite believe it. And it was hard to judge her voice. Did she sound glad at the prospect? Or frightened? Or wary? Maybe it was a generous mixture of all three. "Why would he want you to talk to me?"

"Can we come in, Miss Duvall?" Dex said. "If we could have a few minutes of your time, we'll explain everything." I looked at Dex, trying to catch his eye while keeping the panic out of mine. Did we really want to go in there? *Just a slender broad* I could almost hear Dex say. *Nothing to be afraid of.* And yet.

The door opened wide and we could see her fully for the first time, but that single look at her brought it all back. Though she hadn't made a motion picture in five years or more, I could recall a time when she was both a great beauty and a significant star. She had always been cast as *that* girl: the delicate flower, the girl left behind or the one who suffered in silence while the world moved on. She was almost painfully thin, with a swanlike neck and the trademark mop of yellow curls for which she had been known. In her youth, the combination had heightened her vulnerability and legendary beauty.

Now it combined to create a look that was at once delicate, breakable and slightly odd.

She brought us into a foyer that under different circumstances and perhaps a few years earlier might have been beautiful. Cobalt blue tiles lined the floor. Beautiful tiles. The ceiling was coffered in dark-stained beams and soared to a height that was at least twice that of a normal room. The proportions, the dimensions, the appointments were all elegant and lovely. The overriding feeling, however, was one of confinement and lack of space. Newspapers and old books were stacked precariously high in every corner. The windows were grimy. The pictures on the wall were not askew, but the unkempt nature of everything around them made it feel as though they were, as though everything in the space might topple down in a dirty heap at any second.

That was not the worst, however. What was worse, by far, was the smell. Now that we were inside, we were getting the full force of what had only been hinted at on the stoop.

I couldn't place it at first. Until I was right inside the foyer and the door had been closed behind us. Then I recognized it as the smell of cats. Not a few but many. And it wasn't the smell of cats themselves, but the deposits they leave behind. I've got nothing at all against cats. I've quite liked them when I've encountered them. But this was something beyond two or three or even four pet felines. My eyes would have told me that even if my nose had not.

Four cats reclined in various poses on the stairway we passed as we followed Lorena Duvall to the drawing room. I could feel sharp, green eyes regarding me without much curiosity as we moved out of sight. Two more lounged on an antique breakfront in a hallway. When we got there, the huge and well-appointed drawing room held at least fifteen. They were on overstuffed horsehair chairs, on settees, on rugs in front of the fireplace and one with a tidily marked black and white body perched on the piano keyboard seemed to regard us with a smirk as we entered the room. Under different circumstances, I might have smirked back. As it was, and with perhaps two score eyes watching us, I felt an odd little finger of fear.

As Lorena Duvall tried to make space for us—gently suggesting to the cats on the sofa that they move, trying in vain to remove cat hair from even a single piece of furniture in the room, clearing away stacks of newspapers and books—I tried to align the idea of Laird Wyndham—vital, vibrant, virile and very much of the world—with this woman, his wife. It was impossible to imagine the two of them together, even at a dinner or a party, never mind sharing life. That accounted for the fact that they seldom seemed to spend time together any longer. Wyndham had told us she had withdrawn. From the little I had so far seen, it appeared to be so much more than that.

With the sofa cleared, she offered us tea or a drink. Dex and I declined hastily, perhaps neither of us prepared to drink from a cup or glass that had spent any time at all in this house. With all these cats.

She indicated we should sit on the newly emptied sofa, then perched awkwardly in an armchair against a large calico cat who had been unwilling to move.

"You said," she started. Then stopped. Cleared her throat. Started again. "You said you were here to talk about . . . talk about my husband. Has something happened?"

"You haven't heard from him at all?" Dex asked, drawing out a pack of cigarettes, offering one to Miss Duvall, who declined with a barely perceptible shake of her head, both the smoke and the question.

"Well then," Dex said, "I'm afraid this may come as something of a shock. I'm not going to pad it, though. You're a grown woman, after all, and have a right to know. Miss Duvall,

I'm sorry to be the one to tell you that Mr. Wyndham is being held for murder."

At the sound of the word, one of her pale little paws flew to her mouth. It was a theatrical gesture—something the woman in the silent film would do if she discovered the same thing about a loved one. Considering her background, I suppose she'd come by it honestly.

"Murder," she repeated now breathlessly and, though it really wasn't funny, I had to steel myself not to laugh.

"Yes, yes," Dex said, lighting his smoke with a careless match that he tossed into the ashtray on the table in front of us. "That's right. So first of all we wanted to ask if this is something you know about."

"No, of course not," Lorena said. Dex looked professionally skeptical. It's a knack he has. For my part, I had no trouble at all believing her and I didn't care if she could tell that from my face.

"When's the last time you were in the city?" Dex asked.

"Los Angeles?"

Dex just nodded. With a grunt.

Lorena cast her eyes ceilingward, deep in thought. I followed her eyes, then forced them back down again. The reality of the massive cobwebs right above our heads was a little too much to take.

"Three, perhaps four months. I remember, more or less, because it's been that long since I had a driver."

"You don't drive, Miss Duvall?"

She shook her head, her eyes wide and childlike, odd in a face no longer young. "I never had reason to learn."

"But you're all alone up here?" This was Dex and he said it as though pressing home a point.

Miss Duvall surprised me by smiling at him. The smile warmed her entire face. She pulled a cat from the floor next to her, tucking it comfortably onto her lap. "Hardly alone, Mr. Theroux."

"Quite," Dex agreed dryly. I wondered what was eating him and what he thought he was up to. This wasn't getting us any-place fast.

"But, yes: I'm mostly alone. Laird fixed it so I have someone come in and see to the horses and someone comes to do the pool. But they answer to him, not me. I . . . well I'm off people just now."

"Ah," Dex said conversationally. I couldn't find anything to say at all.

"Did he do it?" she asked suddenly, thankfully alleviating the need for the construction of small talk.

"Do what?" Dex asked.

"You said my husband is accused of murder." She stroked the cat now curled tightly into her lap. If it was a nervous gesture, she gave no sign.

"Ah. That. We think he did not."

"And who," she stopped again. Cleared her throat again. "Who is he supposed to have murdered?"

"A girl," Dex answered. Then corrected. "A young woman."

Duvall's eyebrows arched but she didn't say anything. I thought I saw something in the look, but I didn't quite know what.

"You don't look surprised," Dex said without a question in his voice.

"Don't I?" she said thoughtfully, still stroking. "It's too far away. I'd be very surprised if I discovered such a thing were true. Laird may be many things, but he's no killer, least of all of young women." She allowed herself a small smile. I wondered at its source. "But the life he leads? In the thick of things, as it were. That's what robs my surprise."

"That was once your life," I pointed out.

"Was it?" she said as though considering. "I suppose it was, in a way. And yet, it never was."

"That's very cryptic," I said softly, willing Dex not to interject. "Was that what you intended?"

"You're observant," she said. "I like you. Him I'm not so sure about," she said, looking at Dex, though she smiled to take the bite out of her words. "I'm sorry. I didn't intend to be cryptic, though you're right: I probably was. It's just . . . it's not a part of my life I speak easily about, me and Laird. I don't even think about it much anymore."

"You talk about it like it's all in the past," I said. "He's still your husband. You're still his wife."

"Till death," she said so softly I wasn't sure I'd heard.

"Are you . . . are you estranged?" I said, suddenly bold. What did we have to lose? And we'd come such a long way, the question needed to be asked. Dex seemed to know I was the one to do the asking. He sat quietly on his side of the sofa and smoked.

"No, no. Nothing like that. We're friends. Friendly. You understand." She said this with a sophisticated little wave of her hand. An insouciant toss of her head. Yet I felt myself dangerously close to something painful. Perhaps it was because she was acting, I thought, as though I could suddenly see beyond the mask.

"Not quite," I said, still softly. "You're not estranged, yet you don't live together as husband and wife. You say you're friendly, yet there are other women."

She laughed at that. The laughter wasn't something bitter, something that stung. "Other women were never the problem," she said, looking me full in the face. "Other people is what it always was with Laird."

I had the feeling there was something I should have understood then, but to my shame, I did not. I thought it was words only and I was aware of Dex on the other side of me, mashing out his smoke. And I knew I was out of time.

"Miss Duvall," Dex said now, "here's the long and the short of it: Your husband has hired us to try and prove his innocence. Do you know of any reason why we wouldn't be able to do that?"

She shook her head. "Not off hand. No."

"So you don't think he's capable of murder?"

"That's not a real question," she said with a distracted air. The calico had come from behind and joined the other cat in her lap. It was a small lap and it was now very full. "Or maybe it's a philosophical one. Which one of us is *not* capable of murder? Under the wrong circumstances. I would say Laird no more or less than most."

Her voice had a rare calming quality. Almost like a purring. I had to force myself to focus on the words she spoke, not the shape of them, or the way they fell on the room.

If Dex was similarly affected, he gave no sign. "That's not really much of an answer, Miss Duvall," he said.

"Why, whatever do you mean? Of course it's an answer. The only one I've got."

He tried a different approach.

"Is your husband a violent man, Miss Duvall?"

Lorena looked at Dex closely before answering. "I would not characterize him that way, no."

"Is he . . . is he capable of violence?" I tried.

"Again, Miss Pangborn. Who among us is not?"

"Indeed," I said, "but have you seen signs of it in Laird?"

She took her time about answering, and when she did, her words surprised us. "Have you talked to Steward? Asked him that question?"

"Your husband's mouthpiece? Why would we talk to him? What are you saying?" Dex wanted to know.

"I'm not saying anything. Just asking, is all. Or suggesting, maybe. If there's things that need knowing, Steward is the one to ask. He tends . . . he tends to know things."

"What kinds of things, Miss Duvall?" I asked.

The smile she focused on first me and then Dex was be-
atific. Combined with that mop of hair, it was like the sun had
come out. I knew then that she had no intention of answering
our questions.

"Ta da," she trilled, spreading her hands wide in a theatrical
gesture that indicated quite clearly that our interview was over.
"Thank you so much for your visit, both of you. But I'm tired
now. I must retire." When she stood, both cats dropped to the
ground, one looked surprised, the other annoyed and Lorena
herself unconcerned. "You can see yourselves out."

CHAPTER TWENTY

"WHAT DO YOU make of her?" The noonday sun slashed at the car and the fields we drove through. It reflected off the swaying sugar beets and the white ribbon of highway. I knew that, if we stopped for a moment and I stood beside the car, I'd feel the sun on my shoulder, on my head. I'd feel the sun and maybe I'd feel warm again. But just then, for whatever reason, I felt fingers of damp; a chill. I felt cold.

"Nothing to make," I said. "She's nuttier than Marjorie's fruitcake."

Dex laughed. "You know, I haven't had that pleasure—your Marjorie's fruitcake, that is. But I would imagine it's a nutty delight."

"I'll tell her you said that."

"Please don't," Dex begged. "I have a hard enough time with her already. So," he said at length, "do we think about what she said?"

"What Marjorie said?"

"No. Silly goose. Forget the fruitcake for a minute. Or think about a different one: Wyndham's wife."

"Do we think about what she said about Steward Sterling, you mean?"

Dex grunted his reply.

I considered before answering. "Thing is, I'm still confused about what she meant, are you?"

Dex nodded. "Like, did she mean Steward *did* it or did she mean Steward would know if Laird did it?"

"Yeah," I agreed. "Like that."

"Well, either way, I figure she's barking up the wrong tree."

Dex held the wheel with both hands. His knuckles were white. But he looked calm in all other regards. Calm and completely in control of the big car.

"Could be. Still, she's the one that was married to Wyndham. That's why we went to see her, right? She has reason to know more than we do. I think you have to talk to Steward."

Another grunt. "I think you're right," he changed tracks. "Could be she was always a fruitcake."

"Don't know, Dex. Takes a while to work up to that many cats."

"Could be that's why they're still married," Dex said in a way that made me realize he was thinking it all through for the first time as it came out of his mouth.

"Why?"

"Maybe it's what it always was. She needed . . . I dunno . . . protection, maybe? From the world . . ."

I saw where this was going. "And maybe he did too?"

Dex nodded as he drove. "A wife would save him a lot of scrutiny."

"And not everyone would have been happy about all those cats."

"You got *that* right, sister. Five minutes in that house and I felt like they were sizing me up for a hot meal."

"Now what?" I said.

"Now we go back to the office and pick up where we left off: try to find someone who knows something about what's happened to our boy."

"But you don't think the wife had anything to do with it?" I pressed.

"I don't think she could do the crossword if it was already filled in."

"So I'm back on the phone this afternoon."

"Yeah. That and I want you to find Rhoda Darrow."

"Who?"

"The woman who tangoed me around at the party."

"What do I need to find her for?"

"Well, lots of reasons. Xander Dean hired her, for one. So it would be good to know what was in his head when he did it."

"How am I gonna find her?" I asked, honestly perplexed.

"You're going to detect."

I raised an eyebrow. "Listen buddy," I said, "that's your job. I just answer the phones and type up fake letters to nobody."

He looked at me sitting next to him in the car and grinned. "Yeah. And I'm sure they appreciate it."

"Well, if you suddenly need an assistant, maybe you oughta hire one of those," I suggested.

"Like a junior detective?" Dex asked.

"Yes," I said. "Like that."

"Yeah, I *could* do that, couldn't I?"

"You could."

"But let me tell you something," he said with a smirk.

"What?"

"You come cheaper."

CHAPTER TWENTY-ONE

FIND RHODA DARROW he'd said, making it sound easy. Like finding a good pastrami or a place to see a movie. In reality, though, we were back to needle in haystack time. All I had was a name that both Dex and I realized might or might not be real. And I had a description, through the observant but not entirely unjaundiced eye of my boss.

I thought Dex would tell me how to detect, but he just dropped me off and swanned away, which I supposed was how I was getting stuck with this assignment in the first place. Many hands make the load lighter, so they say. My hands just didn't have any actual experience doing this sort of thing.

"You're a smart girl," Dex said when I tried to stop him. "You'll figure something out. Can't be any harder than me figuring out how to make a cuppa joe, right?"

He was right: I *am* a smart girl, but I know there are easy ways to go about things and there are hard ones. Sometimes the only way to tell the difference is by having someone tell you which is what, but Dex didn't seem in the mood for that. Not today.

After Dex dropped me at the office, I had the little lunch Marjorie had packed for me in the morning. While I ate my kipper and brown butter sandwich, I thought about all those mixed up files again. Then, after lunch, I got to work on finding Darrow, because clearly the filing was going to be even less fun.

Anyone watching the first fifteen minutes or so of my search wouldn't have thought I was doing very much at all. I just sat quietly at my desk thinking about the little I knew about Rhoda Darrow—and where would be a good place to start looking. Finally I looked in the book for the number of Metro-Goldwyn-Mayer, where Wyndham was under contract. Then I called them up. It seemed like as good a place as any to start.

When I got the switchboard, I asked if an actress named Rhoda Darrow was on their roster. The switchboard patched me over to the publicity department and when I said her name, they said they knew who she was. She had been under contract a couple of years before but now she was not. Did they know what had become of her? They did not. Did they know where she lived? No, but the nice woman I spoke to at MGM publicity went away to check their files. When she came back, she told me that Rhoda Darrow was represented by Wally Garris at the William Morris Agency, did I want that number?

I did.

Garris was apparently not available to anyone calling regarding Miss Darrow. I waited another hour, then tried again. The secretary was sharp. Sharper than I was about these things, I suspected, though I figured maybe she had more reason to be.

She recognized my voice right away.

"Listen," she instructed, "I'm done talking to you about Rhoda Darrow, see?"

"But," I pointed out helpfully, "you haven't told me anything at all."

"Right. And that's what I'm done telling you. Don't let me hear you on this phone again." With that she slammed the receiver down so hard, I imagined it rocking in its cradle.

Her instructions had been explicit—"Don't call here again." I had no intention of doing so, either. Instead, I decided it was important enough and the office was quiet enough that I'd get me some air.

Grabbing my handbag, a light coat and my hat, I locked the office and set off for the subway station, just a few blocks away on Hill Street. I risked the ire of the ticket taker in the grand lobby by asking for a receipt. But I reasoned that this wasn't going to be a pleasure ride. It was business, after all. Dex could pay me back. If he was going to make me detect, he could darn well give me my expenses, too.

I went down a series of stairways and ramps to catch the Hollywood train. I sat on a bench while I waited, thinking carefully about what I'd do when I got where I was going. I had a destination, I realized, but I didn't have much of a plan.

It was mid-afternoon when I boarded and the train was mercifully uncrowded. A light smattering of businessmen, no doubt headed out to appointments, shoppers on their way back home, laden with packages and tired satisfaction. A harried young mother traveled with two small children—one firmly attached to each hand. The smaller of the two, a little girl, coughed violently while her mother patted her back, wiped her spittle and looked concerned. I felt bad when I seated myself at the very back of the car, as far from this little family as I could.

When we got underway, I didn't pay any attention to the series of bells or the clacking of the tracks under us as we changed from one set to another. I knew that the two were related—the bells, the clacking, the destination—but I didn't know how and I figured there are some things in life one just doesn't need to know.

Before long—perhaps only a mile and after what felt like only a slight ascent—we emerged from the darkness of the subway into a visual cacophony of light and wires and the general melee that was Toluca Yard, where the extra trams were kept and, I imagine, other various bits and bolts needed to keep the whole complicated electric car system running.

I got off at Hollywood and Vine. A half dozen people got off with me. Not all of them were headed for the Equitable Trust Building, but a clump of us trooped into it together. That suited me just fine since entering the imposing structure on my

own would have been a bit nerve-wracking, especially considering my mission.

The lobby was big, shiny and impressive. I know that it cannot have been marble from floor to ceiling, but that was the impression I was left with: acres of marble worked to a finish so
fine, the surface reflected my face back at me with all the au-
thority of a mirror.

There was a building directory in one corner of the marble-
festooned lobby. It indicated that the offices of the William
Morris Agency were on the eighth floor. The elevator was swift
and new and smooth and if either the elevator or its operator
smelled of anything but clean I could not detect it.

On the eighth floor, the operator directed me to follow the
hallway all the way to the left where, just as advised, I found a
door marked with the name and trademark of the agency. It was
a big operation, one of the most important of its kind. I had a
tough time reconciling what Dex had told me about Rhoda Darrow and the name and reputation of the best-known talent
agency in the business.

At least, that's what I thought when I stood in the hallway.
Inside the office itself, I changed my tune. The William Morris
Agency didn't look greatly different from Dex's operation. Oh
sure: it was bigger, more bustling and a lot more was going on.
But there was no more opulence than Dex and I enjoyed and no
one was just sitting around on their keisters eating bon-bons
and shooting the breeze. I got the feeling that you had to work
with a lot of Rhoda Darrows before you hit a payday like Laird
Wyndham or Lorena Duvall. At a certain level, then, like so
many others, the movie business was a numbers game.

"How can I help you?" the receptionist said brightly as I entered. I was encouraged.

"I'm here to see Wally Garris," I said.

"Is he expecting you?" she asked, pulling her appointment
book toward her as she spoke. I knew the move. I always did it

that way myself. Thing was, there were probably actual appointments listed in the Morris Agency's book. Dex's tended to be as empty as a Sunday school teacher's bank account.

"No," I said. "I just thought I'd pop in and see if he was around."

She pushed the book back to its place thoughtfully. I could almost hear the reevaluation going on in her head. She pulled her sweater closer to herself protectively while pushing a doubtful eye over me. There was no part of me that looked like a glamour puss and I fit into that reception area the way a bear fits into a dinner party.

"Are you one of his clients?" she asked at length.

I shook my head.

"I see. Can I tell him what it's about?"

I thought about it quickly, then shook my head again. Mentioning Rhoda Darrow's name on the telephone hadn't brought me any traction, I had no reason to think it would be different now.

"What have you done?" she asked, pulling a form toward her from the other side of the desk. I could see she was prepared to put together some sort of resume on me. That wouldn't get me an interview with Mr. Garris. My theatrical resume wasn't very impressive, unless you counted my Desdemona in the senior girls' production of *Othello* my last year at Mrs. Beeson's School.

"I'm afraid I haven't done much of anything."

"I'm sorry," she said, but I could tell that she was not. "I'm trying to help you here, but you really have to do something to help yourself."

"Look," I said, "I just want to see Mr. Garris. On a personal matter."

The young woman sat back in her chair with an exasperated look on her face. "Unless you tell me what it's about, you will not get in to see him."

"It's just that . . . well, I called and . . . I wanted to talk to him about one of his clients. Rhoda Darrow?"

"That's not exactly a personal matter, is it?" she said coldly. I could see the last vestiges of the gentility she saved for real clients falling off her in chunks.

"Well," I said, kind of hemming, "I do want to see him. Personally," I said with a haw. "If Mr. Garris could just give me a few minutes of his time . . ."

She drew herself to her full sitting height in order to look down her nose at me. The pose looked most uncomfortable. "Have you any idea how valuable Mr. Garris's time *is*?" she said, clearly understanding that I did not. "If he just gave it away . . ." She let her voice trail off tantalizingly, leaving me to guess what calamities might be possible if such a thing should happen.

"Look, if you would just ask Mr. Garris if he would see me."

She looked at me as though astonished that I was still standing there, still breathing her air. "Close your head and pipe *this*, sister," she said, all of the veneer cracked away by now. An intercom buzzed and she ignored it in order to finish her tirade, "Mr. Garris will *not* see you, we do not have time for whatever it is you're selling, we—" The intercom buzzed again and she broke off with an exasperated gulp and picked it up.

"Yes, Mr. Morris," she said. "Of course. I'm sorry. Right away."

She hung up the phone, looking distracted. She grabbed her steno pad and got up, at which point she seemed to notice me, still standing in front of her desk.

"You're still here," she said without patience.

I nodded.

"Scram," she barked at me, backing me toward the door. I let her push me out into the hallway and watched as she closed the office door in my face. *The bum's rush,* I thought to myself dully. *This is what it feels like.* It was a new one on me.

I stood there, in the hallway, my heart pounding, and counted thirty. Then I counted another ten. When I was done, I opened the office door a crack and peeked inside. There was no sign of the secretary. There was no sign of anyone at all.

I entered the office again and stood in front of her desk for a heartbeat. Maybe two. I had no idea how long she'd be gone. On the other hand, I'd seen her leave with her steno pad after Mr. Morris's call. It seemed likely she was off somewhere taking dictation. Clearly, I had an opportunity. Just what I was to do with it was less clear.

Instinct guided me, I think, because I had no clear plan. Mindful that someone could come at any moment, I moved to the long row of filing cabinets lining one wall. "Darrow" was in the D's, just where you'd expect. I did not think things through, but I knew what I was doing. Whatever was going on with Rhoda Darrow, she no longer had the support of her agency, that much was clear. I thought about just peeking inside and getting Darrow's most recent address, which was what I'd hoped to find here. But, in the end some gremlin guided me to double the whole file up and stuff it into my purse. The handbag was really too small for this additional cargo, but I shoved the file around until no bits of paper poked out to give me away.

Back on the street I looked straight up, beyond the buildings on one side and the construction on the other. I looked straight up at a fat gray cloud scudding across a pale blue sky and said a quick prayer to the god of small things. The Broadway-Hollywood was catty-corner to the Equitable Building. I decided that what was needed was the department store's tea house. It would provide a place to take a load off while I looked over my spoils.

My heart settled into an easier patter once I sat at a wood veneered table with a cup of tea and a tiny crustless sandwich in front of me. Before I brought the file out of my purse, I checked over both shoulders and all around to see if anyone seemed intent on observing my movements. I don't know why. I had no reason to think so.

Reassured that no furtive watchers were watching, I reached into my purse and pulled out the file. There she was: Rhoda Darrow. The studio photograph in my hand showed a beautiful young woman with a creamy complexion and a shy, white smile. The photo was undated, but her clothes and the hat she wore told me it was at least ten years old: the girl in this photo was a jazz baby, plain and simple.

In addition to the photo in the file, there were a few contracts, but nothing more recent than 1927. Apparently Miss Darrow had been another sacrifice to the gods of sound. She'd never worked in a talkie. Not, at any rate, while Garris was her agent.

The only other thing in the folder was her personal file. Her date of birth—it indicated that she had been born in 1898, which would have made her roughly 33. But I knew that might or might not be true—her measurements, her next of kin, her doctor, her address: all the information that your proxy in the entertainment world would need to know about you in order to do business on your behalf. Only Garris hadn't been doing much business for her of late, or so it seemed.

I realized as I sat there, sipping my tea, that the home address on Ivar Avenue listed in Rhoda Darrow's file was not far from where I now sat. I lifted my head and looked more closely at the faces of the shoppers resting near me. Based on how close that address was, the tea house at the Broadway-Hollywood would not be an unthinkable place for Darrow to take a meal. If she was there, however, I couldn't detect her amid the aging dowagers and wives of young swells. I decided to finish my tea and sandwich and hit the bricks.

The day was cool but not crisp. I looked at the address again, only three, maybe four blocks out of my way. I decided to walk there, then catch up with the Red Car again down the line, closer to downtown.

The apartment house was fairly new. It appeared to have been built in the mid-twenties at the very latest and sported the quasi-opulence associated with that optimistic time. Everyone could be wealthy and if not, everyone should live that way, with marble floors and ornate fireplaces—in Los Angeles often beautiful but strictly ornamental. Carved angels and gargoyles guarded such homes and other signs of apparent wealth associated with the grand of other ages.

This is what I wonder: Had the stock market *not* crashed in 1929, where would it have gone? Because, for a time leading up to 1929, money seemed to breed; seemed to grow unaided. If you had a pile, all you had to do was spend all night dancing and drinking with your friends, and in the morning you'd be worth more than when you went to bed. As a result—at least, this is what I think—the houses grew ever grander, the accoutrements more opulent and impressive, the skyscrapers higher, the engineering more delicately wrought. There seemed to be no end.

At the time of the crash, there was a lot of construction going on. Buildings all over town—and all over the country, I guess—were going up that had been conceived and designed to be the biggest and best ever. With the crash everyone's expectations had to change overnight. If they did not know it—if they denied it for a time, as many did—then they knew it within a few weeks or months. Things just were not the same. Many of these buildings and houses and other types of construction that had been going on at the time of the crash were reconsidered. Some that hadn't gotten very far stopped altogether, abandoned, never to be completed. But others that were well underway were reimagined with a sensibility more appropriate to the time. We were beginning to see what I suspected would be the design of a new era: a more Spartan look.

More conservative. The wild imaginings of the jazz age—the sky's the limit, forget the cost—were relics. New realities affected every aspect of our lives.

But Rhoda Darrow's apartment building had been affected by none of this.

At the impressive front entrance, I buzzed 307. I could hear the door unlatch almost instantly and I went on up.

At the door to the apartment, I steeled myself before I knocked. I hadn't anticipated she'd be home and now here I was and here she was. What on earth was I going to say?

I didn't get much time to think about it. The door opened and a man stood in front of me—a nice looking man about my own age. He was newly shaven and the scent of soap clung to him as though he'd just stepped out of the bath. This impression was increased by his bare chest and the towel wrapped around his waist.

I was so shocked at his appearance—and lack of covering—that I nearly fainted, right there in the hall. Perhaps I only did not because such a move would have been extremely ill-advised—naked man, towel, strange apartment and hall and all.

He looked at least as surprised as I did, and perhaps even more mortified, if that were possible. "I was expecting someone else," he said. His hand clutched at the towel helplessly, as though he would cover more of himself with it, though that would have just made matters worse.

"So was I," I said, smiling despite myself as I turned my eyes away. "I'm looking for Rhoda Darrow. Is that who you were expecting, too?"

He shook his head. I caught the motion of it out of the corner of my eye. It was obvious that it wasn't a name he knew. "No. I was expecting my brother."

"Ah. And I'm sure your brother isn't named Rhoda. But is this Rhoda Darrow's apartment?"

Another shake of the head. "No," he said. "It's mine. I've

only lived here for about six months though," he offered helpfully. "Maybe she lived here before me? If you like, you could
ask the manager. She's at 101."

I did as he suggested. The manager was a sallow-skinned
woman of middle years. She might have been blond once, but
now her hair was a dull, yellowish pewter. The small child that
gripped the edge of her housedress looked like a permanent
fixture. She told me she had only been in the building a year
herself and had never met Rhoda Darrow. "But I do got a for-
warding address," she said, meeting my eyes and not volun-
teering anything.

"Wait: are you saying you *do* have a current address for
her?"

The woman ducked her head slightly, nodding in the affir-
mative.

"But you won't give it to me, is that what you're saying?"

"Oh, I never did say that."

"Yes, but . . . oh wait," I said, remembering Dex's folding
money at Number 11. "Are you saying you'd give me the new
address for a price?"

"Could be I'm saying that," the woman said. "I wouldn't
say no."

I opened my purse and drew out a half-dollar, wondering as
I did so how I'd manage to get Dex to reimburse me for it. It
was fairly obvious I would not be getting a receipt.

The woman just snorted at the sight of the coin and the
child rocked on its heels, as though agreeing with its mother's
dry mirth.

"I was thinking more along the lines of a sawbuck."

"A *sawbuck*?" I said, shocked. "I'm not giving you ten
whole dollars for an address. That's crazy!"

The woman shrugged. Clearly she'd had to try. "All right,"
she said agreeably, "a fin then. I'll give you the address for
a fin."

"That's better, but we're not quite there yet. I don't even have five dollars on me."

"What *do* you got then?" the woman asked, looking at my handbag as though she might see right inside it if she stared hard enough.

"Let me . . . let me check. Let's see here," I said. "I'll give you a two-spot and four bits, all right? That's all I've got. I have to leave myself enough to take the streetcar."

The woman grunted her acknowledgment and held out her hand.

"When I get the address," I told her. I may not have been a big fancy detective, but that much I knew. I'd hold onto my money until I at least got a load of what I was buying.

The woman made a face and disappeared back into her apartment, closing the door without another word. I stood there for a full minute wondering what I was supposed to do. Had I insulted her? Had I breached some arcane informant etiquette? But no, soon I could hear the scratch of the door again and she was back, this time without the child.

The exchange took thirty seconds. Less. And then I stood there, two dollars and fifty cents lighter, looking down at a Santa Monica address written in a scrawled but legible hand. I felt a small surge of pride. It wasn't full success, but it was definite progress. It was too late in the day to head out to Santa Monica but I'd gotten what I'd left the office for. I'd detected and was coming home with the meat in my fist.

CHAPTER TWENTY-TWO

DEX WAS WAITING for me when I got back to the office.

"Where the hell have you been?" he said when I showed up around five. But he interrupted me before I could answer, "Never mind. Sterling called. While you was out gallivanting."

"I wasn't gallivanting, Dex. If you would just hold the phone for a minute, I'd tell you."

But Dex had been waiting long enough. He wasn't about to wait for me to finish talking now.

"You know," he said as though I'd asked, "Steward Sterling. Laird Wyndham's shyster?"

"Sure."

"Well, he called. He said Wyndham wants us to go and see him. Today. The sooner the better."

"Us?"

"Yeah: us. He's got some idea you're at every meeting I ever have, I guess. Taking notes so what we're talking about doesn't fall out of my poor, simple head. Anyway, I figured if I didn't ask if you wanted to come along, there'd be hell to pay."

"You got that right," I said, smiling. So even though it was late in the day and that day had been a long one, we prepared to head out to Number 11. Dex had already gotten hold of Mustard and picked up a car so getting out to Number 11 was less painful than it had been on our previous visit. Since Dex already knew the drill—a bit of folding incentive when he showed his P.I. ticket—we got to do pretty much what we wanted. This time the elevator was working so instead of trudging up and down hallways and new stairwells still soiled with construction dust, we were delivered speedily almost to our exact destination.

My optimism that things were going our way was dashed when Wyndham was brought into the big visiting room to meet with us. He looked haggard and worn, as though he'd been spread on the road and had a truck drive over him. Several times. Both Dex and I tried not to show how shocked we were by his appearance. But it was hard. And though Sterling had made the call, he didn't join us. The table seemed bigger without him and Wyndham seemed much reduced.

"Glad you two could come," Wyndham rose when he saw us. He pumped Dex's hand and smiled broadly at me and, in both of those small things, you could sense his relief at a visit from the outside. "Dex and the lovely Miss Pangborn," he said, his voice lacking none of its courtly grace, even if it was raw on the rest of him.

"Sterling said it was kind of urgent," Dex said, dropping into a chair and getting straight to business.

"It's just that, I did as you asked and really started thinking—hard, you understand?—about people who might be able to either clear my name or who will lead us to . . . to whoever actually did this thing."

"Great, Wyndham. That's just jake," Dex enthused. "I take it you dreamed something up?"

"Well, yeah. Now that you mention it. Dreamed up is a good way to put it. See, I got to thinking about what you'd said: about wanting to talk to people about me so you could prove I was innocent. That got me thinking some more—and I've got nothing right now but time to think—it got me thinking that if I could get you behind the scenes at the studio, that would maybe do some good."

"The studio?" Dex said. "You mean a movie studio?"

"Laird is on contract at Metro-Goldwyn-Mayer," I explained. "In Culver City."

"Right. And I got to thinking it would be a pretty easy matter to get you behind the scenes there." He spoke to Dex, but then seemed to include me almost as an afterthought. "Or both of you, if you wanted. Actually, figuring out what to do with her is even easier than you."

"How so?" Dex wanted to know.

"Well, they're always using extras, for one thing. Fact, *Journey of the Long Night,* the film I'm supposed be working on right now, is shooting and I know for a fact that they'll have a need for a lot of young attractive female extras for that movie."

I felt myself blushing—quick and hot. *Young and attractive* is what Laird Wyndham had said. And he'd said it about *me.* My head swam.

"What about me?" Dex asked.

"I figured it might be better for you to pose as someone whose role is behind the scenes," Wyndham said. "I told you I have a lot of time to think, right?"

We nodded.

"So, Dex, I was figuring you could pose as a financier. Someone with money to spend on the business. People like that get an open door to just about anyplace they want to go."

"You really *have* given this some thought," Dex said.

Wyndham nodded and grinned. The cadaverous look he'd worn when we got there seemed to fall away a bit under this new animation. "Like I said . . . what else do I have to do?"

"That all sounds good. I mean, it sounds like we could get in there all right. Under the radar, like. What I need to work out is why."

"Why?"

"Yeah. Like I said, it all sounds perfectly reasonable. That is, it sounds like something we could do. But I'm just not seeing how you figure it will help you."

"Well, you said you wanted to talk to people. People who knew me, right?"

"Right."

"I'm well known at the studio. I spend a lot of my time there. You could talk to people about me. Get the straight dope, as they say. And more, too, I'm thinking. One of the things you asked me first time we met was did I know anyone who had it in for me. Now I've been sitting here wracking my brain on that one, let me tell you. I can't think of anyone. That's the other reason I thought that you, a professional investigator, might be able to get more out of people than someone else could. And maybe you'd get a feel for it if, say, that someone had an axe to grind with me. Maybe even an axe I don't so much as know about."

"Actually, that does kind of make sense, Dex," I said.

"I can see what you're getting at, Wyndham. It's just, this isn't the sort of investigation I generally do. You understand that? I've already had to wear a mask. Now I'm going to have to play dress up? Play pretend? It all sounds a bit silly to me."

"Well, maybe if I take you through it, tell you what I've dreamed up, you'll see it's not silly at all. See, for Miss Pangborn, she doesn't really have to pretend anything, other than wanting to make some dough. It's really just a matter of Steward telling her where to go and who to ask for. They hire extras by the busload at MGM. For you though, Dex, it'll take a specific invitation. Steward will take care of that as well, of course. He's done it before."

"Helped people pose as something in the movie business?" Dex asked.

"No, no: introduced money people to studio people. On the up and up. So, you see, it won't be much of a reach for him to do it in this case."

"So, in a way," Dex reasoned, "I wouldn't have to really pretend to be something I'm not. I could just be me but rich."

I couldn't resist commenting on this.

"And that's not pretending?"

"So you'll do it?" Wyndham asked.

"Look, I'll be honest. This kind of deep cover operation might look pretty in the movies, but in real life? It tends not to get you very far," Dex said.

"So you *won't* do it?"

"Well, I didn't say that either. I'm just suggesting you not get your hopes too far up. I fully expect that the whole thing will be a big waste of time."

Wyndham blinked first at me, then at Dex. He looked a little confused. Truth be told, I felt that way myself. But the disappointment had fallen away.

"So you *will* do it?" Wyndham said.

"Put it this way: you paying?"

Wyndham nodded.

"And," Dex went on, "you're prepared for us to turn up nothing at all. What I mean is: you'll pay whether or not we find anything, right?"

Another nod.

"Well then, what the hell, right? If you're buying, I'm selling. I guess we're going to be in the pictures."

CHAPTER TWENTY-THREE

DESPITE THE MATINEE idol looks he came by honestly, it was never in the cards that Dex should be a movie star. It's even possible that the things about his features that women found compelling weren't really the sort that the camera can pick up, that the things that burn in Dex, burn from within. How could a camera see that anyway?

No, if we were going to play this game, setting Dex up to be someone away from the lens was a good idea. He's comfortable in all those roles: the watcher, the drinker, the guy who pulls the strings. He'd be less successful pretending to be the guy who dances to the music, the guy with the dangerous looks who does what he's told.

We worked all of these things out at the office: me and Dex, Steward Sterling and Mustard, who Dex had asked to come along as extra eyes and ears.

We sat around Dex's battered desk and tossed ideas around until deep into the night. I was tired and, truth be told, did less of the tossing than the others. It wasn't expected of me, in any case. It was easy for me to lapse into the kind of silence I'd learned when I was a child and was often overlooked by adults deeply involved in their own conversations. So it was on this night.

Wyndham's connections would, it seem, get us in just about any place we could ever want to go. Just as we'd roughed out in Wyndham's company back at Number 11, the plan was for me to turn up at the studio the following day like any other extra, coming to the big front gates on Washington Boulevard with the others who were working on *Journey of the Long Night*. I would be one of a huge crowd and thus the chance for detection was unlikely. It also seemed unlikely I'd ever be in a position to discover anything of note, but that was the chance I'd have to take. To me it seemed worth the chance, in any case: I'd get to see behind the scenes at the most important movie studio in Hollywood. And I'd get paid.

Dex's part would require more finesse, which was fine by me. Sterling's office was giving Dex a letter of introduction to the business office. He was going to roll up to the studio in a limo, posing as an investor—from Canada, of all places. So Dex would spend the day talking to bigwigs and getting the ten-dollar tour which would put him in a position to see all sorts of things and talk to all kinds of people. They decided that Mustard would ride along as Dex's assistant—also from Canada, thus able to get to people and initiate conversations on a different social level than the ones Dex would be playing at. I was only sorry it was unlikely I'd ever be within earshot of the two of them to hear them overpronouncing words and showing off their legal whiskey, but there wasn't much chance I'd even see them during the day, let alone get the chance to laugh at their antics.

Steward Sterling dropped me off on his way home to Hancock Park, the long Packard he drove reflecting the night.

"They seem quite filled with hilarity," he said to me at one point on the short ride.

"Mustard and Dex? Yeah. And that's not all they're full of," I said, thinking of the large quantities of bootleg bourbon they had made disappear over the evening.

"I just hope they take it seriously enough," Steward said, sounding concerned.

"You can bet they will never take it seriously," I assured him. "But that shouldn't stop them from getting the job done."

Steward laughed at this, but I thought he had a nervous

sound. Hoping for the best and expecting the worst, I would have said that summed up the lawyer's mien on this night.

"You and Laird are pretty good friends, huh?" I asked, mostly just making conversation.

"Pretty good, yeah. We've known each other a long time."

"He seems like a nice guy."

"The best," Steward said without hesitation.

"That's how it seems to me, too. Which is why it's been so odd, sometimes in this investigation, hearing stuff about him that doesn't line up with how he seems."

"How so?"

"A couple of people, I won't mention any names, but a few of them have said, well, they've said Laird can have a bit of a temper."

Steward didn't answer right away. In fact, for a few moments, it seemed as though the road demanded all his attention, though from what I could see all was quiet and handling the car didn't seem to be challenging his driving talents.

"That's true of all of us, I guess," he said after a while. But to me his voice sounded deliberately casual, as though he was working hard to inject just the right note. "Under the right circumstances, can't we all be pushed to that?"

"That's true. You're right," I replied. "That's how it seems to me. This . . . this was a bit more than that, though. More than everyday aggravation, anyway."

Another silence. Then, "Perhaps you'd best just tell me."

"I can't, really. I would but, as you well know, I'm nothing on this case. Dex's secretary. Hardly in a position to tell you anything at all."

"Yet you brought it up."

We'd reached my house by now, though neither of us acknowledged that. Sterling pulled the car to the curb and we sat there, engine idling. Now Steward reached across me to the glove compartment and pulled out a pack of smokes. He pulled one out and lit it in the mad glow of the car's cigarette lighter. The light did odd things to his features. It seemed, for a moment, to pull them askew.

"I guess I did, didn't I? Sorry. It's just all so much on my mind just now. So you don't think so, do you?"

"Think what?" Steward asked, rightly confused by the track change.

"Think Laird, you know, *did it*. You don't even think he's capable of it."

"No. You're right there. I know Laird pretty well—maybe as well as anyone—and I don't think he's capable of . . . well, of that."

"Someone did it though."

"Well of course," said Steward, back on solid ground, "that's what we hired you for."

"He hit a woman," I said it softly.

"Pardon?"

"I think you heard me."

"All right. I did," he admitted. "I just couldn't believe my ears."

"Couldn't you? That surprises me. From what I heard, you knew all about it."

"Hey, what is this?"

"It's nothing, Mr. Sterling. Exactly nothing. Call it a probe, if you will. A test."

"A test? How did I do?"

I opened the door in a single motion. Hopped out onto the curb.

"I'll let you know," I said, closing the door behind me, moving toward the house, not looking back.

It was after midnight when I let myself in. I was careful to be mouse-quiet and crept along the carefully oiled floors as soundlessly as possible. Though a part of me wouldn't have been surprised if Marjorie had waited up, I was hoping this would not be the case. I didn't want to have to explain myself. I didn't even want to have to talk anymore and I was more relieved than I would have thought to make it to my room without encountering anyone. In my room, I took off my shoes and sat at the very center of my bed with my legs crossed beneath me.

Sitting there, I calmed my heart; asked my pulse to be still. And I asked myself what I thought I was doing. No matter if Steward's boss was shaping up to be a bit of a louse, it didn't follow that he was a murderer. I'd had no business talking to a client like that, none at all. Especially since there had been no direction from Dex to probe in this way. Not even a single hint. Yet I'd wanted Steward to know what I'd discovered, at least the outside shape of it. I'd wanted to see his reaction when he heard the words, when I dropped my bomb.

What had I discovered with this little bit of independent detective work? As my heart moved toward its normal rate, I sat there and considered. When it came to me, it was humbling to realize, the only thing I'd discovered was this: I was not a shamus, a gumshoe, a P.I. If I were—and, say, if I were Dex—there might have been things about this interview with Steward Sterling that would have been enlightening. But I was no detective, and I certainly wasn't Dex. If there'd been anything to discover in my talk with Sterling, I'd missed it completely.

CHAPTER TWENTY-FOUR

WHEN I FINALLY fell asleep, it was not to peaceful slumber. Shadow figures followed me in and out of dreams. It was meaningless. Disconnected. I woke feeling less rested than I had when I lay down.

I contemplated going back to sleep, thinking it was still the middle of the night. But when I reached over and fumbled around on my nightstand for my alarm clock, I discovered it had fallen on its back like a sad little turtle. I righted it and gasped: It was six fifteen. I hadn't gotten a full night's sleep, but I'd slept longer than intended. I'd have to get the lead out if I was going to get to Culver City anywhere near the correct time.

By the time I got all organized with subways out of downtown and streetcars to Culver City it hadn't gotten any earlier and when the Red Car disgorged me in front of the grand MGM gates on Washington Boulevard, it was close to eight.

"Extras is s'posed to get here at seven in the morning," the guard at the gatehouse told me.

"Yeah," I said with a smile. "That's what they told me. But I slept in."

The guy shook his head but let me pass, telling me to keep an eye out for Mary Watkins at Stage 17.

Watkins proved to be a rotund woman with a fluffy halo of yellow hair. A long cigarette dangled from her lip as she spoke and yellow stains on the index and middle fingers of her left hand told me the smoke wasn't an aberration. Still, there was something warm about her. Something likeable.

"Krikey, but you're late," she admonished when she discovered who I was. She sounded lightly exasperated but not unkind.

I had the feeling this sort of thing happened on a regular basis and anyway, she told me, she was short a couple of girls.

"You're going to need to move those pins if you hope to catch up, though," she said. I watched fascinated as smoke seemed to spill out of her nose as she spoke. She looked like a fat blond dragon.

She sent me to the costume department. She said the film was "high concept, high art." I needed to be properly attired. The filming itself was taking place on Stage 32. She told me she'd have a car pick me up from the costume department and deposit me at the sound stage because, "you ain't gonna be able to ankle around in that getup. Not far anyway."

Though her words filled me with dread, I did as she said and "moved my pins." When I told the head costumer what film I was working on, my dread deepened when the woman laughed. "Oh, you're gonna love this one," she said in a voice that careened off the ceiling. She took my measurements then went away. When she came back a quarter hour later she had an assistant with her. Both women were bowed under the weight of the box they carried between them.

The dress they drew out of the box was made of lead. I asked them why, but both women just shrugged and smirked. The senior of the two said, "Ours not to reason why . . ." and though she didn't continue the quote, both women laughed as they finished fitting me into the complicated costume. None of this made me feel any better, and I never got the feeling it was supposed to.

When she was done, the senior of the two led me to a mirror. I gasped when I got a load of myself. The dress was fitted to me in segments and while one woman had fit me, the other had added smoky, exotic makeup. The end result was astonishing. I looked otherworldly even to my own eyes. The straw boss had been right: there was no hope at all of me getting very far in this space dress.

"What's the idea?" I said to Mary when I stumbled toward her slowly. "What am I supposed to be?"

"Well, the movie is a re-telling of Ulysses' epic journey." She looked approvingly at my costume. Turned me around. I was glad for her help. I wasn't sure I would have been able to manage the operation on my own.

"Ulysses?"

"Right. You know, Virgil, Homer, the *Odyssey,* that kind of bushwa." She bundled me into one of the studio's cars, and sat next to me on the back seat while indicating the driver should get a move on. I couldn't sit, exactly, but I managed a sort of semi-dignified sprawl that Mary nodded at approvingly.

"Wow," said I as the car lurched ahead.

"Yeah. Only it takes place twenty-five thousand years in the future."

"Twenty-five thousand?"

"Yeah. And, to answer your question," though I'd forgotten I'd asked one, "you're one of the legion of handmaidens to the god Zeus."

"Zeus. Right. A handmaiden. Gotcha."

"Only he's not called Zeus in this picture. I can't remember what they call him. Cherniak? Something like that. It doesn't matter. But it's something appropriately futuristic."

Journey of the Long Night was shooting on a huge sound-stage near the back of the lot. Outside it was just a big, featureless building painted beige. No windows, few doors, all of them currently closed. Mary waited until the lights that indicated shooting was in progress were off, then she herded me into the building. No mean feat: if the "dress" I was wearing weighed an ounce it weighed seventy-five pounds. It was like carrying around a Packard.

"Ah, yet another handmaiden." No one had to identify the speaker as the director. It was like he'd gone to some directorial supply house for every item of clothing, every mannerism and vocal inflection. He was wearing jodhpurs and high black boots, polished to perfection. He wore a black beret. It slouched on his head just so but I suspected that, without the hat, he'd be bald as a newborn rat.

"Who is that?" I asked quietly.

"Horst von Rauschenberg," Mary told me,

"That's a real name?" I said.

Mary shrugged. "Probably not."

As was appropriate, he paid me no attention, but indicated with an impatient motion of his hand—one, two, three fast chops—that Mary should lead me off to the right. She seemed to know what he wanted because she urged me forward again. I followed her down a hallway at a painful shuffle. Normally I would not have seen it as a great distance, but the lead dress changed my perspective.

After a while she stopped in front of a closed door that, when opened, proved to be full of young women dressed almost exactly like me. When they saw Mary, a universal whine went up, not directed at me but at my escort.

"Ladies," she said, trying to pierce the sound, "ladies, *please*. I know this is uncomfortable and probably no fun at all, but it's what we have to deal with today."

"How does anyone even know what people will wear on planet Zircon?" a lissome blonde complained.

"Yeah!" a striking redhead chipped in her two cents. "And why do the costumes have to be so heavy? It's not like anyone else can *feel* them."

"Ladies," Mary said again, "*please*. It's not as though I have control over any of this. You know that. Oh, I could say, 'Oh, oh! How horrid. I'll look into all these things.' But the reality is: my voice is very small. And, really, my advice is this: pipe down and put up with it. Don't get me wrong: what you're doing here today doesn't strike me as a whole lot of fun. But it's what we have, all right?"

It was clearly not all right, but the lead-dressed women understood what Mary was saying: it was out of their control and at least it meant there'd be a paycheck at the end of the day. I wagered that several of these young women were lugging their lead dresses around in order to feed children—offspring in some cases, siblings in others. Spending the day in a lead dress would, in the end, be a small price to pay. One of those things you look back at and tell people about. Maybe laugh. But while we were wearing them? Man, it was hell.

"Easy for her to say," a tough looking brunette said once Mary had gone.

"Yeah, but she's right though, ain't she?" said another blonde. "She didn't invent this damn getup."

The exotic planet Zircon makeup obscured the speaker's face somewhat, but I was fairly sure I recognized the sultry phrasing and the creeping dissatisfaction that featured in her voice in equal measure.

"Rosalyn?" I said.

"Hmmmm," she said, giving me the up and down. "I figure I'd recognize your face if you didn't look like you were ready to blast off. As it is though, kid, I don't have a clue."

"The other night. The Masquers' Ball? We ate fish in aspic together."

I saw recognition light her face. "Well, well. She of the lovely name. I thought you weren't an actress."

Rosalyn Steele was resplendent in a getup almost identical to mine. I grinned at her, oddly pleased to find someone with whom I had some kind of connection.

"I'm *not*," I insisted. "That's why I'm wearing the goofy two-hundred-pound dress. I thought you were an actress. What are you doing here dressed like that?"

"Ah well, you know how it is."

I shrugged knowingly, but I did not.

"I didn't have anything lined up and my agent told me about this . . ."

"And here you are with us untalented types."

"Exactly," she said with a smile that held no sting.

I shuffled over to stand next to her. There were couches and chairs around the room, but most of the girls were standing. I understood why. The lead was stiff and ungiving. Even though it wasn't solid lead, just sheets of the stuff fitted around a frame of light wood, it was difficult to move freely in them.

"If we're just going to hang around in here all day," I said, "why don't we just have the dresses nearby then put them on quickly when they call us?"

"That would be sensible," Rosalyn said. "But they want us ready in the blink of an eye. And so . . ." she indicated the stiff pewter-colored sides of her own heavy frock.

"I'm going to be pooped tonight," I said.

"You don't know the half of it," Rosalyn warned. "Anyway, I'm glad to see you. You know, after we spoke at the party, I looked around for you. I wanted to apologize."

"To me?" I said. "Whatever for?"

"Oh, you know. I'd had a lot to drink," she said. "Maybe said some things that could have been better thought out. And after you'd gone, it struck me that I'd been horrible to you."

"I wouldn't have said that," I said truthfully.

"Well, I'm glad. Just, I don't know, the topic you got me started on wasn't right for my mood, I guess. But maybe I can make it up to you."

"How's that?"

"You look a little lost, for starters. Maybe I can show you the ropes?"

"Sure," I said. "That would be swell."

The day was endless. *Endless.* I cannot convey to you how mind-numbingly endless it was. A score of times—a *hundred* times—I asked myself what I was doing there. Because, clearly,

I wasn't going to make any big discoveries stuck in a room with between thirty and forty other young women, all set to revolutionize the movie industry with our lithe bodies pressed into lead-covered frames.

True to her word, though, my new friend Rosalyn stuck with me to show me the ropes. So it was that when we were finally herded onto a set that looked like a bleak, metallic beach on some unimaginably bizarre planet, while the shot was being set up, Rosalyn nudged me in the region of my metalized middle.

"Psst," she said, "lookit the swell." I raised my head in time to exchange glances with Dexter J. Theroux, resplendent in an expensive suit I'd never seen before. He was just as eloquently disguised in a cloak of keep-your-distance. He looked beyond the reach of normal mortals, an impression increased by the manservant who obsequiously dogs his master's heels. I wanted to laugh out loud, but instead tried to strike an appropriately interested stance.

"Yeah," I said. "Swell."

"You know, he looks familiar. I feel like I've seen him before."

"Hmmm," I said as innocently as possible, "I wonder if he could have been at the Masquers' Ball too?"

"Yeah, yeah, that's it," she said as though relieved to have solved the puzzle. "I came across him in the garden with a long-legged redhead attached to him. I wonder who he is."

"It's the boy wonder, Irving Thalberg," a gorgeous brunette offered up. "If you ever wanted to impress someone, you'd do all right to impress him."

"No it's not," said another girl. "I've seen Mr. Thalberg. He's not as tall. No, no: I think it's the producer, Hal Roach."

"No it ain't," scoffed still another girl. "Hal don't have that much hair."

The girls continued on in this vein, quietly, so it couldn't be heard outside our group, until the director shushed us with a loud, "Quiet on the set!" We all piped down and waited for him to say, "And . . . action!" at which point we were meant to file out of the screened-off area that had been designated "stage left" and meander around in a sinuous line until we reached our marks at "stage right." Somewhere in there the director had told us he would cut when he had what he wanted. It sounded incredibly fast. Incredibly easy. Of course, it was not.

For one thing, the "sinuous line" the director had envisioned was made difficult by costumes that were heavy and awkward. Though the girls wearing them had been chosen for their athleticism and fit young bodies, it was as though all of us were suddenly fifty or seventy-five pounds heavier than when we'd woken up in the morning. Only it was dead weight, not to mention pounds we just didn't know what to do with. So while the director had envisioned a jaunty line of lead-clad maidens meandering across his set, what he got were girls who walked heavy-footed, with the grace of baby elephants. We were no doubt cute, but lithe? Not so much.

He would holler "Cut!" into his megaphone and all of us would rejoice internally at the prospect of upcoming freedom, only to have him, once again, instruct us on how we should be walking and what sort of mood we were trying to achieve and what we should be feeling and who we should be in our heads. What none of us told him—though perhaps we should have—was that mood-casting was quite beyond our abilities right then. Some of us were having trouble just standing upright and moving ahead.

At some point, I lifted my head and saw that Dex, Mustard and entourage had gone. I tried not to let my brain fill with sour grapes while I thought of him in a cushy bungalow on the lot somewhere, sitting under a parasol, while some girl peeled grapes for him and poured champagne.

"God no! *Cut!* What on earth am I to *do* with you? What's wrong with you? You should be like *gazelles* not *water buffalo*! Like little *rabbits* not *armadillos*!"

And so on. It was endless.

Midway through shooting what was growing to be the scene from hell, and after shouting "Cut!" in what seemed like a less violent way than usual, the director said, "OK. Let's take five. Someone get Sutherland down here. We're ready for him."

Though all of us handmaidens were relieved to have five minutes of rest, only a couple of girls actually left the set and I suspected that a few had shuffled off to find a ladies room someplace. I pitied them their need. I had thus far been avoiding even thinking about what I'd do with all that lead if I had to go to the bathroom.

When Baron strode onto the set, I nearly collapsed in shock. Then it made sense. I worried for a moment he would see me, give me away. Then I nearly laughed aloud at the thought. He didn't know anything about me. He didn't know where I lived or worked or who I was. More to the point, though, aside from the fact that I'd been wearing a mask when we first met, it seemed likely I'd be invisible to him, camouflaged as I was by a full bouquet of lead-clad handmaidens, not to mention the weirdly exotic glamour-puss space-girl makeup. I wasn't even sure Marjorie would have recognized me.

"Baron Sutherland is working on this movie?" I said to Rosalyn.

"Hmmmm," she nodded. "That's right."

"I thought Laird Wyndham was the star?"

"Didn't we have this conversation at the party?" she asked.

"Not really."

"Laird Wyndham is in jail."

"I know *that*," I said. "But I thought he'd been meant to star in it."

"Well, he was. Baron was going to play the aging inventor."

"Well *that's* a step up," I said. "An odd one in a way. I mean, you'd think they'd have other up and coming stars on contract."

"Oh sure," Rosalyn said. "Sure they do. But I heard Baron has it in *his* contract that if anything happened to Laird, he'd get the starring male lead role."

"But they're both contract players, right? Don't they just go where they're told?"

"Sure," Rosalyn said. "That's right. But they still sometimes have billing clauses in their contracts. Like, it wouldn't have just been for this one film. But for the duration."

"For the balance of their contracts, Baron walks into the place where Laird was supposed to stand?"

"That's right."

"Are you sure?"

"Not really," she admitted. "It's just what I heard."

"Isn't that unusual? It sounds hinky to me."

"I guess it's unusual. But it seems like it was a safe bet for production, right? I mean, what was going to happen to Laird?"

It was a good point. Young, strong and in his prime, it would have been pretty good odds that nothing would happen to the main star; meanwhile it secured a seasoned professional for important but less visible roles. Not the starring, romantic role.

So that was something like a motive. But was it enough to kill for? I didn't think so. I looked over toward the place where Baron sat in a director's chair with his name painted on the back. Two makeup girls hovered around him trying as much as they could to repair the damage time had done. The director was chatting with him earnestly, even anxiously; in fact the whole set seemed focused on Baron's happiness and his presence. He was once again a star.

"So who did they get to take Baron's original role?" I asked.

Rosalyn pointed to an old man, erect but definitely grizzled; handsome but decidedly gray. I looked back to the place where Baron sat enfolded in the palm of stardom. In comparison he was the very picture of a man in his prime.

Was it enough to kill for? Not for everyone, certainly. Not

for me. Perhaps not for you. But maybe—just maybe—for someone who had once held it all, had seen time wash it away rather
than reward the effort of a lifetime, maybe for someone like
that, it would be enough.

CHAPTER TWENTY-FIVE

THE SCENE BARON shot with us was a quick one, mercifully. And he didn't even come close to recognizing me. The director had him run up a ramp between us as we undulated
here and there. Then he ran in a different direction while we
looked after him adoringly, waving him away. Honestly? What
we were doing—*everything* we were doing—felt ridiculous to
me. Quite beyond the suspension of anyone's belief. But I'd
read enough movie magazines to understand there were several layers of magic between what was happening there on that
soundstage and what an audience would eventually see in a
theater. Still. It felt just plain goofy and if I hadn't been so mis-
erable and uncomfortable it would occasionally have been difficult not to laugh.

Once Baron was gone—presumably back to some bungalow
with a star on the door—the director put us through some
more handmaidenish paces. I gathered from the type of things
we were being made to do that these scenes wouldn't appear in
the movie back to back, but rather would seem to be happening
over the course of years. The film's story "had a huge canvas."
It was a phrase I overheard a couple of times that day and I understood it to mean the director was building what he hoped
was a Cecil B. DeMille-style epic, though it seemed to me he
was certainly no Cecil B. DeMille.

When the director was finally done with us, he said he was
settling for a few second-rate scenes, but made it clear he'd already spent too much time on the footage he'd shot with us in
it. This imperfection was the fault of his forty incompetent
handmaidens. By then, all of us handmaidens were well past

caring. We just wanted the lead dresses off, off, off so our bodies could begin to recall what normalcy felt like. A funny little bus came and took us back to wardrobe in shifts and we climbed aboard one at a time dispiritedly. Oh, it really had been a long day.

Rosalyn and I stuck together through all of the shooting, and we stayed together after we were through. "Now I know what it must feel like when someone loses a lot of weight," she said, executing a neat little pirouette on the street between soundstages. We both looked smaller and felt lighter, but the exotic makeup remained, for the moment. That would take special care at home.

"I know what you mean," I said, enjoying the light feeling of just walking around without struggle. I'd never appreciated the plain dress and light coat I'd chosen that morning more.

"You wanna go to the commissary? Get a bite?" Rosalyn asked as we walked toward the Washington Boulevard entrance to the studio. I was tired and had only been thinking of beginning the progression of streetcars that would be required to get me home, but her question got my tummy rumbling.

I looked at her, wide-eyed. "I don't think it's for extras." I didn't know much, but I knew that. The sheer number of extras around would have made it impossible to feed all of them.

"I'm no extra," she said defensively.

"You were today," I pointed out.

"True. But most of the time, I'm not. And, anyway, I know a guy . . ."

"Yeah well, sure," I said. "If you can get us in, I'm game." I was enjoying Rosalyn's company. Anyway, I wasn't about to turn down either free or reasonable food.

I followed her through the studio streets. To me it all seemed nonsensical and labyrinthine, but she seemed to know where she was going. One building out of many appeared normal in that it had windows and doors that could not be driven through.

I could tell it was an office, because you could see people through the windows working at desks.

As we passed one office, I was surprised to see Dex, reclining on a comfy looking leather sofa, a long and elegant stogie in his hand. He was pontificating about something or other—I could see his lips move. As he spoke, he gesticulated with a low-ball glass in the other hand. I was close enough to see a generous portion of amber liquid sloshing around over a couple of rocks and a couple of other men seated with him in the room— Mustard not among them—with expressions of frozen good humor on their faces. They must have pretended that Dex was really wealthy in order for studio bosses to be putting up with as much as the faces of these men told me they were. I stopped myself from groaning. Depending on when *this* had started, things might not be going well.

Rosalyn followed my glance. "Hey," she said, "that's the swell we saw when we were on-set this afternoon. Wonder what he's doing here?"

I didn't look and I didn't answer and I just kept moving her along.

A long low car was parked behind the building, and I recognized Mustard in the driver's seat, his nose buried in what might have been a racing form. This didn't bode well either. Mustard wouldn't have liked being relegated to the role of manservant or chauffeur.

The commissary was bigger than I'd expected, taking up what looked like the entire lower portion of still another building. For some reason, I'd also expected it would be cafeteria style. Maybe just the word—commissary—put me in mind of it. But it was not. Waitresses in carefully starched pale uniforms and tidy matching hats gave the room an almost military presence.

"It has to be a bit like the army," Rosalyn said when I mentioned this to her. "I've heard they serve close to three thousand lunches here every single day."

We took an open table at the center of the room and I tried to keep my eyes from darting around to see who was there. For the most part, though, the people I *thought* I was recognizing I wasn't sure about. For instance, I thought I saw Norma Shearer and Joan Crawford sharing a pot of tea at a corner table, but admonished myself for the thought. The two women were known to be jealous of each other, I'd read all about it in movie magazines. Tea and biscuits between them seemed unlikely.

"Oh you're close, though," Rosalyn said. "Half right. The one on the left *is* Miss Shearer. But the other woman isn't Miss Crawford: it's Florence Eldridge."

"It is? She looks different in person."

"They all do, don't you think? But yes: it's definitely Miss Eldridge. The two of them got chummy when they were making *The Divorcee* here last year."

A waitress arrived at our table, diverting my attention from the two stars at their tea party. "You ladies eating or yakking?" she asked pertly.

"Eating, I think," Rosalyn said. "We've been encased in lead all day."

The waitress looked at us like this was the most natural thing in the world. I suppose, to her, it probably was, in this place where space creatures, cowboys and circus performers might sometimes lunch together. We took the menus she offered and she moved off on her round of the dining room.

Sitting there, finally, with the weight off our bodies and being bossed around off our minds, I discovered I was famished. At least, I was as soon as my hand touched the menu's plasticized page. I was so hungry that everything looked lovely, too, but I settled on an egg salad sandwich; Rosalyn opted for grilled cheese and we decided to make like the big stars in the room and split a pot of tea between us.

It was close to five o'clock and the commissary would be

closing soon, but that just seemed to make this visit all the more memorable. I was here, late lunching in a room I'd only ever heard about, with stars of the silver screen all around me. I wasn't sure the sandwich would be delicious, but the feeling certainly was. For a moment, I felt like a star.

The smell was like a dash of cold water on my feeling of hungry tired contentment. The smell alerted me as much as his voice or the sight of him ever could have.

Rosalyn was in mid-sentence—though what she was saying has now fled from my mind. The scent of him washed it right away. I looked up—Rosalyn suddenly forgotten—in time to see him lumbering past our table. And he wasn't alone. Xander Dean was being led across the commissary by none other than Joe, the man on the oxblood sofa at the Masquers' Ball. I tried to have that information make sense to me—that the two of them not only knew each other, but would choose to meet here of all places—but I could not.

"What?" Rosalyn said when she noticed my face. "What is it?" She indicated Dean and the other man, now taking a seat on the other side of the commissary. I looked at them carefully, but neither seemed to have noticed me. For Dean I would be totally out of context, and the only time Joe had seen me, I'd been wearing a mask. Now there was that space makeup, or what the day had left of it, possibly obscuring my identity. Rosalyn was still speaking. I pulled myself back to hear what she said. "You look as though you've seen a ghost. Do you know those men?"

"I . . ." I had no idea where to begin. "I can't explain right now. I'm sorry. You don't know who they are, do you?"

Rosalyn took a pair of eyeglasses from her handbag. Before she put them on, she looked around carefully to see if anyone was watching.

"No," she said when she'd looked at them both as closely as she dared. "I don't know either of them. Sorry. What is it, Kitty?" she said again.

"I'll tell you sometime. Right now, though, I really . . . I really need to hear what they're saying." I looked at her fully to see if she thought this a horrible thing. Invasive. Or just mad. But her face held no such judgment. Little Rosie Stein had chosen to be an actress, after all. She'd been waiting for the excitement in her life to begin. I could see that excitement reflected now in her eyes.

"Well," she said helpfully, "our sandwiches haven't arrived yet. Couldn't we just, you know, move over there? Sit near them?"

This close to quitting time the commissary was almost empty. We had our choice of tables. Would either man recognize me? It was possible, though I doubted it. In any event, each looked focused on what the other was saying. I decided it was a chance I was willing to take. After all, I told myself when I might have quailed: wasn't this exactly why Dex and I had finagled this opportunity? We'd been looking for something, even if we hadn't known exactly what. I thought of Dex back in that office, sloshing his drink and telling his tales. If anyone was going to discover anything today, it was going to have to be me.

"That's a good idea," I said to her.

"And you'll explain it all to me later?"

"Maybe not later," I promised. "But sometime."

When we changed tables, I was careful to keep my face away from the two men. I took the seat closest to their table, with my back to them.

As soon as I was seated, I discovered that even if I strained all my attention to their conversation, they were speaking so quietly that I could only make out the occasional word.

"You can't hear it either, huh?" Rosalyn said, looking disappointed, fully in the spirit of the thing now.

"Ah well," I said. "We'll just eat our sandwiches and see where it all leads."

"Sounds good," she said, just as the slightly disoriented waitress arrived with our lunch.

Rosalyn and I chatted, though I was careful to speak quietly, fearful that one of the men at the next table would hear my voice and recognize it. That seemed unlikely as both of them were intent on their own conversation. I could determine that Joe was in charge. I wouldn't have gone so far as to say he had power over Dean but, at a certain level, that was very much what it sounded like.

I heard the word "Chicago" a couple of times, though I couldn't tell which of them said it. I thought I heard "Laird Wyndham" and I thought I heard "the league" but I might have been mistaken. Such was the way the sound was carrying. When I peeked round at them, though, I thought both men looked uncomfortable, as though they'd rather be anyplace else.

"I'm sorry," I said to Rosalyn at one point, "I'm ruining our lunch."

"Well, I wouldn't say ruining," she assured me. "But we sure were having a better time before those two showed up."

"I need to find out what they're doing here," I said. "Any ideas?"

"That one's not much of a looker," she sniffed, indicating Joe. "The other one's not bad. A bit beefier than I usually like, but he sure smells good."

I laughed, despite myself. "He does at that."

"I'll go see what I can find out," she said suddenly, surprising me and leaving her half-eaten sandwich as she crossed the dining room, engaging one of the young men bussing tables in earnest conversation. This, then, would be the person at the commissary she'd said she knew. I wondered if he was an actor, too. I figured he probably was.

After Rosalyn had spoken to him for a while, he went into the kitchen and she stood outside the door. While I waited to find out what she was up to, I focused hard on the conversation at the next table, even surreptitiously moving my chair slightly closer to them, trying to catch a different air current, one that would do a better job of bringing their words to me.

The little I heard made no sense. "Dead is dead" was one phrase I caught and I thought I heard "won't stay bought," but this might have been my imagination. When I heard a long, low whistle coming from their table, I figured Rosalyn was heading back. I watched as she looked at them coquettishly and, when she reached me, she stopped quickly and dropped a bag on the table. "Bones for my dog," she said, then kept going, sitting herself down with them and engaging them in conversation.

I figured now that the visit with her kitchen pal had been a ruse to put distance between herself and the men at the next table. She'd wanted to make eye contact, I guessed. Establish a connection before she sat down with them. Maybe she'd also wanted bones for her dog.

I was flabbergasted at this bold move on her part, not quite sure what to make of it, and though I strained like mad to discover where all of *this* might be going, I could hear next to nothing beyond Rosalyn's laugh; a warm, merry sound like rain on glass. Then I could hear the cadence of her voice, the texture of it, but I couldn't make out a single word.

After a while, I heard the scrape of her chair as she rejoined me.

She smiled. A beautiful smile. Her teeth were extraordinarily white. "So I asked them."

"Of course you did. And?"

"They said they're just business pals, here having a late lunch."

" 'Natch," I said.

"But the not-so-good-looking one? Not the fat one, but the other? Joe? He says he's only been out here a little while. I think he was fixing to work up the courage to ask me on a date." She made a face. "He's from Chicago. Used to be."

"You got all that?" I asked, incredulous.

"Sure. A bit more, too. Like, I don't know that the big guy works for him, but I kind of got that, do you know what I mean?"

Sure I did. That had been my impression as well.

"I also got that they go way back. But how far and to where I really couldn't say. But listen," she started collecting her things, "maybe I can fill you in later if I get more. You got a number?"

I dug in my purse quickly for paper and a pen so I could write down the office number. "Sure. But why? Where you going all of a sudden?"

She looked sheepish for a second, but only just. "Joe's gonna give me a ride home. Since I live out in Tarzana, it'll save me about three years on the streetcar."

I handed the number across to her. "Do call me. I've enjoyed your company," I said. She took it, but I stopped her when she would have been on her way. "And Rosalyn, please. Be careful. I think . . . well, I'm not sure but I think he might be dangerous."

"Honey," she said with a smile, "all men are dangerous. I'm always careful. I'll give you a call tomorrow. Let you know what's what."

Then she picked up her bag of bones and was gone, and they were gone, too. I sat in the commissary feeling oddly bereft. As though I'd allowed something to happen. Allowed something to swing out of control.

CHAPTER TWENTY-SIX

WHEN I BACKTRACKED my way past the office where I'd seen Dex, he was gone. Mustard and the car were gone, too. I had no way of knowing if they were still on the lot somewhere or if they'd headed on their way. I regretted that; I would have liked to have caught up with them. After the day I'd had, it would have been nice to hitch a ride.

By the time I found the right streetcar, it was after seven and quite dark. I thought about going back to the office and seeing if the guys were there or if they'd left any notes but once I was underway I realized I was bone tired and just wanted to go home. If anything exciting was happening, it could keep until the morning. I needed my bed and a bath and a bowl of Marjorie's good soup.

The following morning, there was something nice about being in the office. Something pleasant and reassuring. It seemed that, lately, everything had been so very busy, I'd barely had a moment to myself. So it was satisfying to spend half an hour alone in the office's morning quiet, straightening the already tidy rooms, making coffee and trying not to listen through the open window to Hartounian's secretary on the phone with her boyfriend.

When the phone rang, I answered it cheerfully. "Good morning, Dexter Theroux's office. How can I help you?"

"Help me, sheesh! But do I need help." I hadn't known her long, but I recognized her voice right away.

"Hey, Rosalyn, I'm glad to hear you got home safely."

"Boy, but barely. Your man Breen is quite the piece of work."

"Breen?"

"Yeah. Joe. I thought you knew him."

"I've *met* him. I barely know him. And don't call him 'mine.' I was avoiding him yesterday, remember?"

"I can see why."

"You can? Why? What happened?"

"You know, it's a pretty long drive out to Tarzana."

"I'll say," I told her. "I can't imagine why anyone would want to live out there."

"It's pretty. And I have a dog. And family, you know. But, yeah: it takes plenty long on the streetcar. That's why I was glad of the offer of the ride."

"I worried about that, though," I admitted. "Busy guy wears a suit like that, he's important. He doesn't just give rides for nothing. Especially out to *the moon*."

"Tarzana is *not* the moon but, yeah, I know. There was something about him, all right?"

"Well, it wasn't his looks."

"No," she agreed, "it wasn't his looks. But I got the feeling he was someone with some weight to throw around, you know? And I could tell right away that he liked the looks of me just fine."

What was there not to like? Rosalyn Steele was the very picture of a starlet. She even had that extra dash of something. She was slender and tall and blond and beautiful. Funny and smart, too. It didn't take much imagination to work out why a man like Breen would be quickly smitten. Rosalyn was the whole package. I figured it was possible that one day she'd be a star.

"Yeah," I said wryly, "I could see that part wasn't going to be a problem."

"So we're driving out there and we're chatting, you know, like people do when they're in a car and they're getting to know each other."

"Sure."

"And he sez to me, he sez," here she pitched her voice low in a terrible approximation of Breen's way of speaking, " 'So, you're an actress, huh? Have I seen you in anything?' And I tell him yeah and I tell him what in, but I also tell him they were small parts, right? And I'm waiting for my big break. And he nods like he knows a thing or two about that and he puts his hand on my knee while he says, 'Well, maybe that's something I can help you with.' "

"He did not," I said.

"He did! And, I'll be honest with you, Kitty: that's what I was there for. You know that, right? I mean, I figured he was someone could do me some good and now he was telling me that was so. Everything was just fine. And a girl can always close her eyes."

"But you said . . ."

"Wait. I'm getting to it. So we're driving along. We're getting pretty close to home by now. And his hand is inching up my thigh. And I'm letting it, right? I know where this is going. I'm a big girl. Only he's a talker, right? And he starts making conversation."

"What do you mean? A talker?"

"You don't get out much, do you? Never mind. A talker is a guy what likes to hear his own voice. Breen was like that. It wasn't enough he's got his hand moving ever closer to my place of business, now he's gotta yak."

"About what?" I said, still inwardly shuddering over the 'place of business' remark.

"Empty yakking. Just to fill up the space with the sound of his voice. Breen seems to like his voice just fine. So he sez at one point, he sez, 'Well, Rosalyn Steele. That's a real pretty name. A blueblood name. Where do you hail from?' Something like that. And I laughed, of course, and I tell him my real name and tell him I was born on the Lower East Side but my family moved out here when I was a kid. And, Kitty, I tell him this and his hand drops right off my lap. And he says, 'You're a kike?' "

"He did not!"

"He did. And not like he's asking, you know, but like he can't believe he sullied his hand. And came close to sullying other things."

"What did you say?"

"What could I say? I drew myself up and I said, 'I *am* a daughter of Israel.' I wish my mother would have been there to see it. Well, not the hand in lap part. But the part where I said that with pride. It would have surprised her, I think."

"And then what happened?"

"Not too much, let me tell you. He pulled the car over to the side of the road—pitch black it is, out in the middle of nowhere, someplace on Ventura. He pulls over and he sez, 'Get out.' All cold like. And just that. 'Get out.' " She made the impression sound dark and ominous now, though it still didn't sound much like Breen.

"So what did you do?"

"What do you think I did? I got out. Slammed the car door as hard as I could—not that he cared. And he hurtled off into the night, leaving me out in the middle of nowhere."

"Hurtled?"

"Absolutely. I left Steve's bones in the car, too."

"Steve?"

"My dog."

"Your dog is named Steve? Sorry. Never mind. So, then what?"

"Then what? What do you think? I ankled it off toward Tarzana. Not a lot of traffic heading out that way that time of night, but I stuck my thumb out and I got a lift before long. Some nice couple coming back from the city. I was lucky they came along: you saw my shoes. They weren't meant for hiking."

I thanked Rosalyn for calling with the update and we said we'd get together for coffee soon. I meant it, too. Even though we were geared pretty differently, I genuinely liked her and figured we could be friends. We were about to hang up, when she interrupted our good-byes.

"Oh geez, I nearly forgot something. That guy he was with yesterday. The big one?"

"Xander Dean."

"Yeah. When we first got going, I asked how they knew each other. Were they friends or whatever. I figured you'd want to know."

"You're right. Thanks."

"Don't mention it. Anyway, he didn't say much, just said the guy was nobody. 'Just hired muscle,' was what he said. Now I'm no dope, Kitty. I know a guy can lie about a thing like that to a dame to make himself look bigger. But you pretty much figured that anyway, didn't you? So I kinda thought that confirms it."

She was right, it did. After we hung up on another promise of coffee or perhaps lunch, I thought about it. The fact that Xander worked for Breen came as no surprise. But, as Rosalyn had said, it confirmed things. I tucked the information away to tell Dex when he came in.

I had just given my attention back to my now nearly cold coffee when the phone rang again. Ours is not generally a busy office, so two phone calls back to back were cause for a raised eyebrow.

"Dexter Theroux's office," I said. "How can I help you?"

"Hi there, is Dex in?" A masculine voice.

"I'm sorry. No. Can I take a message?"

"Yes. OK. Yes. Thank you. This is Samuel Marcus from the *Courier*. Dex and I spoke a few days ago."

"Mr. Theroux mentioned the conversation to me."

"He did? Ah, well. In that case, please tell him that he probably won't be able to get me on the phone all day."

"All right, I'll tell him."

"And that, near as I can tell, there's nothing to that theory of his. That mean anything to you?"

"Yes, actually, it does."

"Good, good. Well then, also tell him this: for what it's worth, the people in *my* office are taking bets that it ain't Wyndham at all."

" 'Not Wyndham,' " I repeated as I wrote it down. "All right. Go on."

"Yeah. The smart money here is on a broad."

"What? But there hasn't been even a hint of that. Where does *that* come from?"

"Well, the figuring is this: the killing was coldly calculated, yet wouldn't have taken a lot of strength."

"I don't know . . ." I said.

"We've talked it all around. Here's the thing though: your boss is on the case, right? If he finds anything, he has to call me up and give me the straight dope. I mean, he knows that. We talked about it. But that was our deal and that's why I'm calling. You got all that down, sugar?"

"Sure, sure," I said, looking down at my notes. "No newspaper conspiracy. Not Wyndham. Money's on a broad. I got it all."

"Great, well that's just jake. Tell him to call and leave a message any time. I'll get back to him fast."

Mustard arrived noisily just as I was hanging up the phone. Two telephone calls and now a personal visit?

"It's like a train station around here today," I said by way of greeting.

"Huh," Mustard said, looking over both shoulders theatrically. "I don't see any rattlers around here, do you?"

"No, Mustard, I didn't mean there were actual trains around here. It's just that . . . never mind. What can I do for you?"

"Ask not what you can do for me . . ." he said mysteriously, then plunked a folder the color of clotted cream onto my desk. It was about an inch thick, held together with an elastic band. The package looked as though it had seen some miles. The corners of the folder were dog-eared and I could see what appeared to be a coffee stain on the side facing me.

"What's this?" I said, inexplicably reluctant to touch the thing.

"Open it up and see. Is he in?" he said, moving toward Dex's closed office door.

"No. Haven't seen him. Haven't heard a peep. And I wanted to hear how it went at the studio yesterday."

"Well, it went."

"I know that, wise guy. But specifics. And I've got some of my own."

Mustard looked interested but would not be diverted. "We'll get to all that when he shows up. Meanwhile . . ." and he poked the folder another inch or two closer to me on the desk.

"All right already," I said, before doing what he suggested, opening the folder and looking at the first page of a thick sheaf of mimeographed paper.

"The Motion Picture Production Code of 1930," I read. "Wait, the name is familiar. Why?"

"Read on, just a bit," Mustard said. "I think you'll see."

" 'If motion pictures present stories that will affect lives for the better,' " I read, " 'they can become the most powerful force for the improvement of mankind.' " I looked at Mustard again. "I don't understand."

"Skip to here," he said, indicating a section a bit farther down the page. And then, "Out loud," when I would have read it silently.

I complied, treading lightly over it until I got to this part: " 'Motion picture producers recognize the high trust and confidence which have been placed in them by the people of the world and which have made motion pictures a universal form of entertainment.' Mustard?"

"Keep going."

I sighed, but did as he asked. " 'They recognize their responsibility to the public because of this trust and because entertainment and art are important influences in the life of a nation. Hence, though regarding motion pictures primarily as entertainment without any explicit purpose of teaching or propaganda, they know that the motion picture within its own field of entertainment may be directly responsible for spiritual or moral progress, for higher types of social life, and for much correct thinking. . . .' Wait. Why are you having me read this?"

"Who do you figure wrote this document?"

"These people," I skimmed back to what I'd already read, looking for the salient bit, "these 'motion picture producers.' I know something about that. I was talking to this guy at the Masquers' party . . ."

"Yeah, but you're wrong," Mustard interrupted me.

"Wrong about what? I haven't told you anything yet."

Mustard grinned. A bit sheepishly, I thought, but he grinned nonetheless. "No. You haven't. But I know you're wrong anyway. It was written *for* the motion picture producers. But it was not written *by* them."

"Oh-kay . . ." I said. I could tell there was something Mustard wanted to say, but he was getting to it in his own sweet time. I let him amble.

"The actual writing was done by a Catholic priest."

"A Catholic priest."

"Right," he hesitated a beat. I waited things out. "A Catholic priest," he repeated, "named Daniel Lord. From . . . Chicago."

I sat there for a minute, waiting for the import of what Mustard was telling me to sink in. Obviously, there was something here he wanted me to see. Something he'd already gotten loud and clear, but it just wasn't coming through.

"Listen, Mustard, I don't wanna say 'big deal' but . . ."

"Don't you see it?"

I shook my head while still scouring my brain. "I'm sorry, Mustard. Maybe there's something here I'm missing. We've got . . . what? Some kind of rules written by a priest who wants movies to be moral. And you're acting like it's some big missing piece."

"Well, it's the Chicago thing, for starters."

"It's a big place, Mustard. Chicago is a city. There are a lot of people there. I'm pretty sure they don't all know each other."

"Sure, I know that," he said impatiently. "But, see, I told you: a guy I know in Chicago—a horse racing guy—gave Xander Dean my name. But Dean, who does he work for? Did he ever tell you?" Mustard watched my face for a second, then looked slightly triumphant. "See, he never told you, did he?"

"Are you asking me if he told me? Or are you asking me if I know?"

"There's a difference?"

I nodded.

"OK then, I'm asking did he tell you."

"In that case, no."

"There you go," he said triumphantly.

"Are you kidding me?" I said, feeling the end of my rope drawing near. "What are you *talking* about, Mustard? I'm completely lost."

"I'll draw you a picture."

"Do that."

"We'll just play pretend. Let's say that, back in Chicago, Daniel Lord hires Xander Dean . . ."

"Wait," I interrupted. "A Catholic priest hires local muscle? Already that's a stretch."

"Just pipe down and listen up, will you? And, anyway, it's not as much of a stretch as you might think. See, Father Daniel Lord has spent most of his career in St. Louis."

"All right," I said.

"And things with him seem pretty quiet up to 1926."

"Then what happens?"

"He was made a director of the Sodality of Our Lady."

"The Sodality of Our Lady," I said the words. Tried them on. "What's that?"

"OK: I'm still working on that," Mustard admitted. "They don't seem to go around publishing manuals on what they do."

"No," I said wryly, indicating the copy of the Production Code on my desk, "just on what others should do."

"I do know that it's not just priests what are members though. Peter Paul Rubens . . ."

"The artist?"

"Yeah. And Leopold of Austria . . ."

"Ummm . . . is he the one they called the Holy Roman Emperor? Maybe that's not such a leap."

"Maybe even Cecil B. DeMille."

"Really?"

"Maybe. Anyway, you get the idea: not just people you'd think of as belonging to religious organizations."

"Let me say it again: Holy Roman Emperor."

Mustard ignored both the crack and my tone. "So, like I said, this Daniel Lord was made national director of the Sodalists in 1926. In 1927, he consulted on *The King of Kings* for DeMille."

"Who was also a Sodalist."

"Maybe. But, see, that's Lord's first Hollywood connection. And maybe, from his perspective, the first time he finds himself thinking about how he could affect the morals of the nation."

"But that's conjecture, right?" I said.

"Sure."

"All right. Then what?

"In 1929, Lord starts work on the Production Code more or less under the direction of Cardinal Mundelein of the Archdiocese of Chicago."

"More or less."

"Sure," Mustard admitted, "probably one or the other. I'm just not sure yet which one. Anyway, from what I can tell, these guys put the Production Code together and then give it to the Hays Office."

"I've heard of that," I said.

"It's not really called that. It's the Motion Picture Producers and Distributors of America," Mustard said. "Will Hays is the head of it. But, from my digging, I gather it's kind of a shield. The studios formed this organization in the 1920s. They gave Hays a lot of money to quit his post office job and run it for them."

"He was a mailman?"

"Kinda. He was Postmaster General."

"Of the *United States*?" I've never claimed to know much about either business or politics, but even I know that's a pretty important job.

"Yeah. And before that he'd been chairman of the Republican National Committee. But he'd only been Postmaster General for a year before the studio heads hired him to head up the Hays Office. . . ."

"Which wouldn't have been called that then."

". . . word is they offered him $100,000 a year."

I just looked at Mustard then, finally speechless. Mustard allowed the quiet, perhaps enjoying my stunned expression.

"That's a lot of mazuma," I said. "And it would explain why he gave up the cushy postal thing."

Mustard nodded. "It would indeed. Anyway, they put the Production Code into action, but no one would listen."

"What do you mean?"

"Well, the studios figure they've done their part, you know, they've hired Hays and he can pay lip service to whoever and make the pesky government types who would inflict rules on things just go away. Only it's not enough, right? It's not enough for anyone: the government wants real censorship, not just lip service. And the church wants morality. So something's gotta give."

"I have no idea where any of this could possibly be going," I said.

"Well, the Hays office brings in an enforcer. Someone whose job it will be to make everyone toe the line."

"Xander Dean?" I ventured.

"Not even close," Mustard said. "They bring in Joseph Breen."

"Who is also from Chicago?"

"No," Mustard admitted. "Pittsburgh. But there's a Chicago connection."

"Of course there is," I said dryly.

I looked at Mustard for a full fifteen seconds without saying anything. Who would have expected that his long convoluted story would actually have a postscript that I'd be able to write?

"What?" Mustard said. "You're burnin' a hole in me."

"I know him. I know Joseph Breen," and all the bits I'd been inadvertently collecting on him came tumbling out. "I met him at the Masquers' Ball. And I saw him yesterday. At the MGM commissary. He was there with Xander Dean. And he gave a girlfriend of mine a ride home and it turns out he hates Jews."

Just then the door opened and Dex came in. "You two look chummy," he said. "There a reason for this party?"

Mustard and I looked at each other, then we both looked down at the Production Code, still on my desk.

"Yeah, there's a reason. Let's go in your office, buddy,"

Mustard said, leading the way, but indicating I should follow. "I've got a lot to tell you."

"A lot," I chimed in.

"And you're gonna wanna drink. A big one."

CHAPTER TWENTY-SEVEN

"WHAT THE HELL does any of this have to do with our guy?" It was a bellow. I could hear that it came from Dex's heart. It was fueled by the bourbon he'd been topping his glass with every ten minutes or so for the last three quarters of an hour, but it hadn't been born there. That place was a different one entirely.

Mustard looked almost comically unconcerned about Dex's outburst. He and Dex had been friends a long time and they'd been through a lot together. The trenches in Europe during the War, for starters. They'd watched each other's backs. Lots more since, I guessed, and though neither of them ever talked about it, the bond they shared ran deep. They were connected in that strange distant-close way that only men who have faced bullets together ever are.

"No, really, Mustard, you come in here with some cock and bull story about secret religious organizations—in Chicago of all places—and political leaders and the Holy Roman Empire . . ."

Mustard shot me a look at that one and I shuffled my feet apologetically. I probably *should* have left Emperor Leopold out of things, since I could barely remember that lesson from Mrs. Beeson's school myself and I was fairly certain that Dex had retained even less of the tale than I. Plus, strictly speaking—as I'm sure Mustard would have pointed out given the chance—the emperor's position as a Sodalist didn't have much to do with anything at all.

"But don't you see," Mustard started to say, "it's the Chicago connection . . ."

"Don't start that again."

". . . and it comes through Xander Dean."

"Right. And Kitty saw Dean and Hays' right-hand being all chummy at the studio yesterday," Dex supplied. "And Breen told a girlfriend of Kitty's that Xander was hired muscle. And all of this doesn't prove anything at all."

"On the other hand," Mustard said, "you have to admit it's a little odd."

Dex nodded agreement. "You're right. It's certainly at least a little odd."

"What about you two," I prompted. "I haven't heard how your day at the studio went."

"Well, I'll tell you one thing," Dex said, "they serve a very good grade of whiskey at MGM."

"The best," Mustard agreed.

"And the Cubans! I haven't had a cigar so good since I don't know when."

"No, really you guys. Did you find anything useful?"

The two of them looked like small boys, caught in the act of something nasty . . . and delicious. They did not scuff their feet on the floor, but I caught an impression of that just the same.

"Well, we discovered one thing," Dex said. "You shouldn't wear lead."

"That's right," Mustard chimed in. "The color doesn't suit you. I've seen you move more elegantly, too."

I did my best to ignore their jocularity. It was hard. Sometimes when the two of them got going, it was difficult to get them back on course. And sometimes they were obviously having so much fun, you didn't want to try. "Well," I said, "I actually have still more to impart."

"No kiddin'?" Dex said.

"One of the people I saw on set yesterday was Baron Sutherland."

"Your boyfriend," Dex put in knowledgeably. Mustard's ears perked right up when Dex said it, too.

"Hardly that," I said. "And he didn't see me and we didn't talk. But one of the things I learned yesterday was that it's possible, though not definite, that Baron had his contract drawn up so that if anything happened to Laird Wyndham, he himself would step into Laird's roles."

Dex sat back in his chair and seemed to contemplate this. For his part, Mustard said, "How good is your source?"

"Not terribly," I admitted. "Still, it might be worth looking into."

"Definitely, Kitty. Thanks. Anything else?"

"Well, I already told Mustard: I saw Xander Dean at MGM yesterday. In the commissary with Joseph Breen. I got the feeling that Xander was working for Breen."

"And they're both from Chicago," Mustard said, sounding pleased with himself.

"Working how?" Dex asked, completely ignoring his old friend.

"I don't know," I admitted. "I couldn't hear what they were saying. Well, I did . . ." I shot a quick glance at Mustard, "I *did* hear the word 'Chicago.' Least, I'm pretty sure I did."

"Oh good God," Dex said.

Mustard beamed.

"But a girl I was talking to, Rosalyn Steele? From the Masquers? She was an extra with me yesterday. And she got . . . well, she got Breen to give her a ride home."

"Wait: you got a girl to go home with Breen in order to get information?" Dex looked incredulous.

"No," I said. "No, never. She actually wanted a ride home— she lives out in Tarzana—and he was offering, so . . ."

Dex didn't say anything for a moment. Just looked at me piercingly. "Anything else?" he said after a while.

"Well, it gets ugly."

"Go ahead, Kitty. I'm a big boy," Dex said. "I can take it."

"He put the moves on her, before they got to her place."

"There's a shock," Mustard said.

"Only when he found out she's Jewish, he almost pushed her out of the moving car."

"That doesn't sound very nice, Kitty, but it doesn't have anything at all to do with our case, does it?"

I shook my head. "No, you're right. I wouldn't think so. But I wanted to pass it on, anyway. Plus, in the course of all this he told her that Xander Dean is in his employ."

"Which may or may not be true."

"That's what I thought, too."

"Anything else?"

"Just one thing. And it's nothing I found, just a phone message from Samuel Marcus at the *Courier*." I relayed the message and both men sipped their drinks while they contemplated what it might mean.

"They think it's a broad, huh?" Dex said.

I shrugged. "I told him I didn't think it was likely, but they have other ideas."

"Well, like I said a few days ago," Dex said, "I think we need to find Rhoda Darrow."

"So much has been happening, Dex. That's what I forgot to tell you. I found an address for her. In Santa Monica." I hit the highlights of my sleuthing and was warmed by Dex's approving smile.

"That's just swell, Kitty. Great work. That'll save some steps. Course we won't know until we get there if this is her current address. Still, it's a better lead than we had before."

"But do you think Rhoda Darrow might have done it?"

"Do I?" Dex said. "To be honest, I'm not sure I do. But I'd like to know what she knows, in any case. And we *do* know that Dean hired her so, if nothing else, it's another connection to

Dean. I'll go out there in the morning and see if she's still around there. Thanks, Kitty."

"I could do that part," I said.

"Do what part?"

"Drive out to Santa Monica and see if that's still her address."

Dex looked at me speculatively before answering. "I guess that's not a bad idea," he said. "Divide and conquer," he tipped his glass. "We've got this Chicago thing to check up on. Xander Dean. The priest guy."

"And Joe Breen," Mustard put in.

"But you hafta promise you won't actually *do* anything," Dex said. "Just find out if that's still where she lives."

"Sure, Dex."

"And don't be disappointed if she doesn't live there anymore. Chances are she doesn't. You said she left the apartment, what? Six months ago? She seemed the type that might already have moved on."

"But if she did, there might be a new address for her, right?"

"Right. And it'll save me some steps. Me and Mustard have got things to work through around here, so take Mustard's car."

"Hey!"

"Why not?" Dex said. "You ain't going far. We can't have Kitty going all the way out to the beach on the streetcar when there's a perfectly good heap sitting right outside."

"You can drive a car?" Mustard said, sounding astonished.

I choked back a sigh and the impatience I felt creeping in. Dex had taught me to drive. Mustard had sat in cars while they were being driven by me. Yet both of them always forgot I could drive.

"Sure," I said, feigning innocence. "You just point it in the direction you want to go and push the pedals, right?"

"It's not a gun," Dex said. "You can't just aim it at a target and expect to get to where you're going without hitting a few innocent bystanders."

"Dex, you taught me to drive. I know what I'm doing."

"Ah. Well then, I should definitely be able to vouch for you. If I taught you everything I know, then you should be better than Mustard here."

"Will you bring it back tonight?" Mustard asked.

I shook my head. "Tomorrow morning."

"All rightee then," he said jovially enough, "why not? But make sure when you bring it back, it's still got all four wheels and the radio works." He handed across the keys. "It's parked on Spring."

CHAPTER TWENTY-EIGHT

I'D FORGOTTEN ABOUT the dark maroon Marmon Sixteen until I stood in front of it. When I did see it, I nearly lost my nerve. You didn't need to be a mechanic or look under the hood to know that this was a more powerful kind of car than the ones I was used to driving. It was longer, lower and altogether meaner looking. Mustard had told Dex it was the world's most advanced car. He hadn't told what he meant by that, but he and Dex had exchanged a look like they were sharing some secret only men would understand and I hadn't bothered asking. Anyway, the Sixteen *looked* like the world's most advanced car. You didn't need to ask questions.

What got me moving was turning the alternatives over in my head. Well, *alternative* really, because there was only one, and it ran on tracks. I swallowed my fear, got up my gumption and climbed behind the wheel.

Once I got the car moving I spent a few minutes getting used to the sensitivity of the controls. The dashboard looked like it belonged in something you could fly to Pittsburgh. I thought the Marmon felt lighter than other cars. And more powerful. It was a distinctive car and I felt a weird and possessive pride to see heads turn as we drove past.

Rhoda Darrow's former landlady had written down an address on Palisades Beach Road and the information that the house was called Bella Luna. I couldn't help but wonder how an out-of-work and apparently down-on-her-luck actress had ended up in such a swell neighborhood. Would that be another clue? Another hint toward Mustard's much-ballyhooed Chicago connection? I pressed ahead.

I found the place without much difficulty. The golden mile isn't even a mile long and, what with Marion Davies' huge and glistening beach house taking up five acres of that mile, it was simple enough to narrow down where the house was. Especially with a name like Bella Luna. I could only see one house that would fit that description and when I stopped the car and went in on foot for a closer inspection, I saw that I was right: a tiny mosaic sign announced to visitors that they had arrived at the house of the beautiful moon.

Bella Luna was small, charming and walled like a tiny Mediterranean fortress right there on the beach at Santa Monica. A gate with a bell greeted visitors on the street side and the same high wall surrounded the whole place.

For a while I pondered how to discover if Rhoda Darrow was still in residence. It was possible Dex had some highfalutin' detective trick for this part of the investigation. The only thing I could think to do was approach the front door.

A uniformed maid opened the gate not long after I rang.

"How can I help you?" she asked.

"I'm here to see Miss Darrow."

"Who shall I tell her is here?"

"Miss Katherine Pangborn," I said, drawing myself up to my full height and shifting my body so that the Marmon would be easily visible.

"Please wait here," the servant instructed. "I'll see if Miss Darrow is receiving."

So that was that, I thought to myself as I stood there on the stoop. I had my confirmation. Rhoda Darrow did still live here. I could leave now, mission accomplished, and tell Dex what I'd discovered. I peered into the door the girl had left open. The garden the wall surrounded was beautiful—I could see it through a massive window—and a swimming pool glistened in an unreal but beckoning shade of blue. Inexplicably, though, boxes were stacked neatly next to the front door.

Someone was moving, though if it was in or out, I could not be sure. What if she was leaving? What if Dex came tomorrow and found nothing but dust bunnies? Then where would we be?

"I'm sorry," the girl said on her return. "Miss Darrow is indisposed this afternoon. Perhaps if you check in with us in the morning. By telephone," she added pointedly, handing me a stiff piece of cardboard, on which there had been written a phone number in the Gladstone exchange.

"Is Miss Darrow going on a trip?" I asked, indicating the boxes.

The woman's face might have shown surprise at the question, or maybe alarm. Whatever it was, I didn't have the skill to read it properly and she didn't answer my question. Just looked down her nose at me and shut the door.

I went back to the car and drove a few blocks before I found a phone booth. When the office phone rang and rang and rang I cursed myself for my optimism. What had I been thinking? Of *course* Dex and Mustard wouldn't be there. The two of them in the mood they'd been in, there were any number of downtown dives where they might have taken their self-satisfied joviality to kill the rest of the afternoon in mutual congratulations.

While I drove back to the beach, I thought about what to do. I was all the way down here and, from what Dex had said, slightly taller and stronger and healthier-looking than Darrow, and no doubt several years younger. Mustard would have said something like, "In a clean fight, you could take her easy." He would have been half-kidding, but he'd have meant it just the same. That was the place from which he viewed the world. Simple-like. Most of the time it didn't seem like such a bad thing.

Now that I was all the way out there, I had no doubt but that it ought to have been Dex there thinking about his next move. But it was not. It was me. This left me with a sort of sadness for my beautiful, broken boss, but it also sprang the steel in my spine. A thing had been thrust upon me. Was I big enough for it? I thought maybe I was.

I decided that I owned enough of that steel to at least walk the perimeter of the property, keeping close to the wall at first, but just seeing what I could see. That proved to be pretty much nothing. The wall was taller than I with no openings. The sand was hard going in my medium-heeled pumps, but I didn't dare take them off for fear of ruining my stockings. I negotiated the sand in my shoes as well as I could, hoping that Dex would appreciate the lengths to which I would go for the good of his business, even while I knew that there was no way he'd really be able to.

In the wall farthest from the street there was a gate that was no doubt intended to allow residents the easiest possible stroll to the surf. I could see the gate was locked. For one awful moment, I thought that was it, I'd have to turn around and shuffle back through the sand to the car. At the last minute, though, I noticed that the gate was not locked at all, but had merely been made to look that way. I just had to reach through and unlatch the bolt from the inside.

Then I was inside the wall in a garden that seemed, at first, like a fantasy or something from a film. The swimming pool I'd gotten a glimpse of through the house dominated the space and was surrounded by beautiful tile work. A Moorish bath of Roman design, that was the feeling one got.

Inside the walled garden, you could not see the ocean, though you could catch a sliver of the view by way of the wrought iron door through which I had come. You did not have the feeling of being at the beach, virtually on the strand. Until you listened. That was an odd sensation, strangely soothing. Not seeing the view, but hearing it. It was like being on another plane in a different world. It was a lovely garden. I could have spent a long time there.

Then I saw her where at first I had not. She was reclining on a chaise at the far side of the pool, under the shade of a huge orange umbrella that cast a reddish glow over her skin. Though I'd never seen her before in person, I didn't need anyone to confirm that this, finally, was Rhoda Darrow.

She was thin. I could see this through her swim costume. Almost bizarrely so, with pointy little elbows and bony little knees. She looked as though she might break. Thin as she was, she had the pallor most of us gain only in illness or even in death. It was something beyond the pink alabaster so admired in maidens, a ghostly glow that increased when she caught sight of me.

Rhoda Darrow brought herself to a standing position in a single movement that managed to appear both lithe and painful. "What do you want?" she said in a voice that was surprisingly smooth and well-modulated. I had expected something else from an actress who had never "talked."

Her question was itself telling. She didn't ask who I was or what I was doing there. With her question, she assumed a desire. That meant something. She was scared.

It was actually a good question. I'd spent so much time tracking her down, now that I had her, I didn't know exactly what to do.

"I work for Dex Theroux," I told her. I saw a flicker of something, but not full recognition. She remembered the name, her look told me, but not the context. "He's a private investigator," I told her. "His office is downtown."

"What's a shamus want with me?" she said, but I thought I could see full recognition now.

I tried again. "You were his . . . date the night Fleur MacKenzie . . . died."

"At the party," she said quietly.

"That's right. It is my . . . my understanding that you were told to have him see certain things."

A spot of color to those pale cheeks. But no denial. "How did you get in here, anyway? I should call someone." She started to move toward the house but I stopped her easily with my hand on one frail arm. I could feel her little bird bones moving beneath the skin. I held fast. Mustard was right: if it came to it, I could take 'er easy. My heart clenched at the thought.

"You're not going to call anyone," I said quietly and, fortunately, she wasn't putting up much of a fight. Then something emboldened me. I gave her a little push and she fell back into her chair. I controlled the rush of excitement that flooded through me and found I couldn't quite. As a result, I felt a flush of embarrassment stain my cheeks. That together with the glitter the excitement this no doubt put in my eyes, combined with the slight shake of my hands—pure nervousness—probably combined to make me appear more dangerous than I ever had before. I could see that danger reflected in her eyes.

"What do you want?" she said tremulously. I tried to feel pity for her but I just couldn't muster any. Instead I started grilling her, while keeping on eye on the door that led into the house. It wouldn't do to have a servant come out here while I was browbeating her mistress. I could imagine police being called, paddy wagons arriving and me in handcuffs being marched off to join Wyndham at Number 11.

"Someone hired you."

"Someone *always* hires me," she said, with some of the waspishness back in her voice. Maybe she thought I was as harmless as I looked? She was right, but there was no sense in letting her know that. I moved toward her threateningly, relieved when I saw the fear flood back to her eyes.

"Someone hired you to incriminate Laird Wyndham." There. I'd said it straight out. The thing I hadn't even been sure was the case.

"Don't be ridiculous," she said, but I thought I heard the catch in her voice.

"I know who it is anyway," I lied. "I just want to hear it from you. How did Fleur fit into this?"

"You know so much," she said, "you tell me."

"Don't play with me, girlie." Even while I said it, I thought the words sounded straight out of a bad movie. In a way that made sense. I was working on pure instinct now. Instinct fueled by a lot of films. The little I knew about tightening the screws, I'd learned from watching in the dark. I pressed on. "You don't tell me what I need to know, I'm going to hurt you good."

"You wouldn't dare," she said, but the fear was back in her eyes.

I dropped my voice down to a dangerous place. "Oh, but I would. Now I'll ask you one more time: how were you and Fleur connected?"

"We . . . we were both under contract for a while. At MGM."

"What happened?" I asked.

"What always happens? Our moments passed somehow, I guess. We fell out of fashion. It happens," she added defensively.

It did happen. I knew that. I realized at the same time that her looks—and in a way the late Fleur's, as well—were similar to Lorena Duvall's. That thin delicacy, the pale locks and skin, the swan necks and flat chests. The three of them could have been sisters, in a way. Then I realized that the three of them *were* sisters: discarded for the fuller, richer, lustier models that movie-goers wanted today.

"So you were friends," I said.

"Friends," she said the word with something like contempt. "Yeah, sure. We were 'friends.' Then when we were down on our luck, we helped each other when we could. I thought I could help her that night."

"How?"

Her face closed up at the question. She turned her head away.

"How?" I repeated. More forcefully this time. Even to my

own ears my voice sounded harsh. Like the shot of a gun. I shook her again when I said it and I saw the fear rise in her eyes, while I could have sworn I felt her bones rattle.

It was a strange thing, to see that fear. Fear of *me*, someone who has a tough time deboning a chicken. I must have been convincing, though. Her fear was the desired effect, but I was still surprised. Nor did I quell the thrill of excitement that came with recognition of that fact. I'd deal with that emotion later.

"Please . . . please don't hurt me. I'll tell you, I swear I will. But you mustn't tell—please promise you won't tell? He told me he'd kill me if I did."

"A lot of people might be standing in line to kill you, Rhoda. What do you make of that?" Honestly, it was like I was reading a film script. The words? It does not seem possible that I was thinking of them by myself.

"He . . . he asked me to get a girl to come. To the party. Someone young and pretty, he said," she dropped her voice. "A hophead. He said that was important."

"What?" I said, wanting clarification. I'd barely been able to hear her.

"The girl," she said, her voice only slightly stronger. "He wanted her to be a hophead."

"And so you arranged for Fleur to come?"

She nodded.

"But I didn't know what he had in mind. Honestly, I never did." I believed her. She was an actress, but she wasn't this good.

"How did she die, Rhoda?" My voice was soft now. Comforting. I knew I didn't need to coerce her anymore. The words were tumbling out of her like they craved escape.

"But I don't know that, don't you see? I wasn't there. She was alive when I left her. . . ." Her voice trailed off and I understood something.

"You weren't surprised though, were you, by her death?"

"Oh, but I was. I *was*," she insisted. "I never thought she'd die. I thought it was just, you know, sex."

"You sold your friend as a prostitute?"

"Sure," she said coldly now. "Why the hell not? We used men, Fleur and I, every chance we got. And why the hell not?" she said again. "It's not like they wouldn't use us if they had half the chance."

The venom in her drained all the mad out of me. What would it be, I wondered, to be this injured? To be this mad? And to hate people so much you put your own life and that of others on the line to perpetuate that anger?

"You made the arrangements," I accused, my voice softer now. Quieter. The mad might have drained out of me, but a cold, hard anger remained. "You might as well have killed her with your own hand."

"No, no," and now she met my eyes. Twin pools of blue, threatening to overflow, or so it seemed until she'd looked at me for moment and realized that tearful tactics were unlikely to work. "It . . . it wasn't like that. I never thought it was a game."

"You talked to Laird Wyndham. At the party."

"I was to tell him that someone wanted to see him," she choked back a sob. "In the bedroom. Someone wanted a word."

"And that someone was Fleur?"

"She'd been told to wait for him. That he would come in and that all she had to do to get fixed was seduce him."

I played this back in my mind. Ran it against what Dex had initially told me. It fit. It also painted a lurid portrait. Wyndham, who didn't want to be there in the first place, is told someone wanted to meet him; perhaps even *needs* to meet him.

He enters the bedroom and the girl is naked and desperate. "Hungry" was how Wyndham had put it. She wants her fix and she thinks she knows how to get it. Wyndham is repulsed. How could he not be? He, who could have had any woman he wanted, accosted by a junkie. And then . . . then I ran out of scenario. A few pieces were missing, even if I now felt closer than I had.

"So you killed her?"

"No," she sobbed. Sank back onto the chaise. Dropped her head into her arms. "*No.*"

"Someone did. And there's good money riding on it being a woman." Then I added softly, "You."

She shook her head violently in denial. Again I feared the slender neck would give under the strain. "No, no. Not me. Not. Me."

I let it go for the moment. "So you were upset when they found her. I know you checked her pulse. And then what?"

"Then nothing," she said sadly. "It was over. She was dead."

"Rhoda, who hired you?"

"That I won't tell you. You know I won't. I *can't*. He told me he'd kill me if I did."

"Rhoda, you must tell me. Don't you see? The way things sit now—based on what you've told me—it's you who are responsible for Fleur's death." She shook her head, but did not interrupt me. "And make no mistake about it: I will tell people what I know. And then *you* could be the one in jail, not Laird Wyndham."

She started to cry then, quiet sobs that began somewhere deep inside. "It doesn't matter. You can say whatever you like, *do* whatever you like when it comes down to it. He told me he would kill me if I didn't do everything he said. I believed him. I believe him still."

"But Rhoda," I sat on the chaise lounge next to her, stroked the back of her arm, "if you help us, he won't be able to hurt you. If you help us, *he'll* be the one going away."

"How can I be sure?" she asked, but I could tell she was wavering.

"We'll take care of you. And we . . . we can hide you until all of this is over." No one had said anything about this, but

I knew I could make it true. Dex had given me fifty dollars—
fifty dollars—in order to buy the right outfit to work this case.
Surely we could hide one desperate actress until the matter
was dealt with?

She raised her head to me then, looked at me with something
like hope in her eyes. It didn't look effortless there. It looked as
though hope was something she hadn't worn in a while.

"Do you really think you could keep me safe?"

"I do," I said. "I'm sure of it. Now tell me: who was it that
hired you? Tell me his name?"

"You told me you knew who it was," she said.

I shook my head. "I lied."

She sighed and I could almost hear her thoughts. Here she
was, at the point of no return. There really was no going back.
And then acceptance. She'd come this far, after all.

"I never knew his name," she said. "When he . . . when he
called me, he just said to call him Slim."

"Was that a nickname?"

"I don't think so. I think it was more of a joke. See he isn't
skinny. Not by a long shot."

But a light had dawned. Of course. I wasn't even sure why I
was surprised. "No, he's not skinny at all, is he?" I said with
confidence. "He looks more like a baby grand in a good suit."

CHAPTER TWENTY-NINE

THERE WAS NO question of me leaving Rhoda Darrow alone in the walled house by the sea. She was going to cooperate. I had no doubt about it at all. But I knew she was frightened. And she was weak. That could be a deadly combination, so I asked her to dismiss the staff at the house and tell them she was going to Chicago, without even wondering about my choice of false destination. She packed an overnight bag and I took her with me in the Marmon.

"Where are we going?" she asked as we drove. "Not Chicago, right? That was just something you wanted me to say."

"No. Not Chicago," I said. But, beyond that, I didn't know what to tell her because I wasn't sure myself. In the end, I took her to the office in the hope that Dex and Mustard would be back, maybe three sheets to the wind but still affable and full of ideas.

I was disappointed to find the office empty, though I had the feeling the guys might not be far off. Wreaths of smoke still lingered in the heavy air and though Dex's glass was drained—of course—what must have been Mustard's glass still held a finger of bourbon and the end of a couple of rocks. They had probably gone for dinner. At least, that was what I hoped. That they'd gone out to get a bite or some fresh booze or both and they'd return in short order so that I could get Rhoda to tell them her story and we could figure out what it all meant and what to do.

"What a dump," Rhoda said as she looked around the office, wrinkling her nose slightly.

"Nicer than a jail cell though, don't you think?" That shut her up.

Rhoda seemed interested in snooping around Dex's office, and I didn't stop her. I had a collection of Agatha Christie short stories that Mustard had brought me called *The Mysterious Mr. Quin* and I had a dog-eared copy of William Faulkner's *The Sound and the Fury* that had made me weep when I'd read it the month before. I figured *Motion Picture* or *Photoplay* would have been more her style but they weren't the kind of thing I kept around the office.

In lieu of anything real to keep her busy, poking around would at least give her something to do. For a while. After all, there wasn't *that* much to look at. Snooping through it might be interesting for a couple of minutes, but I could foresee limited entertainment possibilities in that area.

I kept my eye on her as she moved around the room. She inspected the motley collection of pictures on the wall—a washed out ocean scene on one. A poorly executed still life on another. She tested the furniture, ran her fingers down the spines of the books on Dex's shelf and generally had a good look around. I kept an eye on her, but I didn't stop her. I didn't know what I'd do with her when she ran out of things to keep her entertained.

"Mind if I nibble one?" she asked, eyeing the heel of the bottle of bourbon.

"Sure," I said. "That's fine."

I got her a clean glass from the stash in Dex's desk. She plunked herself down behind the big desk, and I sat at my usual place in front of it. It wasn't that I felt like having a big chin wag with her—we weren't going to be girlfriends, I could tell that straight off. I just didn't know what else to do—either with her or with myself. With all our business talk out of the way, it wasn't like she and I had a lot to say to each other or a lot in common.

When I heard the outer office door open, I tried not to let Rhoda see my relief. "I'm in here Dex," I called out, not bothering to get up. It had been a long day and, anyway, I wanted to be in a position to see his face when he got a load of Rhoda Darrow, not just in our office, but in *his* chair.

It was the voice that alerted me. I could feel the welcoming smile die on my face.

"Well, well. Well. What do we got here?"

Then the business end of the biggest gun I'd ever seen. And it was pointed at my head.

"Slim!" Rhoda's voice. "I can explain. It ain't . . . it ain't what it looks."

It took me a moment to process everything that was going on and once I did, I realized how the most natural thing for me to do—bring Rhoda back to the office—had also been the most dangerous. Why couldn't I have left a note for Dex and just taken her home? Yet that hadn't even occurred to me. It was only with a gun in my face that I realized how shortsighted my actions had been.

I couldn't even begin to imagine how he'd known where to find her. Then I remembered that I'd introduced myself to the woman who had opened the door at Rhoda's house. Perhaps she had told him that I had taken the mistress away and Xander had done the math and followed us here. I realized, though, that the how didn't so much matter. Xander Dean was here and he was larger than life.

"And what does it look like, sugar?" He was beautifully dressed, a deep blue silk hankie peeping from the breast pocket of his jacket today, a well-creased fedora just so on his head, but any pretense of gentility was gone, so far gone, in fact, I wondered that I hadn't seen through it before. I wondered about my own motivations. Had I been so blinded by the possibility of a paying job for Dex that I hadn't seen what now seemed obvious? Here was Mustard's Chicago connection, with the very worst connotations those words could have. At that moment I felt as though I would have spotted that if he were getting off a bus.

"Well just . . ." Rhoda hesitated. Tried again. "Well, just . . . it don't look good, maybe. But it ain't what it seems."

I kept my yap shut and he paid me no mind. He'd seen Rhoda sitting behind the desk, and just now he didn't want to see anything else. How quickly it all can unravel, that's what I figure he must have been thinking as he crossed the room, tucking his gun into his holster once he'd seen it was just us girls and we were unarmed. How quickly it all can come apart, as he snaked out one long, thick arm and grabbed a big mittful of Rhoda Darrow's hair.

She yelled then, I can't put it any other way. She did not scream, which is what I would have done. Screamed out of surprise and maybe fear. Rhoda Darrow yelled, as though with all that had happened, this single thing—a hand wrapped painfully in her hair—had pushed her past her breaking point. Angry. That's how she sounded. So angry that when she tilted her head up and sank her teeth deeply into Xander's wrist, I was barely surprised to see the blood begin to squirt between her lips.

It was his turn to yell then—a low, animal sound. While he yelled, he wound up and hit her so hard with his left, uninjured hand that she was jolted out of Dex's chair. I heard a crack as her head hit the bookshelf behind the desk. Then there was nothing. I couldn't tell if she was alive or dead while she lay there still and pale and Xander Dean bled all over Dex's office floor.

Your thoughts surprise you at a time like that. You'd think that all you'd be able to keep in your head are pure animal responses—fight or flight. But that's not strictly true. Or it is on a certain level, but that level is pretty near the surface.

As Xander stood bleeding and Rhoda lay either dead or dying on the scuffed hardwood floor, I found myself calculating the space between the door and the place where I stood. At the same time I wondered if Dex had remembered to take his piece—I tried to picture him with or without it—or, as he occasionally did, if he'd left it hanging in its holster behind the door on the coat tree against my advice. Would this be the one time he listened to me? Or would I make a grab for the gun only to find it was not there?

At the same time my mind cast about for another type of weapon. What could I hit him with? The wastepaper basket? A chair? Dex's ashtray, dirty but made of stone. And, were I able to grab one of those things for such a purpose, would I have what it took to get the job done? There was nothing in my background that let me think this might be the case.

As I stood there I realized—weirdly, oddly, unexpectedly—that this was a version of the thing you hear: *her life flashed before her eyes.* In a sense, all these things flashed in front of my eyes. Or, maybe behind them. Not my life, though, but ways I might prolong it. The whole of it took just a few seconds, and all of the options looked grim.

How long did we stand there like that? I don't know. Time slowed down. Stopped.

Xander Dean stood looking toward Rhoda's still form, his blood running down his arm, pooling oddly by his feet.

So much blood. How was that even possible?

Me, still in the chair opposite the desk, crouching now, as though I might bolt or attack. Take your pick because it didn't matter; fear stayed my hand.

We stood there for an hour or a moment, I'm not sure. We stood there and time did not matter.

For a while, time stood still.

CHAPTER THIRTY

IT WAS THE tick, tick, tick of the clock on the bookshelf that made me focus on reality; on the situation at hand. The same bookshelf, I thought almost idly, that had caused that awful crack to Rhoda's noggin.

I could hear the rising sound of an ambulance. Increasing in volume, coming closer. I remember thinking—ridiculously—that it must be coming for Rhoda. But of course it was not. No one had called for an ambulance. No one even knew we were there.

Before long the sound of the ambulance began to recede, just as it had grown. My heart turned over. I felt it. My heart turned over with a sigh.

I knew I had to do something, but I seemed unable to formulate even a single cohesive thought, let alone anything so well considered that it could be called a *plan*. From the looks of him, Xander was facing the same challenge. Lucky for me, in his case there was all that loss of blood to deal with and lightheadedness to blame. I'd take it any way I could get it.

Left to our own devices, I wonder how long we might have stood there like that, Xander and me. A half hour? A day? Eternity, though on the way there we'd be turned to stone. It was like we were caught in a spell, only partly of our own design.

In the end what got us moving was the slam of a distant door. I recognized it as the door at the top of the stairwell, though I figured Xander probably would not. I also knew what it meant. In our building, the elevator stopped running when the operator went home. Our elevator was as old as the building: the elevator operator wasn't just there for his good looks and witty banter. The sound of the door closing could have meant Hartounian had come in to repackage olives or one of the accountants had come in to do some late night figuring or perhaps the dentist had come in to contemplate the meaning of payne. But I hoped it didn't mean any of those things and that Dex was on his way back to his office at that exact moment. I hoped some more that Mustard would still be with him.

The door at the top of the stairs slammed. A hollow, echoey sound.

Xander and I looked at each other. Our eyes locked over Rhoda Darrow's pale, still form.

I'll remember that moment always. Xander's eyes seemed impossibly blue and I could see the pulse jump at the base of his throat, the shadow late afternoon can leave on a man's chin, the way his mid-section strained against his good suit.

I was not aware of gathering myself up, of collecting myself like a racehorse at the gate, but I must have done—and Xander? He saw it too because both of us sprang into motion in the space of a single beat of our hearts. He came toward me but I—lither, younger, faster, lighter and fueled by the possibility of death—I sprinted toward the open office door, praying that the door to the hallway had been left open as well.

It had. I scrabbled through it without hesitation while Xander thundered along behind me. I imagined him losing ground, perhaps regretting that extra cheesecake or six, while I sprinted down the hallway, around the corner, and straight into Dex and Mustard.

"Kitty. What the hell?"

I didn't explain. Didn't need to. My eyes would have been wide with fear, my breathing ragged. Later I'd realize that the front of my dress was ruined with a splash of blood. Xander's or Rhoda's? I'd never know. It didn't matter anyway. Not in the end. Except it alerted my boss and his friend that something serious was afoot. Xander, for his part, pulled up when he saw them, shifting from pursuit to retreat.

Dex and Mustard catching Xander Dean? It was no contest; none at all. They cornered him in the office, like some wild animal. He tried to use Rhoda's still form as a hostage, a shield, but it didn't do much good.

"I'll kill her," he said, his gun to her head. "I swear I will."

I saw Mustard cock his head this way, then that.

"Ain't she already dead? She looks dead," Mustard said.

"She's *not* dead," Dean said through gritted teeth.

"Whaddaya think, Dex? Dead?" said Mustard.

"As a doornail, looks like," Dex replied.

"She's *not* dead," Dean said again.

"And we're gonna take your word for it?" I was standing behind Dex and Mustard in the hallway and, at this point, I saw both men raise their guns, level them at Dean's chest.

"It's over, Dean." This was Dex. "You'd best put the gun down. The girl's body, too. It wouldn't take much for me to make a few alterations to that nice suit of yours." He waggled his gun at him. "Alterations even the best tailor couldn't fix."

There was a moment's hesitation. A moment when it seemed as though Dean might take his chances with getting to the gates of hell before his time. In the end, though, he threw down his gun with the sort of casual familiarity with which I might discard a chicken bone or yesterday's newspaper. Without being asked, he raised his arms and linked his hands behind his head. Later Dex would say it was because of something in Mustard's eyes. It wouldn't have cost Mustard much to kill Dean right there. I think Mustard was disappointed he wouldn't get the chance.

As soon as Dean was neutralized, I pushed past the boys to Rhoda's side. At first I couldn't feel the beat of her heart and I figured she was dead. The copious amount of blood bore this out. But then I felt it: a reedy pulse, barely there. But still.

We called an ambulance. We called the cops. While we settled in to wait for both, Mustard and I did what we could to staunch Rhoda's bleeding, while Dex watched over Dean and drank from the bottle of scotch he and Mustard had been bringing back to the office.

We took a breather then. That is, we caught our breath. We took a breather because we thought that, with Xander Dean in custody and Rhoda Darrow damaged but safe and in our hands, something was finished. Complete.

We were wrong.

CHAPTER THIRTY-ONE

"I DIDN'T KILL her, don't you idiots understand that?" Dean had been pushed into a chair in Dex's office. The cops would show up, probably sooner rather than later. Meanwhile, we had to listen to him mewl.

That was how Dex put it:

"Quit your mewling, Dean. Save it for the jury. You're gonna need all the help you can get." Then he pushed his face up close to Dean's and said in a deadly stage whisper. "You're gonna need it, else you'll be doing a little jig at the end of a rope."

"Gee-zuz, what does it take?" There was desperation in the big man's voice now. As though we held a key to the rest of his life. Maybe, in a way, we did.

"Are we idiots?" Dex looked from me to Mustard, then back again, as though asking our opinion on an important question. I didn't say anything. Mustard kept his own counsel, too. "When we first saw you today, you were holding a woman in front of you—a woman you probably thought you had killed, by the way. You held a gun to her head. Told us you were going to shoot her. To *shoot* her, Dean. And we're supposed to believe you're innocent?"

"He ain't innocent," Mustard said with distaste. "This mook was born not being innocent."

Mustard hated Dean now. I could see that, plain as anything. From Mustard's perspective, Dean had abused some sort of network of trust. It was an abuse that Mustard could never forgive.

"What do you take us for?" Dex wanted to know. "You set me up. You hired the girl," he indicated the place where we'd made Rhoda as comfortable as possible on the floor. "You made sure I saw Wyndham go in with the other girl you hired. Now stop me, please, when I get to the innocent part."

"But you're already there, don't you see? We didn't want the girl *dead*. That wasn't the plan. Think about who I was working for. You've been detecting. You've figured it out, right? She wasn't supposed to *die*."

"No?" Dex said, skeptical, but listening. "What then?"

"It was supposed to be scandal. That's all." He looked from me to Mustard, then his eyes went back to Dex, so obviously in control. "That's *all*. I mean, hell: why would we have wanted the girl dead? We didn't need her dead. Dead was worse. Look what it did: with the girl dead, of course you're going to think I did it. Everyone is. And everyone's going to look at the whole thing real hard, too. Much harder than for scandal. Geez," and here his voice rose and I was surprised to hear it touched by anger, "we didn't want *any* of this. Think about it: the girl can't testify if she's dead. She'd be more useful to us alive, all around."

"You're saying *we*." My voice sounded overbright and overloud in the electric atmosphere of the room. The others must have thought so, too, because three heads turned to look at me. "Who is *we?*"

"But you know."

"Tell us anyway," Mustard said, shaking Dean up a bit by the lapels for good measure.

"I don't know much," Dean said and Mustard gave him another shake. "I *don't*. The guy what hired me is called Joe Breen."

"From the old neighborhood," Mustard said with distaste.

"Sure, sure. I knew him from Chicago. That ain't against the law."

"You said Breen was from Pittsburgh," I said to Mustard.

"But he came here by way of Chicago," Mustard shook Dean up a bit more for good measure. "These mooks all did."

"Who was he working for?" Dex asked.

"That I don't know," another shake. "*I don't,*" he insisted. "But I got some ideas."

Quickly then, before the cops came, he sketched out what he knew. In some ways, Mustard hadn't been far from the truth. In others, he'd been whole planets away.

Joe Breen had been hired by the Hays Office some months before. Breen's job was to get the movie studios to self-police the administration of the Production Code that had been written a year or more before.

"They weren't playing ball, see? That's why the Hays Office hired Joe: to make the studios play ball. Least, that's what he said."

Breen decided that what was needed was a big stick. He had many to offer. He hired Dean to be one of them. Dean's job was to highlight—at a grassroots level—what was wrong with the movie industry. Not the technical details, of course, but the rotting core at its moral center. Dean's job was to bring that to light. It was understood, though never outlined, that he could use any tools available to make this happen provided no one could ever connect him with the Hays Office or anyone *connected* with the Hays office.

"It was a conspiracy?" I said, shocked.

"Well. That word . . ." Dean said. I didn't know if I should be amused or annoyed at the look of distaste that he wore.

"You were part of a conspiracy to make the movie industry look bad—corrupt. But to what end?"

"Better movies," Dex said. "Jesus, that's it, ain't it? All of this . . . conspiracy . . . was so the studios would start producing better—cleaner—movies."

Dean might have said more on this—I'm pretty sure he had more to say—but we could hear the sound of many feet, some of them flat, approaching down the hall.

I was glad when the ambulance people arrived right behind

the cops. Before they moved Rhoda, the nurse leaned over, wide-eyed because there was a lot of blood, and examined her quickly. Then the nurse and driver transferred Rhoda to a gurney. I noticed all of this medical activity only at the periphery of my consciousness because I was focused on what was going on with Dean and the cops.

I wasn't terribly surprised to see O'Reilly and Houlahan again. They seemed to have been assigned to us and whenever a cop was called, the two of them would pop up like bad apples. I was kind of getting used to them by now. With them was a fresh-faced kid the other two called Kesterson. They ordered him around like a lackey.

"Is he injured?" said O'Reilly, putting rough hands on Dean. "There's blood on him, but he seems okay."

"Check his hand," Dex supplied. "The twist he hurt bit him pretty good." He indicated where the still unconscious woman was now being wheeled out of the office on her gurney.

"*Bit* him?" this was Houlahan. "Well I never. From the looks of her she was tryin' to get a meal into her. Can't imagine the fat boy would be too tasty, though. Well, cuff him anyway, kid," he said, addressing Kesterson. "He may be injured, but he's a big 'un, too. We don't want him getting away."

Dean grimaced while Kesterson cuffed him gently, but he didn't holler. He knew things could get worse and he was past the point of making any trouble.

"So he's the one killed the girl? Not Wyndham?" Houlahan said.

"He says not," Dex said.

"Ah, he'd probably say his mother was a call girl, too, if he figured it would save his neck." Houlahan again.

"But I didn't kill her," Dean spoke up for himself now. There was a desperate edge to his voice. I could have told him to save his energy. I could have told him desperation wouldn't help him with these bulls. It would only make them meaner.

"Think about it: why would I have killed her?" His eyes scanned from the three cops to Dex, Mustard and me. He was testing his audience. I could feel it. He was testing which way we were gonna go. It didn't matter. I could have told him that, as well. He could be as convincing as anything. He was going to get a free ride down to their clubhouse whether he liked it or not. And I had a sawbuck leftover from my shopping trip to Blackstone's said he wasn't going to like it much.

Once the cops had bundled Xander Dean off to put him under glass, Dex asked me to call Sterling. To tell him what had happened. He wanted me to set up an appointment for him and Mustard to see both Wyndham and his lawyer at Number 11.

"I'm coming with you," I informed Dex. The office was strangely quiet in the wake of cops and ambulance attendants and Chicago mobsters with their broken molls.

" 'Course you are, Bright Eyes. But you're going to be making the appointment. I figured you'd take care of that part on your own."

I smiled at him. My best smile. *Course I was*. He sometimes acted like a souse and, when pressed, could be a bit of a louse, but there were worse bosses than Dex Theroux.

Even though it was eleven o'clock at night, I got Sterling on the phone in no time. I heard Mustard talking with Dex in the background. He wasn't surprised. "He's a shyster, ain't he? A lip. He don't need no sleep. They gotta keep moving or they die."

Sterling listened while I briefly told him what had happened, then reiterated Dex's desire for a meeting at Lincoln Heights.

"If what you've said is true," Sterling said, the beginning of jubilance coloring his voice, "maybe we should hold off for a few days. With this man in custody, I should be able to secure Laird's release in no time."

"I only know Mr. Theroux requested a meeting with you and Mr. Wyndham tomorrow, Mr. Sterling. Shall we say ten in the morning?"

"Well, that's done," I told Dex when I got off the phone. "But he didn't go easy."

"Course he didn't," Dex said, looking satisfied; like something had been confirmed. But he didn't explain.

Mustard drove me home that night in the Sixteen, but we didn't talk much. We were tired. More than tired. It had been the kind of day that sucks the goodness from your soul.

When I got in, the house was in silence and I was glad. It was possible I heard the radio going in the living room, maybe Marjorie and some of the boarders were listening to a late program, but I didn't peek in to see. I went to the kitchen and prepared a small plate of "kippers" and a few crackers and a glass of milk to take up to my room, creeping through the house as quietly as I could. I didn't want to disturb anyone, sure. But, more than that, I really just wanted to be alone with my thoughts.

And my thoughts. What did I think that night? It's hard to pinpoint now. I know this: I felt a hollowness of soul I'd seldom felt before or since. A kind of emptiness where a happy fullness most often is. I know that I believed in evil on that night. I believed in all the great evil in the world. And I saw it in places where it's normally invisible. I saw it reaching for me in spots that were usually safe.

Despite my exhaustion, that night it took the sandman a long time to send me over. Several times as I reached the bridge that leads from consciousness to sleep, I felt a hand reach for me. And I stepped back.

When I finally slept, it was a deep, dark sleep. I didn't dream at all.

CHAPTER THIRTY-TWO

THE FOLLOWING MORNING, Dex, Mustard and I were uncharacteristically quiet. There was none of the joking and horsing around that usually marked Dex and Mustard's relationship. And none of the cheerful reprimands from me while trying to keep them in line.

Dex and I were having coffee at our own desks when Mustard came in. Out of habit, he made himself a cup, then left most of it steaming on Dex's desk when we got underway.

The mood continued on our ride to Lincoln Heights, then in the building as we passed through the gauntlet of flatfoot desk jockeys on our way to meet with Wyndham and Sterling. It was exactly the same path Dex and I had taken more than once. But it was different today, something had changed. Neither of us said it, but we knew. We would have been hard pressed to say exactly how.

Wyndham and his lawyer were altered, as well, in quite different ways than the three of us. There was a delicious joy to them both and they did a lot of back clapping and made many congratulatory sounds. For my part, I was surprised to feel myself recoil when Wyndham touched my hand.

No one noticed.

Neither of them saw how subdued the three of us were or that our interactions with them were not quite what they'd been. I couldn't fault them that. To be honest, at that moment it would have been difficult for me to pinpoint what was different. But different it was.

"Thank you both for seeing us," Dex said when the back clapping was under control and we'd found seats around a scarred table in the farthest corner of the room. Even so, their bright mood earned scowls from several inmates chatting softly with their own visitors. There was an unwritten code around visiting at a jail. I'd gleaned that. No matter what the inmate was charged with, and how they likely behaved in other areas of the jail, in the visiting area, everyone was quiet, respectful, on their best behavior. Visits for most were so rare that it wasn't a privilege anyone wanted to risk. If there was a code, Wyndham was breaking it. I doubted that he cared.

"Well, of course, we were happy to see you." Wyndham said, beaming. "After all, what else do I have to do? Though Sterling here is confident all will be finished with this nightmare in just a few days time. Perhaps I can take you three for dinner then? Or out on my yacht. Gosh, but I've missed the water!"

Dex ignored him. He dispensed with any preamble, going straight for the core of the matter. I envied him his nerve.

"Laird," he said, "I asked you once—the very first time we met, right here—I asked you straight out if you killed that girl. And now, I'm asking you again."

"What?" The confusion on Wyndham's face would have been comical if I hadn't known just how serious Dex was about his question.

"You heard me," Dex said.

"I heard you. Yes. But I guess I can't believe what I heard." Laird Wyndham wasn't smiling now.

"Yes, yes," Sterling said, his usually calm demeanor ruffled. He reminded me of a park pigeon getting the bum's rush from a free meal. "What's the meaning of this? These matters have all been dealt with. You told me yourself: they have the killer in custody now. It's all been resolved."

"Well, they certainly have a guilty party in custody. But what's he guilty of? Not murder," Dex said. "I'm pretty sure of that."

There it was; out in the open. The thing neither Dex nor Mustard nor I had said yet out loud. The thing we'd all felt in our hearts. We *believed* Xander Dean, as unlikely as it seemed. We knew what he was and we suspected what he was not. He was capable of many things. Hell: he might even be capable of murder. But did he kill Fleur MacKenzie? We did not think he had. That, of course, left the question: if not him, then . . . who?

"See, it's all in the timing," Dex said. "As you know, I saw Rhoda Darrow approach you at the party. She made sure of that. Her job was to catch you in a compromising situation. There would be scandal and outcry. Maybe you'd even lose your contract with the studio. People would stop going to your films. Only nothing went according to plan, did it?"

Wyndham didn't move at all. He did not blink. His hand betrayed no tic. We looked at him, all of us, waiting for his answer. Finally it came.

"I guess not." It came out a whisper, but it seemed to echo in the space between us.

"Tell us what you found." Dex's voice was gentle now. A father talking to an errant son. A friend. A lover. Someone who cared and would never hurt him. "Tell us," he said again, even softer this time.

"The girl . . . ." Wyndham stopped. Ran the insides of his fingers across a stubbled chin. Began again. "The girl was dead." He ran his eyes over each of us in turn. He was looking, I think, for understanding. I can't imagine what he found instead.

"Dead?" Dex said, as though surprised, but I could tell he was not. Who was acting now? "But how could *that* be? If she was dead, wouldn't you have cried out? Called for help? Why would you just have left her there?"

Wyndham didn't say anything now. Just shook his head, somewhat helplessly, I thought.

"All right," Dex picked up the thread again, "you don't know? I'll help you out, because I *do* know . . . you didn't say anything, because you knew who did it."

"I think this has gone far enough." Steward Sterling suddenly seemed like a child to me. A child playing dress-up in his lawyer father's clothes. It was something in the helplessness I heard in his voice, despite this attempt at subterfuge, at bravado. There was a rub in the timbre; a quaver, though not a break. And there was something loose and suddenly hopeless, though this might be imagining on my part. "My client doesn't know anything about anything. Haven't we been telling you that all this time?"

Dex kicked back in his chair, the very picture of confident comfort. I wondered how much of it was an act. "Oh, I know what he's been saying. And I know what you've been saying, too, Sterling. Now I wanna hear the truth."

"I think you'd better leave," Sterling said, beginning to rise.

"You're going to kick me out of jail? That's rich. But no." Dex's voice was suddenly cold. "Sit the hell back down. We're gonna talk this out."

To my surprise, Sterling took his seat.

"Now I'm gonna tell you a story," Dex said, once again the picture of relaxed comfort. He might have been sitting in his own office chair. He might have been reclining in his apartment, holding forth to the rats and the cockroaches, tipping back a bourbon and saying what was what. "And the two of you? You're gonna listen up. Here we go: once upon a time, there were two men. Maybe, for a little while, they fell in love. Or maybe—just maybe—one of them did. And the other, well maybe he was never capable of it in the first place."

I looked at Dex, really looked at him. What was he saying? I looked at Mustard: his face held the same expression I imagine mine did. Neither of us said anything. No one did. We just wished Dex would get on with it. We wanted to see where this was going.

"But that don't come into it for a while. Here's what does: the one man—the one in love—he gave everything he had to give, and it was a lot. The other man, he didn't reject the first man's love. He took it. But he took love from everywhere. It was never enough. He took it from other men, from women, from crowds of people who went to see him in the pictures and read about him in movie magazines. Everyone loved him."

Wyndham was now eerily quiet. Nothing moved about him. But I noticed he had closed his eyes.

Sterling, on the other hand, looked like a man close to breaking. I felt sorry for him, though it's hard to explain that. Given the circumstances. Given what I know, what I figured right then.

"The two of you fought that night," Dex's voice was quieter now. We all had to strain to hear him. "I don't know what about. I think it was about women, about how Steward needed more from Laird and Laird could only give less. You'd fought and Laird, you went to the party. But Steward, you lurked around, not sure what to do with yourself. You wanted to make it up with Laird—even tried to call him a few times—but he didn't even seem to care.

"You were outside the bungalow when the girl was brought into the room. You saw her through the window. You saw her naked. Waiting. You knew what her purpose was there: knew she was there to have sex with your lover."

Lover. The word thudded into the room like an elephant. Laird and Steward had been lovers. Had, in fact, been in love. Of course they had. I'd never thought of it myself, but now that Dex had said it, it all made so much sense. Laird had chosen a wife who would not encumber him, who would allow him to continue to feed his appetites. And his appetites had been *wide*. Steward hadn't understood that, not really. He'd fallen in love with Laird and had thought Laird returned the feeling. But Laird probably never had. Not really. Steward had, for Laird, been one of many. But for Steward, Laird had been *the one*.

None of this was reflected in their faces. Both men remained unchanged. Laird in that place of calm, Steward looking like a violin string: taut almost to the point of breaking.

"And you knew, too, that Laird *would* have sex with her. He always did, didn't he? You couldn't stand the thought of it. He claimed he loved you, but he could resist no temptation. Not the smallest one. And you were angry. Suddenly you were so angry, you couldn't contain it. You wanted to kill someone. You wanted to kill Laird. But you loved Laird. You could never kill him."

"So he killed Fleur instead." I spoke without knowing I was going to, shocked not only by what Dex was saying, but at how right—correct—it felt.

Had Dex expected he would make these accusations and that one of the men—perhaps both—would break down and confirm all he said as true? I think maybe he *did* expect that. Dex can play at being jaded all he likes. I know him better, though. At heart, he believes that, once you have the answer, justice will be done.

If Dex did hope that, he was left disappointed. There was no weeping confession. No confirmation to aid in bringing matters to their rightful conclusion.

Wyndham never blinked, never moved. In fact, I never heard his voice again. I did hear Steward's though. "I don't want to hear another word of this," he said tightly. "I think you'd better leave before I call the guards and have you removed by force."

Dex didn't say anything more but, for me, he didn't need to. No matter the outcome we knew—the five of us—we knew just what had transpired that night. It was possible that Xander Dean might swing for Fleur's murder and Steward Sterling might remain free to defend a hundred guilty men and Laird

Wyndham might have sex with a thousand willing starlets and still we knew what had really happened on that night.

Is that justice? That's not justice. It's just knowing. Sometimes that's all we have. It just has to be enough.

CHAPTER THIRTY-THREE

I THOUGHT THAT was the end of it. I really did. Dex and I went back to the office. Mustard went off to fix things. We got back to our lives. Mostly insurance claims and cheating wives.

Months later, we heard that Xander Dean had been convicted for the murder of Fleur MacKenzie. I brought the newspaper into Dex's office, plunked myself down and read the item to him. It was short: Dean had been found guilty. There wasn't a lot to say.

I felt a twinge, but Dex saw that twinge and he laid it to rest.

"You and me figure he didn't kill that girl. Fact, we're pretty sure he did not. They got him on the wrong murder, Kitty, but I'd lay money he's killed someone sometime. Probably not just once, either. Life has a way of catching us up when we're not looking. Life has a way of laying us flat when our heads are turned."

"Are you talking about divine justice?" I asked.

Dex shrugged. Took a slug of bourbon, a hit of his smoke. Then he shrugged again. He seemed to be thinking about how he'd answer me, but I could sense the shape of the words before he sent them into the air.

"That'd be a fancy way of putting it, I guess. 'Divine justice.' Sounds almost pretty when you say it like that. And the thing I'm talking about? I'm not so sure it's pretty. But I like to think that, in the end, a man gets what he deserves."

"Do you really believe that, Dex?"

He looked me square in the face and nodded his head. "I do."

It was that look in Dex's eyes I thought about when, a few weeks later, I was flicking through a movie magazine and a tiny item caught my eye. There had been an incident aboard the *Woebegone Dream*. While the boat was anchored off Ensenada, the actor's trusted friend and lawyer had unfortunately slipped into the sea.

"It was a freak accident, so unfortunate," Wyndham was quoted as saying. There'd been a group of people staying on the yacht, including a starlet named Belle Soul who, judging from the photos, had the longest legs that had ever been. The photographer had posed Wyndham and the girl in front of the yacht. Wyndham's face was composed in sad lines and Belle was taking a run at it too, but it also looked like the face of a woman who thought her life was about to begin.

Wyndham had told the journalist that, sometime in the night, after everyone had gone to bed, Sterling had apparently gone out on deck and fallen into the drink. No one had been around to see him and pull him back.

In the morning, when it was discovered Steward wasn't on board, the coast guard had been called and the tender dispatched with crew to look for the missing man. They'd found him a few hours later some ways distant. He was floating. And he was quite dead.

"He was a wonderful man," Wyndham had told the magazine, and there it was in black and white. "A dear friend. He will be missed."

I thought about divine justice again then. I couldn't help it. However it had been dealt out. Had what Wyndham told the magazine been true? Maybe. Maybe Sterling had just wandered out on deck and tripped, fallen overboard. End of story, end of tale. Maybe Wyndham had killed him, to get him out of the way. Or maybe Sterling and his broken heart had taken a chance with the sea.

From my perspective, though, it all amounted to the same thing. As Dex had said: Divine justice.

There were no signs of foul play.

AUTHOR'S NOTE

Death Was in the Picture represents a careful concoction of reality and fantasy. Or perhaps fantasy is too strong a word. More like: a blend of history and what-might-have-beens and even a few perhaps-weres-but-no-one-is-talking-about-them.

Kitty, of course, is fictional, as are Dex, Mustard and the other major characters in the book. A few historical characters have been included, but they skate at the periphery of our adventure and are not central to the action as we experience it. For example, Joseph Breen was a real person, though the situations in which he plays are fictional. He was a noted anti-Semite, though. We have some of his writings and they are as ugly as you can imagine. Daniel Lord was a real person (could I have given the priest that name? I think not), and it is widely thought that the writing of the very first Production Code document was his or mostly so. The Masquers Club exists in Los Angeles and has done since 1925. A splinter of this organization formed the Screen Actors Guild in 1933. The Masquers Ball is my own invention, but the possibility of it was just too delicious to pass up.

What tempted me about this storyline was the fact that the more research I did, the more I realized that not only was it a story worth telling, but aspects of it perhaps *needed* to be told. Fiction being what it is—particularly fiction told by a first person narrator—the book couldn't actually be *about* the themes that give the story heart and pulse. There are shadows of conspiracy here and censorship and sharp loss. But, for the most part, they must remain as hints and shadows, secrets of history, if you will. Certainly, it would be implausible for our Kitty to discover answers to questions that she lacks the inside knowledge to even ask. And so we see the questions at the edge of things, with the darkness swirling about her feet. Mysteries within mysteries. But life is like that.

Many thanks to my editor, Peter Joseph, for helping to pull the essentials from the morass my brain had become while I was working on this book. I cannot imagine a better editor than Peter. In fact, he's so wonderful, I don't even try.

Thoughts and good wishes—and thanks, of course—to my agent, Amy Moore-Benson. May all your dreams, your heart, your world, be clear.

Thanks, as always, to my partner, David Middleton: first reader, sounding board, confidant. Lover, teacher, friend.

Thanks, also, to my son, the actor Michael Karl Richards, whose dreams are contagious and who understands the place where artistic integrity and creativity fuel each other's hearts.

And thanks to my brother, Dr. Peter Huber. You keep me walking toward the light.

I must again thank the L.A. Conservancy—http://www.laconservancy.org/. This remains one of the top organizations dedicated to historic preservation in the world. They have to be: Los Angeles is such a dynamic city, reinventing herself every minute. It's easy for a lot of people to forget the importance of the past. History is sometimes lost in a heartbeat. And though it occasionally seems as though the L.A. Conservancy wages a heartbreaking losing battle in the fight to save pieces of this amazing city, it makes the wins they *do* enjoy all the more sweet. Check out their Last Remaining Seats program for an example of this. Kitty would be glad to know her beloved Million Dollar Theater survives pretty much as she knew it and as we see it in this book.

And you, of course, gentle reader. Thanks for participating in another one of Kitty's journeys. Without you, all of it would be quite without point.